Reviewers on *Nicholas*

"The leading man is the sexiest one this reader has seen in a long time!"
—*Romantic Times*

"Everything about this story and the elements within worked . . . a wonderful book that did not disappoint!"
—*Paranormal Romance Reviews*

"I really didn't want this book to end, and when I finished I knew that this book would stay with me."
—*TwoLips Reviews* (5 lips; Reviewer's Choice; Recommended Read)

"Engrossing and easy to read in one sitting . . . The sex is knock-out hot . . . Sure to please any erotica fan."
—*Just Erotic Romance Reviews*

"On my top ten favorite erotic books list."
—*Night Owl Romance* (5 stars)

"I couldn't put this book down until I finished every delightfully wicked page! . . . Beautifully written."
—*Romance Junkies* (5 stars)

"A steamy, hot tale that scorches the pages."
—*Coffee Time Romance*

Reviewers on *Raine*

"One of the strongest heroines I have ever read . . . great, erotic sex."
—*TwoLips Reviews* (5 lips; Recommended Read)

"Without question the best historical paranormal erotic romance this reviewer has ever read . . . This is a must read book for 2008!"
—*Paranormal Romance Reviews*

"Two thumbs up for another sensual read that will be gracing my keeper shelf."
—*Night Owl Romance* (Top Pick)

Also by Elizabeth Amber

BASTIAN: The Lords of Satyr

DANE: The Lords of Satyr

DOMINIC: The Lords of Satyr

LYON: The Lords of Satyr

RAINE: The Lords of Satyr

NICHOLAS: The Lords of Satyr

SEVIN:
THE LORDS OF SATYR

ELIZABETH AMBER

APHRODISIA

KENSINGTON PUBLISHING CORP.

www.kensingtonbooks.com

APHRODISIA BOOKS are published by

Kensington Publishing Corp.
119 West 40th Street
New York, NY 10018

All Kensington titles, imprints, and distributed lines are available at special quantity discounts for bulk purchases for sales promotion, premiums, fund-raising, and educational, or institutional use.

Special book excerpts or customized printings can also be created to fit specific needs. For details, write or phone the office of the Kensington Special Sales Manager: Kensington Publishing Corp., 119 West 40th Street, New York, NY 10018. Attn. Special Sales Department. Phone: 1-800-221-2647.

Aphrodisia and the A logo Reg. U.S. Pat. & TM Off.

ISBN-13: 978-0-7582-4131-3
ISBN-10: 0-7582-4131-3

First Kensington Trade Paperback Printing: May 2012

10 9 8 7 6 5 4 3 2 1

Printed in the United States of America

For Tamara Marsh, Reneé A. Shook, MJB, Debra Guyette, Tammy Ramey, Amelia Durbin, and Suzanne Vitti, and the many wonderful, supportive members of my e-newsletter group at http://groups.yahoo.com/group/Elizabeth Amber

And for you. I hope you enjoy Sevin's story.

—Elizabeth Amber

The Satyr Clan in Rome
(Descended from Bacchus, the Roman God of Wine)

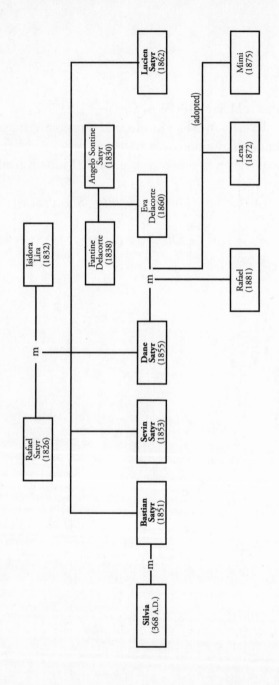

The Satyr Clan in Tuscany
(Descended from Bacchus, the Roman God of Wine)

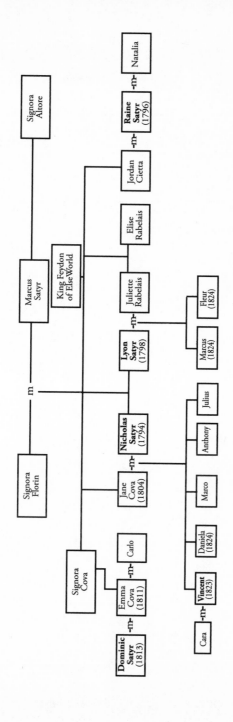

Contents

PROLOGUE

In centuries past, the Satyr secretly dwelled throughout Italy, watching over the vineyards of the wine god, Bacchus. After a Great Sickness arose, few remained to protect a sacred gate between EarthWorld and ElseWorld, a parallel realm populated by creatures of myth.

The corridor of lands extending from Tuscany southward to Rome was once so thoroughly bespelled that ElseWorld immigrants went largely unnoticed. But the recent discovery of their existence by humans threatens a small clan of Satyr lords in Rome.

They are four brothers of ancient Satyr blood—Bastian, Sevin, Dane, and Lucien. Entrusted with safeguarding artifacts created by their ancestors—artifacts that are even now being excavated in the Forum—they are determined to protect their families and holdings in their adopted human world.

Upon the coming of each new month, their blood beckons them to heed the full moon's call to mate. To deny this carnal call is to perish. To heed it, bliss.

SEVIN

1

Capitoline Hill, Rome
1882

"Heathens!" "Heretics!" "Go back where you came from!"

Lord Sevin Satyr braced a muscled forearm on the stone doorjamb at the front entrance to the *Salone di Passione* and surveyed the throng in the street below with disgust. The fearful; the haters; the avid, ethnic purists; and end-of-the-world prophets. Hundreds had come despite the gray drizzle and looming storm, all of them squeezing into the narrow streets of Capitoline. The smallest of the Seven Hills of Rome, it was thick with monuments, museums, medieval *palazzi*, and one very exclusive club where humans could not trespass—his infamous salon.

Rising three stories high, its gleaming marble façade was lined with soaring Corinthian pilasters crowned with carven olive branches. Its magnificent staircase stretched before him, sweeping downward to the street below. All of this grandeur only hinted at the glories to be had inside.

Although it was only late afternoon, some who'd gathered carried torches and lanterns. Either they were planning a long siege or they had visions of burning him out.

Good luck with that, Sevin thought grimly. The centuries-old veil of magic that had protected ElseWorld creatures such as he from human perception in this world had been destroyed only weeks ago, but the Satyr still had the ability to erect an invisible forcewall around something as small as a single building. These hecklers weren't getting through the barrier he'd established around the salon's perimeter, no matter how they tried.

Someone pitched a bottle at one of the high windows and it bounced off the magic shielding it. Sharp gasps of surprise and awe filled the street in reaction. Whispers swelled into fearful shouts and dire predictions.

Knowing the barrier to be impenetrable, he'd opted not to employ extra security tonight, nothing beyond the usual guards. A show of excessive force was the surest way to start trouble. He rarely questioned one of his decisions, but now—

"Fifty hells!" he snarled. "I didn't expect it to be this bad."

"I expected worse," his youngest brother, Lucien, replied darkly. He stood nearby on the landing with his arms folded and surveyed the mob with brooding eyes. "First Calling night since creatures from an alternate world are discovered in their midst? Naturally these backward humans would all turn out to witness the comings and goings."

"That's the Italians for you—any excuse for a celebration," added the muscle-bound, one-eyed sentry who stood guard at the door.

"Or for a riot," Luc put in.

Sevin stepped over and reached upward. With a hard jerk, he unfurled the wine-colored banners on either side of the entrance doors, formally signaling their anticipation of the upcoming Calling night.

More whispers. *What was the significance of the flags?* the humans wondered.

"Next Calling, perhaps we should hand out explanatory leaflets," Luc suggested wryly.

A slight smile curved Sevin's lips, drawing a line at one side of his mouth that hinted at his famous dimples. "They'd pay well for such a privilege, I imagine."

Luc shot him a hard glance. "Surely, why not just invite them all inside to goggle their fill instead of leaving them out here to speculate on what we get up to under a full moon?"

The sentry sniggered.

Luc had spoken in jest, but in actuality Sevin had been thinking along similar lines in all seriousness. This outpouring of fear and hatred was not only dangerous for his family's future here in this world, it was bad for business. Which meant that he was going to have to find a way to get into the good graces of these humans. He had a solution in mind, but tonight was not the time to put his plan in motion.

No, tonight, like his brothers', his thoughts must instead turn to other things. To matters of sensual gratification. For the Satyr had been born to act as carnal followers of the wine god, Bacchus. With the coming of the whole moon tonight, they would succumb to an inextricable sexual thrall. One that called upon them to worship the ancients through the lustful actions of their own flesh. A craving to do so would become a fever in his blood. In the blood of all creatures from his world.

During their collective erotic surrender, all would be vulnerable in the time to come and must seek out a safe haven for the hours from dusk to dawn. Until now, no haven had been safer than the salon. Until now, they'd managed to keep this place hidden from prying eyes. Invisible to humans.

But no longer.

"How are the rest of our clients going to make their way

through this crap?" Sevin muttered. "And where are Bastian and Dane?"

"I doubt many more will chance it, signor," said a feminine voice. "I suppose we'll all just have to entertain ourselves tonight, won't we?"

He glanced over one shoulder. His new hire, Signorina Ella Carbone, had come slinking out to join them. A fey female with long red hair and a rouged mouth set in a perpetual sultry pout, she had a fondness for putting her hands where they weren't wanted.

All three men on the landing watched as she artfully molded her considerable curves along Sevin's side, smiling up at him through long artificial lashes. "You're so tense," she purred. "Maybe I can help you with that, hmm?"

He felt his companions' speculation, but the truth was he hadn't lain with this woman, and wouldn't. When he and his brothers had reached their eighteenth year, each had in turn taken part in their first Calling, whereupon they had been gifted with a different and unique talent.

His lent a special meaning to the act of coition. When he first lay with a woman he would become privy to her closely guarded secrets. It was a talent useful for ferreting out classified information in business dealings and had garnered him a repu-tation—even among other Satyr—for a keen ability to intuit and fulfill a woman's fleshly desires.

But after years of liaisons with women like this, he didn't need to lie with this one to learn her goal. She wanted to rut with one of the legendary Satyr on this special night. To use him for the rare carnal animal he would become. To have him fornicate with her until dawn with not one, but two cocks, his sexual energy and her pleasure never flagging. And later, she hoped to lord it over the others that the powerful owner of the salon had chosen her.

One of her hands slipped under his long coat and flexed brazenly on his rear, her other slipping between the buttons of his linen shirt to stroke his chest. He caught her wrist in a hard grip and shot a dark glance in the direction of the sentry. Sevin was no woman's trophy.

Springing into action, the sentry briskly peeled her away and steered her inside with a determined hand at her back. "It grows dangerous out here. I must insist you go inside, for safety reasons, you understand." Ella found her protests falling on deaf ears as she was finessed off into the depths of the salon where her wiles could be put to more effective use among its patrons.

The uniquely talented men and women who were employed in this house of pleasure were here by their own choice, and they abided by Sevin's rules or quickly found themselves tossed out. He had rules for himself as well, and rule number one was never to show favoritism by taking an employee to bed. It was bad for morale.

A carriage pulled up at the foot of the granite steps, and the woman was quickly forgotten. Bastian, his eldest brother, leaped from the conveyance, then turned to help his new wife, Silvia, alight. As the carriage then slowly waded off through a sea of humanity, Dane, the second to youngest of the four brothers, reined in and dismounted. A light smack on his well-trained stallion's rump sent it pounding off to the stables around back.

The trio then fought their way through the drizzle and the crowd, ignoring cries of "Heretics! Fiends! Murderers!" Passing twin stone griffins at the foot of the stairs, Bastian and Dane moved ever upward, guarding Silvia between them as they headed for the salon's front entrance.

"Murderers? That's a new one," Dane said, nodding a greeting to Sevin and Luc. "Is Eva already inside?" When Sevin shook his head, Dane put his hands on his hips and glared out over the crowd and into the distance, looking disgruntled as he searched for his errant wife. "Damn. I knew I should have insisted on bringing her myself."

Brushing droplets of rain off his wool coat, Bastian eyed Sevin as he ushered his own wife toward the door with a broad, proprietary hand at her lower back. A toucher, this brother was. And then on the opposite end of the spectrum there was Luc, who kept his hands to himself and shrugged off even the most casual touch as if it burned him.

"What's your attendance like?" Bastian asked.

"Half the usual," Sevin told him. "Only the gods know how those who are too afraid to come will fare out on their own tonight."

Beyond the crowd he spotted two furtive figures approaching from an alley. A pixie and a fey, by the look of them. Seeing the threatening crowd, they backed off. Slinking into the shadows where they'd find other less safe accommodations in which to pass this dangerous night.

"Damn it all to hells and back!" Sevin slammed the side of a fist on the stone doorjamb. He was on edge, had been all day. They all were. Already he could feel the temporary changes that were occurring in his blood and body. The tension that was building in him. It would break free only with the appearance of the whole moon. Only a few hours more.

Just inside the door, Bastian murmured something to his wife, and in response she put a hand to his cheek and lifted her face for his kiss. With a smile and a nod to Sevin and Luc, Silvia then entered the salon. Her husband watched her go with a besotted look he took no pains to hide.

Intercepting Sevin's amused glance, Bastian sent him a smug

half-smile. "Laugh now, little brother, but you'll fall one day, too. And you might just find wedded bliss to your liking."

Sevin snorted a laugh. "When hells freeze."

"Ah yes, I forgot. You're already wedded to the salon," Bastian chided.

"And a fine, faithful, and profitable wife she makes," Sevin returned unapologetically. The salon was big business in the ElseWorld community in Rome—the only one of its kind. He'd convinced the ElseWorld Council to allow him to commission it, and he had seen it built against all obstacles when he was but eighteen. It flourished because he excelled at running it. If he had time for little else these days, so be it.

"Finally," Dane said, sounding relieved as another carriage rolled up in the street. The door of this one bore the Patrizzi family crest. Sevin felt Luc tense behind him as Dane took the steps downward. Bastian moved closer to their youngest brother, ready to stop him were he to try anything foolish.

Two feminine faces peered from the carriage windows, both with blond hair. One was Dane's tardy wife, Eva, who was Satyr herself, though this was unknown to anyone outside the family.

The second occupant was that friend of hers, Alexa Patrizzi. A human.

Sevin's gaze cut to his youngest brother. There was nothing subtle in Luc's body language as his eyes pinned Alexa. He wanted to kill her.

Unfortunately, Sevin's reaction to her was altogether different. He ground his teeth against the sharp curl of attraction that speared through him. An attraction for her—a woman he'd never formally met, never even spoken to. A woman whose family had all but destroyed his. He'd heard she'd gone to Venice. It appeared she was back.

As Dane and Eva ascended the steps, the crowd turned surly, rocking the carriage and hemming it in so the driver couldn't proceed. Alexa Patrizzi was still inside. Any friend of a Satyr's wife was apparently to be rebuked. When Eva made as if to go back to her rescue, Dane all but dragged her upward and out of harm's way.

"We have to help her," Eva urged once they reached the landing.

"I'll help her to the five hellfires," Luc growled, making a lunge in the direction of the carriage. Dane and Bastian each grabbed one arm, restraining him.

"There's trouble enough already. We don't need you starting any more," Bastian said through gritted teeth. Then he frowned as something in Luc's face gave him pause. "What's wrong with you? You're unusually pale."

"Nothing. A headache." Predictably, Luc shrugged them and their concern off and they let him. Had they touched his skin instead of the linen of his sleeve, his reaction would have been considerably more violent.

"Dane," Eva insisted, putting a hand on his arm.

"We'll help the signorina, I promise. Now go inside, *cara*, where it's safe. I'll be in shortly." With a brusque kiss, Dane swept her toward the door and handed her off to the sentry whose job thus far tonight seemed to have been reduced to herding women.

"Your wife should choose her friends more carefully," Sevin murmured as the couple passed him. He heard Eva's soft protest, something about unfairness of his statement.

But Sevin didn't wait to hear more. Dane had once been engaged to Alexa Patrizzi, but only through the machinations of her devious mother. It had not been a love match—far from it—but his wife's ongoing friendship with his former fiancée made for an awkward situation.

If Dane couldn't make his wife see reason, Sevin would take care of this matter himself. "Watch things here," he told Bastian over one shoulder as his boots struck the steps downward. "I want to have a word with Signorina Patrizzi."

Inside the rocking carriage, Alexa Patrizzi sat with one gloved hand braced upon the tufted seat and her other on the wall, calmly waiting for the crowd around her to weary of its tirade. She hoped they didn't damage the carriage—she'd planned on selling it to pay off her attorney.

Her mother had chosen the saffron-colored velvet upholstery she clung to, and for that reason alone Alexa would be glad to be rid of the conveyance. However, she had to admit that its thick golden tassels, which sprouted at intervals along its walls, did make for convenient handholds to anchor herself in her current situation.

When a particularly abrupt jostle brought her face nearer to the rain-fogged window, her eyes widened. One of Eva's brothers-in-law was loping down the steps, apparently coming to her aid. And if she wasn't mistaken, it was Sevin, the charismatic owner of the sensual paradise that was the salon just beyond him.

Her calm abruptly deserted her. Half standing, she managed to rap on the interior ceiling of the carriage, a signal for the driver to proceed. But he either didn't hear or had all he could do to control the horses at the moment, because they didn't budge.

She rubbed away the condensation on the window with the heel of one hand. Peeking out through the glass again, she surreptitiously watched the sheer force that was Lord Sevin Satyr make its way down the magnificent staircase. As his dark-coated figure knifed through the crowd and the incessant gray drizzle, he looked neither left nor right, seemingly unaware of the mad scramble to get out of his path.

Her feminine sigh filled the carriage. Watching a Satyr male in the simple act of walking was a pleasure so gratifying that she would actually purchase tickets for it. There was something about the way these beautiful silver-eyed men carried themselves that spoke of brawny masculine strength and an unshakable conviction that the world was theirs to command.

Although she did not regret the breaking of her former engagement to Eva's husband, she did envy Eva her connection to his family. What must it be like to be under the protection of a man such as this? To lie with him and be claimed by him—to be the object of his affections and lustful nature? It was a prospect that both thrilled and repelled at the same time.

As those in the crowd scurried this way and that before him, a small child toddled from among the sea of legs into Lord Satyr's path. Without missing a beat, he scooped the girl into his arms and out of harm's way.

A voice cried out, "He's got my daughter! Oh! Unhand her, you—you *devil!*"

Alexa let out a huff of breath, feeling ashamed of her entire species in that moment. She supposed that to these fearful humans he and his brothers did resemble devils. All of them towered at six and a half feet or more and had those strange, mirrored eyes. And this particular one was more suspect than the others in view of his connection to the mysterious, hedonistic *Salone di Passione. What sort of man created such a place?* she'd wondered, each time her eyes lit upon him. As far as she knew, no human had ever ventured inside it.

Seeming unaffected by the mother's slurs, Sevin deposited the child into her arms, with a charming smile and a flourish. *Lord, the man even had dimples!* Incongruous in such a ruggedly handsome face, they somehow softened him and made him more, well, human.

As he moved on, the woman stared after him, fanning herself in a vaguely stunned manner, a smitten expression on her plump face. Her child could have been trampled, yet she didn't even bother to thank him for rescuing her!

And then suddenly Lord Satyr's hand was on Alexa's carriage door and he was calling up to her driver. "Sit tight. I'll take care of this," he ordered in the tone of one used to unquestioning obedience.

Then the door opened and he swung himself inside, bringing with him the fresh scent of rain and the aura of sexy male. Alexa fought the immediate attraction that swamped her as he crowded inside and made himself at home on the bench seat across from her.

He was certainly the most beguiling of the brothers, in her opinion. From his straight brows, strong jaw, and broad shoulders, to his powerful thighs encased in lightweight black wool— everything about him aroused her baser instincts.

Really, it wasn't fair to let such a man run loose. Just gazing upon him caused a woman to contemplate certain nocturnal matters of a physical nature that occurred between the sexes. Matters that society deemed unfit for a lady to dwell upon.

Before she'd fled to Venice in the wake of her family's shame, she'd often observed Sevin's brothers and him from afar with a girlish longing. But she was past such things now. Older and far wiser about the uncertainties and perils of life and men than a well-brought-up lady of twenty-two should ever have to be.

Still, no man could make a woman more aware of the fact that she was a woman than these Satyr lords. It was an undeniable fact.

Sevin combed his fingers through his rain-soaked raven hair, slicking it back. The woman across from him watched the gesture with thick-lashed dark eyes. Signorina Alexa Patrizzi. At least she didn't shrink away or gawk at him in scandalized fascination as most humans did these days.

Instead, she only glanced outside at the crowd and then leaned toward him with an earnest expression in her soft gray eyes. "I'm so sorry."

His face hardened, lip curling as he sat back, stretching out his boots so she had to move her hem aside to make way. "You *should* be. I wonder that you dare show your face in Rome again."

"Oh." Now she drew back, her posture going ramrod straight as an understanding of his meaning drained the color from her pretty features. "I meant to apologize for this throng's treatment of you. But yes, you are right, of course. I-I should formally apologize as well for the pain my family has caused yours. And I *am* sincerely sorry." She pressed a gloved hand to her breast and leaned forward again as if willing him to believe in her sincerity.

What the hells is she wearing? Sevin wondered. *Sackcloth?* It was an unusually warm early-autumn day, yet she was buttoned up to her throat, every inch of skin covered save her pale face.

"More so than I can say," she went on. "Sorry to the depths of my soul for what happened to your brother. I cannot even begin to imagine what he must have suffered." She drew a shuddering breath and sent him a gaze that pleaded for his charity.

Except for the color of her blond hair she seemed nothing like her family, at least on the surface. But evil in the blood ran deep.

Abruptly, the carriage gave a hard lurch and she threw out an elbow, whacking it against the window to keep from falling.

"Damn annoying humans," Sevin bit out. With a careless flick of his hand he erected an invisible cloak of protection around the conveyance. Then came the startled sounds of those who felt themselves unexpectedly thrust away by his bespelling. The carriage suddenly ceased its rocking.

"We're not all bad," she informed him tartly as she straightened again and righted the little hat perched atop her head.

Ignoring her, he rapped twice on the ceiling of the carriage, a signal for the driver to move on now that he'd made passage possible. Since the crowd was still close, they began carving a slow path.

"Then tell me, signorina. Are you one of the bad ones?"

She froze, her hands clenching in her lap. "What?"

"I think you are. I think you are a Patrizzi with the same blackened heart as your mother and brother had. And I want you to stay away from my family, including Dane's wife," he announced, getting right to the point. "In fact, I want you gone. Tomorrow. Out of Rome."

"What? Why should—?"

"Why?" he interrupted in outrage. "Because your family has done mine unimaginable, irreparable harm. Because the same night my parents died, your family abducted Luc and Dane. Kept them enslaved in the bowels of the catacombs under your family home. Dane may have escaped the worst of what they had in mind, but Luc was tortured in ways he's never revealed. In ways that still eat at his soul."

She drew in a harsh breath, tears welling in her eyes. "But I had no part in that. Eva said your family investigated and found me innocent of any wrongdoing."

"We found no evidence that you were *guilty*. There's a distinct difference. Eva may believe in your innocence, but my brothers and I are of the theory that you could not have been completely unaware of what went on under the earth beneath your own feet for so many years."

"I *am* innocent, I tell you. Bona Dea was my mother's business enterprise. And my brother's. I didn't know what was happening down there. That her cosmetics were created only through the abuse of your kind. And if I could undo everything and put it all right again, I swear to you that I would."

His hand cut the air between them, in an innately Italian gesture. "You cannot put it *right*. No one can. But you can do the decent thing. Go. So that my youngest brother will not be reminded."

Averting her gaze to the window, Signorina Patrizzi visibly struggled to collect herself. Or was it all an act? When she looked at him again, Sevin found himself drowning. He hadn't expected her to be like . . . this. So open and seemingly without subterfuge. He'd always been a shrewd judge of women. And this one seemed . . . wounded, deep inside where it didn't show.

One of her hands was restlessly rearranging the fall of her skirt. His eyes dropped, noting the way the fabric molded slender thighs. He shifted on the bench seat, fighting the insidious arousal that seeped through him. *Damn!* He worked with exceptionally attractive women around him day and night, and was never so strongly affected. What was it about this human that got to him so?

This unwanted attraction to her had plagued him since the first time he'd seen her. She'd been wearing blue that day, he remembered, her skirts and her blond hair lifting in the breeze as she strolled in the distance through the Forum ruins with Eva.

Afterward, he'd found himself listening keenly whenever her name was mentioned in his company. He had been sorely disappointed to learn that she was human. He'd sworn off human women in his late teens, and with good reason. Still, this infernal hunger for her had persisted.

"I've only just returned from several months of travel," she said coolly, refusing to look at him now. "I assure you I intend to live a quiet life, a *respectable* one. No one—not even your brother—will know that I'm here."

As the carriage broke free of the crowd and began moving at a normal clip, his low reply burst between them like a provocative explosion.

"*I'll* know."

2

"W-What?" Alexa's eyes flew to his face. Surely, the provocative note in his voice had only been her imagination. Hadn't it?

"Against all odds, I find myself attracted to you." Sevin crossed muscled arms, eyeing her as if this fact were somehow her fault.

She stared at him in dismay. "You've never even spoken to me before today! And you cannot possibly be enamored of a woman whom you believe capable of the horrors my family committed."

"It's not something I'm proud of, I assure you. But the feeling doesn't seem to be going away. If you remain in Rome, within easy reach, the knowledge that you are near will hound me. Eventually, there will come a Calling night when I will wind up between the legs of my family's sworn enemy," he said, intentionally crude. "And I can't allow that to happen."

She drew in a sharp, offended gasp. "And you think I would let you?"

He smiled faintly. "Males of my kind can be quite convincing in such matters. Especially on a night such as this one. Our passions run high under a whole moon, and human females are particularly susceptible. If you stay in Rome, it *will* happen between us."

"Your opinion of my morals is very flattering, signor. And your intentions toward me so handsomely stated," she said sarcastically. "When we arrive at my home, I beg you please do come inside and make good on them. You make it all sound so . . ."

Alexa fluttered a hand to encompass him. He watched as her eyes flew over his entire frame, then ripped back to the unmistakable masculine bulge at the front of his trousers. Her eyes widened and she swallowed visibly before ending her thought with a single, thready, desperate word. ". . . tempting."

She blushed then, and her eyes darted away from his, the gloved fingers of one hand rising to fidget with a button on her bodice.

Damn, she wants me, too, he realized. If she'd shrieked or swooned over his admission, he might have been able to take his leave of her more easily—as he should do. He was playing with fire here. And if it were to eventually burn his family, the fault for that would lie with him.

She straightened, a prissy look replacing the bemused one. "I believe I am quite safe from any harm from the crush back there," she announced. "So I think you'll agree that it would be best if you take your leave now." She reached up to knock against the roof, preparing to signal the driver to stop and let him out.

Sevin's hand closed on her sleeve. "Wait."

Her eyes caught his. "Why?"

Because my blood is heating and my body urges me to choose yours as its mate for tonight. Because I want to lie with you, not some Shimmerskin conjured from the mist, as I have done of late. Because I want you to prove yourself to be worthless and despicable, so that I can finally forget you.

She tugged at her arm, and after a brief hesitation, he let her go. For a long moment, silence reigned in the rocking carriage. The air between them was taut with indecision and an ill-advised, unspoken desire. With very little wooing, he could have her, he knew. Right here in the carriage, or in her house, minutes from now. But she wasn't a harlot or a woman one took as a mistress. And he wasn't the marrying kind.

Her lips parted as if she would speak any minute and order him out, yet she did not. A delicate, pink tongue slid over her full lower lip; then white teeth sank into it as if she would unconsciously punish herself for wanting him.

What would that mouth of hers taste like? Her throat? The secret feminine heart of her that she kept safely hidden and tucked high under those prim skirts? He shifted, feeling his sex stir.

No! The rule he'd established when he was eighteen was ironclad. He did *not* mate humans. No exceptions.

But you could kiss one.

In that way, he might learn more of what she truly was. Not everything, perhaps—not as much as his talent would tell him if they were to mate. And there were intimate engagements that technically fell shy of mating—embraces that would hint at whether she was as innocent as she claimed in the matter of her family's shame. And he found that he needed to know.

So what was stopping him? He had an hour or two to kill until the moon came. The salon was safe under the protective veil he'd constructed with his talents. His brothers would watch over things there until his return. None of them need ever know what happened here between him and this woman.

Outside the carriage, the storm turned furious. Inside, he and Alexa Patrizzi were intimately cocooned by muffled sounds that seemed distant—lashing rain and the clatter of wheels on puddled cobblestones.

Her face went prissy again, and she took a deep breath, looking as if she had summoned the will to remove him. "Signor . . ."

"Fifty hells," he muttered. He was about to do something stupid.

Signorina Patrizzi drew back, wary when he leaned forward. Resting his forearms on his thighs, Sevin wrapped his hands under her knees and gently eased her forward. Just a few inches—enough so that her legs came between his.

"Signor, stop it." She pushed at his hold, trying to straighten. "I'm not going to—"

"Let me have you?" he finished for her.

She could feel the heat of his touch through the fabric of her dress. The gentle rub of masculine fingers at the tender hollows behind her knees. *Mmm.* The sensation shot a strange ache all the way through her core, making her want to relax her spine against the seat back and melt into him. Instead, she curled her gloved fingers into claws over his wrists.

"Whatever game you intend, do not play it with me," she told him levelly. "You are no doubt only feeling . . . excitable . . . in the way of your kind, due to the impending rise of the moon. I really think it would be best if you return to the salon."

"Don't worry, signorina. Alexa. I won't seduce you." His tone was easy, confident. It made her far less certain of her ability to resist him, should he attempt to do just that. "And do you know why?"

His head lifted and she caught his mirrored gaze, seeing herself reflected there. "Because we're in a carriage? Common decency? Because I'd shoot you if you tried?" she suggested sweetly.

Lord Sevin chuckled, low and dark, as if not wanting to be

amused by her, but unable to help himself. Then he responded with a slow, negative shake of his dark head. "Because my family means everything to me. And because your family was an enemy to mine." His hand caught one of hers, his thumb finding the naked pulse at her wrist between glove and sleeve. "And because you are human."

"Well, that's settled then," Alexa said softly. "We won't be lovers."

His words about his family had deeply affected her. Like him, her family had once been everything to her. Until a few months ago, that is, when she had discovered the truth—that they'd been villains of the worst kind. And then there was her recent unfortunate experience in Venice to consider as well. Really, did she dare trust her disastrously poor judgment of anyone ever again?

"No," he agreed easily. "We won't be lovers."

He'd taken her hand now, and she watched like a rabbit to his wolf as he plucked at the tips of her gloves each in turn, with the fingers of his free hand.

"But," he went on, "for the length of a carriage ride, let us flirt at the edges of such a possibility. Tempt ourselves with what cannot be."

Five gentle tugs came on her fingers, each one sending a sharp corresponding tug of arousal curling through her. And then her bare hand was resting in his larger one and being lifted to caress the line of his jaw.

"A touch," he went on, and then turned his lips into her palm. "A kiss."

It was such a simple occurrence, and yet a monumental one. Her unclothed hand had never been held by that of a man she didn't know, much less kissed. And never by any man so overwhelmingly . . . masculine.

She closed the hand he held and pulled it into a fist at her breast, where her blood beat an erratic drum. Within her palm she could still feel the warmth of his jaw, the soft rasp of the early evening stubble that darkened it, the sweet press of his mouth. "But we're only five minutes from my home—" she murmured, the beginnings of a feeble protest.

"Fifteen." At her surprised look he shrugged, a loose, easy movement that made her want him. "Yes, I know where you live. I told you this isn't the first time I've thought about you in this way."

Her eyes fell to his lips as he spoke. They were beautifully shaped, like those of the Renaissance statues she'd seen in the National Museum. It certainly was not the first time she'd thought of him in this way either. But those were daydreams.

This was real. Did he really wish to hold her? To crush his mouth to hers? A man as beautiful as he could have anyone. Why *her*? And why was she considering his suggestion? After all, he had told her only moments ago that he did not believe in her innocence.

Her attorney had instructed her that it was of the utmost importance that she live a respectable life. Her behavior in the years ahead must be above reproach if the successful resolution of their litigation on her behalf was to stand up to scrutiny.

But she was not meant to lead a lonely life. Despite recent disappointments, she longed to know a man's loving, his embrace, his kisses. This handsome stranger was offering her a brief taste of these things she craved. Fifteen minutes' worth. Then he'd promised to leave her to the decades of respectability and isolation that awaited her.

"Very well," Alexa said briskly. "We will throw caution to the wind until the end of this ride, but no more. So flirt with me—a woman you suspect to be your enemy. I won't stop you, within reason. And I'm curious. You and your brothers have quite the reputation. Though so far you have done little more than a casual suitor might. I'm not really impressed—"

Another laugh rumbled from his chest—a dark sound and a

quick flash of white teeth. "By all means, then. I wouldn't want the reputation of my entire species to suffer on my account."

In a smooth shift of masculine muscle, Sevin joined her on the seat. She scooted aside to make room. Without quite realizing how it happened, she found herself crowded into the corner behind her. He was leaning over her, with her thighs draped over his, so that she very nearly sat across his lap. One of his hands had settled at the small of her back, and his free hand caught one of hers, pinning it to the tufted velvet saffron wall alongside her head.

"Tell me more of our reputation," he bade her. "Tell me the rumors and I will say them true or false."

"*Um...*" Distracted by his closeness, Alexa could hardly collect her thoughts well enough to respond. She could scarcely believe she was being held in his arms and that he was freely offering her information she'd often longed to be privy to! She pressed her free hand to his chest, an unconscious barrier to his scandalous suggestion that she broach matters no lady should with a man she hardly knew. When she didn't find her voice, he found the words for her.

"Do they speak of what my brothers and I are?" he prompted. His mouth trailed kisses along her jaw as he spoke, sending a hot thrill over her skin. "Of how we will pass this sort of night? Of what the ancient blood in our veins will drive us to become? How much has Eva told you? Come now, speak frankly."

Like every other citizen in Rome, she'd seen the urns, the statues, and the fresco paintings that this man's eldest brother had unearthed in the Forum. The ones depicting the Satyr with their enormous, distended phalluses, in lustful pursuit of maenad females.

She gazed at him from under her lashes, her cheeks flushed. "Eva and I don't discuss personal topics of that nature in any detail. But there has been gossip and speculation, even as far north as Venice."

"Go on," he murmured encouragingly.

"It is sometimes . . . I mean, it is generally rumored that on a night like this, when a full moon shines . . ." She hesitated. "That your kind is capable of giving a woman fifty fulfillments."

His lips caressed the tender skin of her throat, just below her ear, and she felt his smile as he spoke. "True."

"Oh? Well. Goodness. I suppose that would mean . . ." The fingers of her free hand toyed with the neckline of her bodice, as she sat momentarily flustered. "In roughly nine and one half hours, that would amount to more than . . . five per . . ." Her voice faded and roses bloomed in her cheeks. ". . . hour." She'd always had a head for figures, but displaying her mathematical skills to a suitor was no way to attract him. *Attract him? Is that what I'm trying to do?*

"It's my contention that the quality of such encounters is more important than the quantity," he went on. His eyes studied her face as his fingers left her spine to unfasten the first few buttons at her neckline. She stayed him, her eyes searching his.

For a brief instant, Alexa saw behind the mirrors to the man. Saw a glimpse of the easy self-assurance that was such a part of him. One that silently whispered to a woman, *I can give you pleasure beyond your wildest imagination.*

Her heart twisted with a wistful sort of longing. She had never known a man's passion.

But she knew all too well what fornication was.

It was sounds and smells. It was Venice. It was the steady ticking of her clock as she breathlessly waited. The *hiss* of a lamp extinguished, blanketing her bedroom in complete darkness. It was her body being summarily flipped so that she lay on her belly. A fist at her nape to keep her still. A cruel masculine weight at her spine. The ripping of fabric. Harsh brandy-soaked breath. Her freshly laundered pillowcase muffling her screams.

Sevin's mouth came again, brushing hers this time. His breath was clean and didn't taste of brandy. His lips were warm, and moved on hers with a studied leisure that quickened her pulse. It was an arousing kiss, one that thrilled and made her yearn to beg him for more. To beg him to place those lips of his elsewhere upon her person, in places no woman of breeding should ever request that a man kiss.

His hand on her bodice turned, its knuckles moving slowly down her buttons and upward again. The movement teased the fabric at her breasts, quickening her breath. She twisted the uppermost button and tugged her bodice open slightly, giving him permission. He took it.

Cool air found her skin as his fingers pressed her bodice open. Her head lolled back and she shivered at the heat of his hand as it traced over the upper swell of her breast. A moan escaped her as he rubbed a thumb over its peak. That beautiful mouth of his found the hollow of her throat, her collarbone, her shoulder . . .

With a soft sigh, she let her eyes flutter closed. She turned her face toward the window to give him better access. Outside, the rain had thickened, pounding them in sheets. Her breath and heartbeat seemed far too loud in her ears.

Then, suddenly everything stopped.

Sevin gazed down at the woman in his arms, feeling as if all the blood had drained out of him. A chill drove down his spine even as a punch of lust struck him square in the gut.

The turn of Alexa's head had revealed a small design inked low on the side of her neck, at the bend where throat met shoulder. A tattoo. It was a perfect flower, yet not just any flower.

It was an *iris*.

Seeing the direction of his gaze, she self-consciously covered it with her hand and shrugged her collar higher again. "An indiscretion. One of many I regret during my recent trip to Venice," she murmured in explanation.

Simultaneously, the carriage reined in. They'd arrived at her fine, stately row house. Their allotted fifteen minutes had flown past. He'd been so intent on his own pleasure that he'd learned nothing of her guilt or innocence during his exploration of her.

What the hells am I doing?

What he'd wanted to do since the moment he'd first seen her in the Roman Forum with Eva that day he'd visited Bastian's headquarters. He was touching her. Kissing her. Glorying in the taste of her, in the soft give of her flesh against the hardness of his own.

He knew better than to tempt himself like this on a Calling night, especially with a human. When he'd been younger, with his family gone and no one to guide him, he hadn't known what the repercussions of bedding human females might be. But at twenty-seven years, he had no such excuse.

Family was not something he took for granted. Having lost his parents when he was fifteen, whereupon all three of his brothers disappeared for years—Dane and Luc abducted by the Patrizzi family, and Bastian fallen prey to an addiction—he would do almost anything to keep them all together now. This female, innocent or not, was a threat to Luc's recovery, and therefore she must be banished.

"I want you out of Rome," he gritted, their faces still only inches apart. A distant rumble of ominous thunder punctuated his words. Outside, the storm was moving off, but the hedonistic tempest inside him still raged for this woman, strong as ever.

She straightened and pushed at him, her nimble fingers going to re-button her bodice. He frowned, wanting to stop her. Wanting the right to sweep her into the house and keep her there, under him, all fucking night. His eyes went to her mouth, reddened by his kiss, and watched it form a single word.

"No," she murmured.

"What?" He pulled back, realizing he'd been staring like some callow moonstruck youth. His jaw worked as anger at himself welled up and burst out in her direction. "If you defy me—if you remain in this city, you'll regret it, I promise you."

Alexa nodded tiredly, not meeting his eyes. "I'll consider what you've said, signor. But I'll need time to come to a decision."

"You have until tomorrow," Sevin informed her in a clipped voice.

Ignoring her protest at this perceived injustice, he flung open the door and leaped from the carriage. Determined to put her from his mind, he welcomed the bracing chill in the air and the half hour of walking it would take him to reach the salon.

In the hours before a Calling, he often formed a strong attachment to a female that would see him through the moonlit night of debauchery with her. That was all he was feeling now. Sexual desire. He would slake that elsewhere soon enough.

But as he made his way through back alleys and narrow crooked streets to the rear entrance of the salon, a decade-old prophecy pounded over and over in his head in time to the sound of his boot heels pounding the cobblestones. *Your beloved. You will know her by the iris.*

He hadn't thought of that old Romani crystal gazer's prophecy in years, not till he'd seen that tattoo tonight. It had been a foolish prophecy, one he hadn't heeded then and would not now, despite tonight's strange coincidence.

The fortune had been told to him during the dark years that he'd been alone, cut off from all family. When he was but fifteen and cast adrift—his parents recently dead and his brothers missing—he'd been taken in by the Romani, a tribe of nomadic gypsies passing through the Italian countryside.

They'd become a surrogate family. And for three years, he'd lived, worked, and loved among them.

Clara had been one of them. The crystal gazer's daughter. She'd been comely, fragile. *Human.*

She'd loved him.

And he'd killed her.

By the time Sevin reached the salon, the crowds outside had dissipated, presumably due to the intensifying of the storm. A few hardy stragglers remained, but he paid them little heed. The forcewall he'd erected would keep them out.

Opening the back entrance, he was immediately greeted with the soft strains of music. Nodding to the guards posted there, he tossed his dripping coat on a hook, and moved down a corridor. Another dozen steps and he was parting velvet curtains and entering the central salon.

It was a massive, splendid room that was the heart of the salon, with a gilded, coffered ceiling that rose three stories high to form a dome. Encircling the vast circumference of the upper floors were rows of balconied seating boxes, including two that served him as office and personal apartments. Enormous candelabras forged of precious metals mined in ElseWorld were positioned between the boxes, bathing strategic areas of the floor in their radiant glow, while leaving others intimately shrouded in shadow.

He took it all in with a calculated eye, noting in satisfaction that everything was going smoothly. Years ago, he'd designed this place in its entirety. Had made it a seductive paradise in which creatures of his blood could engage in concupiscent pastimes away from the prying eyes and suspicions of humans.

In the distance, a carousel turned with mesmerizing slowness. Lacquered dragons, unicorns, and other fantastic creatures pumped up and down upon it, some bearing riders engaged in amatory embraces, and others who rode alone, exhibiting themselves for the voyeuristic entertainment of the room at large.

His new hire Ella was among the latter, he noted, and she had drawn an appreciative crowd of spectators as she undulated sinuously on a demonic dragon. Seeing him, she sent him a sultry smile and reached out in his direction, coyly beckoning him closer with a sly curl of her fingers. He returned her smile with one of his own and a nod, but felt no pull to venture closer.

He had another woman on his mind. Alexa. The remembered shape and texture of her flesh still burned his hands, and her taste was still fresh in his mouth.

But he would not have either woman tonight, or any night. Instead he would lie with Shimmerskins—a breed of insentient females who had serviced the Satyr's lustful needs since ancient times. In recent years when he'd been so busy with building and then operating the salon, they had become familiar companions to him. They were convenient and accommodating sybaritic partners, who simply disappeared into the mist from which they'd come when he had no further lustful need of them.

Yet his engagements with them were becoming unsatisfying of late, and he'd rarely bothered over the past few weeks. If he didn't watch himself, he would become like Luc, foregoing all carnal pleasures except once a month during the Calling, when he had no choice but to yield to his body's demands.

All thoughts of fleshly pleasure were instantly set aside when he was approached by one of the sharp-eyed guards. Two dozen or so were stationed at discreet intervals within the salon to ensure that no trouble erupted.

"There's been an incident in the east wing," the man announced *sotto voce*. "A small explosive device discovered in the liquor bar. Your brothers have gathered there—fortunately they contained it when it went off."

"It went off? Gods, man, don't leave such details to the end next time." All business now, Sevin made for the east wing himself, hurrying without seeming to hurry. No need to draw more attention to this minor disaster. Everyone was agitated enough already with the moon's coming and the upheaval outside tonight.

He found his brothers gathered like three dark pillars around the larger-than-life statue of Bacchus—the focal point in the center of the main liquor bar. Eva and Silvia were nowhere in evidence and presumably awaited Dane and Bastian in two of the many private and semiprivate chambers that ringed the central salon. Likely they were even now being pampered and prepared in anticipation of the sensual rites they would soon enjoy with their husbands.

Upon seeing him arrive, Dane gestured to the statue's pedestal. "You missed the excitement." When he stepped back, Sevin saw that the pedestal and floor tiles surrounding it had been blackened and damaged. An ugly pile of charred and twisted debris was being swept away by servants.

Atop the pedestal, the Roman wine god stood frozen in gold-veined stone, appearing blithely unaffected. Grape vines wreathed his hair and a wine goblet was extended in one hand as he offered a toast, one made in celebration of the fleshly delights all comers might enjoy in this idyll of his making.

Sevin's brothers held no goblets yet, which meant they had not begun the ritual that would initiate the changes that would occur in them with the fullness of the moon. They'd been waiting for him.

Bastian held out a gnarled ball of mangled metal and Sevin took it, turning it over in his hands. "What am I looking at?"

"It's an artifact of some kind. Was, I mean. It's rubble now." Bastian took it back and studied it with the concentrated fascination he typically reserved for two things: archaeological artifacts and his wife. "A rudimentary device, but effective all the same."

"We think the culprit smuggled it in somehow," the guard admitted.

"Looks as if there's a traitor in our midst." Dane went behind the massive, semicircular liquor bar of polished mahogany and brass, finding an ancient cabinet hidden there. Turning a golden key in its lock, he then removed two bottles, which he set on the bar. Finding a quartet of ornate goblets, he began pouring.

"Hard to believe that only a few weeks ago Pretender Galas were all the rage in Rome," he went on. "No fear then. Humans thought nothing of cavorting about dressed as their favorite mythological deities and beasts. Their greatest pleasure on a Sunday afternoon was flocking to the museums to gawk at the statues and urns Bastian unearthed in the Forum. Centaurs, Venuses, Fairies, Satyrs."

"That was before they found out such creatures were real," said Bastian. "Which put a more sinister complexion on things for them."

"I'll be damned if anyone is going to force us out of this world with rioting and arson," said Sevin. "We've been here most of our lives. This is our home, not ElseWorld."

Then to the guard, he said, "Lock the doors for the night. From here on out, I want tighter security checks before anyone is admitted. Weapons are to be confiscated and held until patrons depart. Interview everyone before they go tomorrow to find out what they know about this. And secrete that device somewhere safe for tonight. Lord Bastian will want to take it with him tomorrow for study."

"Understood. Certainly," said the guard as Bastian handed over the artifact. With a quick half-bow, the sentry charged off with the device to carry out his orders.

Once he'd gone, Sevin set a hand at his hip and surveyed the scene. "The guard said you contained the explosion?"

"Luc did." Bastian jerked his head in the direction of their youngest brother, who hadn't spoken a word since Sevin had joined them. "Which is why there was no more damage."

At the moment, Luc was lounging on a chair cocked back on two legs against the wall behind him, his boots propped on the chair opposite. His arms were crossed over his broad chest, chin tucked, and eyes closed. Without opening them, Luc muttered, "Just tossed out a simple spell, is all. Nothing to get excited about."

Bastian sent Sevin a look, which informed him that what their brother had done went far beyond "simple." Knowing how Luc hated anyone marveling over the unusual powers he'd somehow acquired while hidden away for all those years in the Roman catacombs, they let the matter drop. All of them knew he was downplaying what he'd done. They were accustomed to that, and to his moody silences.

Having poured measures of ruby liquid from the first bottle into three goblets, Dane handed them around. Then he poured from the second bottle into a fourth goblet. This was a nonalcoholic elixir, which he served only to Bastian, who could not tolerate spirits. "Drink up. The moon's no more than an hour from coming."

Four golden goblets lifted toward the statue of their god, accompanied by four calls of *"Salute!"*

Then, as one, the four Satyr lords drank of the elixir that was their lifeblood. It was a necessary thing they did now. Without this elixir to commence matters and prepare their minds and bodies for the Calling, they would meet their deaths in the hours before dawn.

This ruby liquid was the sole reason that the Satyr clan in Tuscany still guarded a special, ancient gate on their lands. Through this conduit between the adjacent worlds, grapes were regularly exchanged. Those that came from ElseWorld vineyards were brought into this world, and then a portion were transported to Rome for use in this tradition.

This cross-pollination between the worlds was crucial in

keeping all the peoples of ElseWorld's blood alive. If the gate's location was ever leaked to humans, it could prove disastrous.

Sevin tossed back his elixir and was quickly done, setting his empty goblet aside. Humans considered them to be little more than carnal beasts, he knew. But these Callings were more than an animalistic sexual romp. Nights such as these brought Else-World clans and families together to worship the ancient gods and ways of their ancestors. The ritual tonight would be a time of bonding. A renewal of what they all were. An affirmation of what it meant to be of Satyr blood.

"Is this the last of it?" Dane asked, studying his goblet.

Sevin nodded. "I'll send for fresh grapes from Tuscany on the morrow to get started on fermentation of more stock."

Bastian shook his head. "I'm afraid it will no longer be so easy. There's a travel embargo. Voted into law throughout Italy this afternoon. I don't know the details. But the gist is that those of us with ElseWorld blood are no longer allowed to travel outside the confines of our city of residence."

Dane and Sevin both swore darkly.

"This day just keeps getting better and better," Luc muttered into his goblet. He raised his drink to his lips. But then he grimaced and moaned. His chair legs hit the floor and he bent low, his head dropping between his legs.

"Luc! What is it?" Sevin demanded in alarm, going to him.

"Damned headache." Luc pressed the heel of his hand against his forehead.

The brothers shared a look. Luc never complained unless he was near to dying.

"Has this happened before?" asked Dane.

Luc nodded and then moaned again as if the movement had pained him. "A few times. But this is worse. Like lightning driving through my brain."

He sat up again and let his head drop back against the wall, visibly making an effort to breathe evenly.

"Could the coming of tonight's whole moon be the cause?" Bastian speculated. "That combined with the fact that the protective curtain is now gone?"

"Maybe this will help," said a voice. Sevin looked over his shoulder to see Ella approaching. Other employees and patrons had been filtering into the bar. But she had brought a cool cloth and now made as if to lay it on his youngest brother's brow.

With a snarl, Luc knocked her hand away.

Another of the salon's female employees shook her head sharply at Ella and drew her aside. "That one doesn't like to be touched," she whispered in a voice that carried. "He won't even touch us on a Calling night." She nodded in Sevin's direction. "Unless his brother insists."

Her warning fell into a silence that caused it to hang heavily in the air.

"Out!" Sevin commanded, his gaze encompassing the room. Patrons and employees alike started in surprise at his tone.

As a guard came and ushered them away, Sevin went to Luc and carefully clasped a hand on his shoulder. He and his brothers made a point of regularly making such gestures, trying to accustom him to accepting them again. "Perhaps it's time to retire, Luc. Maybe Shimmerskins will put you at ease."

Goblet still clasped in one white-knuckled hand, Luc grunted a grudging assent and rose. But the instant he stood, he stumbled and let out a guttural cry. His free hand reached out blindly and found Sevin's sleeve, gripping his arm hard, as if needing a lifeline.

Sevin steadied him. "I've got you. You're all right."

But Luc only laughed, a hollow, aching sound that sent a knife of empathy stabbing deep into Sevin's marrow. "No, brother. I'm not all right," Luc muttered cryptically. Something in his tone went odd then, and he bit out three final words. "Not. At. All."

"What the hells?" Sevin heard someone say. Dane. But then

his brothers and everything around him began to waver, like a scene on a distant horizon viewed through the sweltering summer heat. The carousel music sounded garish and tinny to his ears and its spinning made him dizzy. He fought to breathe.

And then, suddenly, Sevin was bathed in darkness. Not the kind in which you could make out shapes once you got accustomed to it. No, this darkness was the black pit of his brother's nightmares.

3

Sevin hunkered down in a crouch, his survival instinct kicking in.

There was movement near him.

"Luc?" he ventured.

"Here."

"Anyone else?"

Silence.

Luc still gripped his arm, he realized. Sevin twisted, reversing their hold so that he now gripped Luc's forearm. With his other hand he reached out into nothingness. Total and complete blackness. He stood and stepped out blindly, tugging Luc behind him.

After a few steps, his fingers made contact with something cool and solid. A rock wall, uneven in places and roughhewn. Somewhere in the distance, he heard the steady trickle of water.

"Where are we?" he wondered aloud.

"Catacombs." The word was a thready monotone from his brother's lips. "The tunnels below the Patrizzi house."

"What? How the fuck did we get down here?" If these were

in fact the very subterranean tombs in which Luc had been imprisoned for twelve years, he had to get them out of here. Luc's grip on sanity was tenuous enough without subjecting him to this abomination.

"Don't know," said Luc.

Still holding on to his brother, Sevin moved forward, feeling along the wall with his opposite hand. "Well, figure it out so we can get back to the salon. Gods, I thought this place had been destroyed when Dane found you."

"This is a different section than the one that caved in," said Luc. "But I well recall the general stench down here."

Other than the smell of cool earth, Sevin detected no such stench. He took the fact that the air was not stale as a positive sign. Perhaps they were close to some sort of exit. But he didn't correct his brother. Luc had had a dozen cruel years to memorize every nuance of this place. If he said he recognized its scent, then he recognized it.

Sevin continued moving down the corridor in what he hoped was the direction of the water sound, pulling an unresisting Luc behind him. "Has this happened to you before?" he asked Luc. "This instantaneous traveling?"

"Some," Luc admitted dully. "Only when these headaches are at their worst."

"And you didn't think to mention it?" Sevin felt rather than saw Luc's shrug.

"I'm freak enough without adding to my repertoire, don't you think? Besides, I've taken inanimate objects for the ride before, but never another person," said Luc. "And never so far in one go."

When Dane had come to Luc's rescue some months ago, Luc had somehow moved an overhead beam support, causing the cave-in that had killed Alexa's mother and brother—his jailers. He hadn't done it with his hands, but with his mind, Dane had said. This had been the first inkling his brothers had of his otherworldly talents. Luc had been tight-lipped when it came to anything regarding those, so they'd learned little more of them in the months since.

"How do you usually get back to where you came from? In the same way? As quickly?" Sevin demanded, his mind racing. They had already drunk the elixir. When the moon came, they would both feel it, even down here where they could not see it. And then they would both require the surcease of a woman's flesh.

This didn't worry him particularly, for he knew he could conjure Shimmerskins. He had done so often enough before in the salon. But he didn't know how adversely a night in this place would affect his brother. Luc teetered on the edge of madness as it was. A night spent here might topple him into the abyss. They had to get out.

"It's not something I can direct," Luc said, sounding frustrated. "It has only happened a few times before. Each time, it has taken longer to return to my starting point."

The wall Sevin had been feeling his way along abruptly ended. Reaching out, he searched for something to hang on to. Finding another wall at right angles, he forged onward. "We can't wait for some serendipitous magic to transport us. We'll have to get out on our own."

But after they'd wandered on for what felt like hours, but was surely far less, he had to admit defeat, for now anyway. The time for thoughts of escape was at an end until morning. For tonight, he needed to find a place off the main corridor, somewhere they could pass the night. A room or cul-de-sac that would afford a modicum of safety from interlopers, should there be any.

After only a dozen or so feet, the wall ended again, this time turning through a doorway. They were in a room now. The splashing sound of water was far louder here. His hand bumped something. A chair, no, it was bigger, ornate and polished. More like a throne. He pushed Luc down to sit on it. As he did so, he realized Luc still held his wine goblet, something he hadn't noticed before.

"Stay here. Don't move," Sevin told him. On his own, he began roaming the perimeter of the room, feeling his way. There were leather trunks stacked along the walls and statues standing taller than he. There were other pieces of furniture and statuary, many of them made of fine cloth or smooth stone.

A few more steps, and Sevin inadvertently kicked something that clanked noisily. Bending, he lifted and felt of it. An urn studded with stones, perhaps jewels. One that hummed with magic. Everything here did.

Luc's strained voice reached him. "Where are we?"

"A storage place of some sort, filled with what feels to my touch like ancient treasures. Every one of them made by Else-World hands and tainted with the magic of that world."

At the back wall of the room, Sevin discovered the source of the trickling sound. An enormous fountain of some kind stood there, bubbling fresh water that sprang from some unknown source into a series of small pools incorporated into it.

Who had brought all of this here and what it all meant must remain a mystery for the moment. Artifacts were his eldest brother's specialty, not his. When he and Luc found their way out of here, he'd send Bastian back to investigate. *If* they found their way out.

At this point, these treasures were less important than the room itself. It was surprisingly clean and well kept, its stone floor covered with rugs. The profusion of ElseWorld magic in these objects had apparently kept the chamber free of rodents, insects, dust, or mold. To find a haven of this quality in which to pass the night was a timely gift from the gods.

For all too soon, his and Luc's minds and bodies must become engaged in hedonistic pursuits to the exclusion of all else. Under the moon's thrall, they would forget themselves. They would become vulnerable.

"Luc?"

"Mmm."

"Unless you can get us back to the salon soon, we're going to have to spend the Calling night here."

Luc let out a harsh breath. "It's not something I can control. Believe me, if it were, do you think I'd have brought us here?" He sounded at the end of his rope.

Fuck. "Stay calm. I can bespell the perimeter, and we'll be relatively safe here. We'll make do with Shimmerskins, just like any other Calling night, so—. Wait, that's it. Damn, why didn't I think of it earlier? Their skin is luminescent. They can serve as living lamps to lead us out of here!"

Concentrating, Sevin gazed into the endless darkness and focused his mind in an attempt to conjure several of the insentient females. At his silent command, the air should have begun to vibrate. Mist should have spun and glimmered, then stilled, shapeshifting. Iridescent forms should have risen from the vapor and solidified into the females who had serviced the Satyr since ancient times.

But none of that happened.

And when it didn't, he was disoriented. The ability to bring forth Shimmerskins had been with him since he was eighteen and in the throes of his first Calling. To a Satyr male, losing this ability was akin to losing the ability to speak or to hear. "They're not coming," he said, trying to sound calmer than he felt. "You try."

"I *was* trying," said Luc. "Same result as yours. Nothing. Has this ever happened to you before?"

"No, but then I've never tried to bring them forth while in the depths of hell," Sevin snapped.

Luc sighed. "Nor I. I was seventeen when I was freed from these catacombs. Didn't yet have the power to conjure them."

Sevin ran a hand through his hair, his mind working to formulate a plan. Any plan. Roman catacombs were known to stretch for miles, with twists and turns that had never been mapped. Men had died in them, their skeletons simply swept into the enclosures with the bones of other long-dead men. Well, by the gods, he wasn't going to let his brother, who'd already suffered so direly in these very tombs, die here in them tonight!

Luc's voice came, stark in the silence. "Damn, I'm sorry, Sevin. I didn't mean to bring you here with me."

"There's no one I'd rather be lost with, brother. Don't worry. We'll get out of here. Even if I have to claw our way out with my bloody fingers."

They'd be dead by morning if he didn't. Judging by the changes he felt beginning in his body, they had only twenty minutes or so until the moon came. If the Satyr didn't mate with females from dusk to dawn on a Calling night, they did not survive. Simple fact.

"Let's go." Sevin found Luc again and pulled him by one arm back out into the corridor.

"I see something," Luc murmured almost immediately. "A light. There."

Since he couldn't see anything, Sevin had no idea in which way his brother was pointing. He plumbed the depths of the blackness around them in all directions. Then, to his right, he saw a winking glow in the distance.

"A shade from the ElseWorld hells?" Luc speculated with black humor.

Smugglers, more like, Sevin speculated silently. But whoever it was held their salvation in his grasp—a gas lamp. Determined not to spook their savior, he clapped a silencing hand over his brother's mouth and shoved him back into the room. Luc shrugged off this touch, but Sevin hardly noticed, for the gesture had become a familiar one since Luc had returned from these very bowels less than one year ago.

The pale vision rushed onward, moving toward them. The lantern swayed back and forth in its hand. Its golden light flickered wildly, alternately revealing the stone walls of the corridor and their visitor's long, flowing gown. A woman? What was a lone woman doing down here? And what was she running from?

His nostrils flared slightly. The Satyr had keen senses, and before he saw her face, Sevin recognized her by scent. It was none other than Alexa Patrizzi! Her pale hair was down and tousled as if she had just risen from sleep.

Alongside him, Luc snarled, recognizing her a split second later.

At the sound, she froze uncertainly. The arm holding the lantern jerked, banging against the cavern wall.

"No!" Sevin leaped for it, but before he could get his hands on it, it clattered to the stone floor, its precious light extinguished.

"Who's there?" Alexa demanded in frightened tones. Soft footsteps, a muffled thud. "Ow!"

"Be still. You'll hurt yourself. Wait till I can get the light on again," he told her.

"Lord Satyr?"

"Sevin," he confirmed as he knelt and searched by feel for the lamp. "How far are we from an exit? Can you lead us out of here?" He purposely failed to mention his brother's presence. No need to spook her even more.

"I don't know. I—" She paused uncertainly.

"You're lost?"

Silence.

"Did you just nod?" His hand touched warm glass and metal.

"Yes."

Damn. "What are you doing down here alone this time of night?" he demanded as he concentrated on relighting the lantern he'd found at last.

A telling silence. "I'm subject to nocturnal wanderings," she said at length. "Somnambulism."

"You sleepwalk?" She was lying. When they'd first seen her, she'd been fleeing something, or someone.

"You're the one trespassing," Alexa countered in that prissy way he now recognized as a shield she put up when she was uncertain or afraid.

"We came to be here accidentally. Not on foot but in an instant, through a burst of unexpected magic," Sevin told her.

"We?"

"My brother is here."

"Which one?" she asked cautiously.

"Luc. The youngest."

"Oh."

Silence thickened the blackness around them as Sevin worked at the lamp, twisting the mechanism to get it to catch. Coaxing it to light again was paramount at the moment, but as he worked at it his mind sorted through their possible options. Trying to figure out how to turn this crock-of-crap situation they were in into something resembling survival, he zeroed in on what was paramount and disregarded the rest.

Fact one: It was now too close to Moonful to search their way out of this place in time for what was coming, even with a lantern. He and Luc were stuck here for the duration.

Fact two: Their Satyr blood would soon rage out of control, their bodies undergoing physical changes that would call them to mate with a female. To ignore this call was to perish.

Fact three: For some reason, the gods had seen fit to send this particular female—his family's enemy—into his orbit tonight. Not once, but twice. And unless a miracle occurred that transported Luc and him from this pit in the next quarter hour, it was going to become necessary for them to mate her tonight. Until dawn.

The minute she'd admitted she didn't know how to get out of here, her fate had been sealed. If he were here alone, he might have chosen a different path. Given her a choice in things. Risked his own life by denying himself use of her if she refused him.

But because Luc was here, the choice was made. For all of them. He would not let his brother die. Not down here.

When the flame finally leaped again, he breathed an inward sigh of relief. The first thing he saw in its glow were Alexa's small, bare toes peeking from below the hem of a gauzy nightgown. As he rose, he held the lamp before him, lighting her shape from hem to a low neckline that revealed the shadowy hint of well-rounded curves.

His brows rose. This was the sort of gown one of his salon employees might select to please a client—lacy, translucent, provocative. Quite a contrast from the prim day dress she'd worn when they'd met earlier. This was what she wore to bed?

She folded her arms over her breasts. He moved the lamp higher still, and studied her features, pale and gaunt in the shadowy catacombs.

Annoyed, Alexa canted her head at him. "Looked your fill, have you?" she inquired in a falsely sweet tone.

Lord Sevin didn't reply, but instead stretched out his arm beyond her, holding the lamp high in an attempt to shed light down the corridor. Her eyes surreptitiously drank him in. Earlier today in the carriage, she hadn't noticed how very tall he was. And his shoulders—they were surely twice as wide as her own. With the lift of his arm, his linen shirt had drawn taut over his brawny chest and shoulders, and she felt the strong pull of his masculine attraction.

Forcibly shaking it off, she looked in the direction of his

gaze. In the distance she saw only more blackness. Though she would have much preferred to be fully dressed, it was fortunate she'd found him. He would offer protection if she were followed and accosted.

After going to bed early tonight, she'd awakened to the sound of intruders moving about her home. She'd heard voices—those of two particular men she'd prayed never to hear again. Having dismissed all the servants from employment due to a decided lack of funds several days ago, she'd been alone.

Certain that the interlopers had planned to make mischief, she'd sought escape. Coming downstairs, she'd slipped past them in the foyer and scurried for the closest door. Cornered in her mother's library, she'd made use of the secret entrance that led to these catacombs. Her mother had shown it to her only once, four months ago. It had been the last time she'd ever seen her mother and brother alive. The next day, Alexa had fled to Venice. And they'd been killed in a cave-in in these very catacombs the following week.

"What were you running from?" Sevin asked, moving the lamp to light her face.

"My past," she told him, with a glib sort of truth.

When he only stared at her, she added, "We're only ten minutes or so from the entrance I used. I was hoping to find another exit, but I think I can retrace my steps. Given a little time." She looked back the way she'd come, unsure.

Foolishly she'd dashed down here helter-skelter, coming some distance into the tunnels and taking random turns with no thought of how she'd get back again. Thinking she'd heard her uninvited guests behind her, her only concern had been escape. But now she wondered if perhaps the sounds she'd heard had only been the echo of her own movements, for she saw no sign of anyone coming this way.

Taking Alexa's lantern with him, Sevin went over to his brother. Her friend, Eva, always referred to him as Lucien. But in the carriage, she had learned that his brothers apparently called him Luc. In the golden lamplight, he appeared pale and beautiful like some dark-haired angel who'd accidentally ventured into hell.

Judging from his expression, he considered her the devil-in-residence. She'd never had anyone gaze at her with such hatred. It was there in his eyes, in the stiffness of his muscled body. A feeling of guilt and shame overwhelmed her for what he'd suffered at the hands of her family. Their blood flowed in her veins.

Lucien held the stem of an ornate wine goblet loosely in his long fingers. Going to him, Sevin took it and tilted it, surveying its contents, and then handing it back to his brother. "Drink," he commanded him. "But leave some for her."

For her? What did that mean? she wondered. "I'm not thirsty."

"I won't take her," Lucien bit out, drowning out her words. "Not *her*. Not here."

"You will. Do you want to die?"

Silence greeted his question.

"Luc, don't be stupid."

Alexa's breath tripped. Watching Sevin's broad back, remembrance slowly crept through her. "This is the night that you both . . . change." Her voice quavered on the last word, and her eyes dropped below his waist, to well-shaped hips and strong thighs encased in light wool. Realizing how unseemly her interrogation was, she quickly averted her eyes.

She scuttled a few steps backward, out of the ring of light.

Sevin glanced at her over his shoulder. Seeing that she was shrinking away, his eyes narrowed. He went to her, approaching her as a hunter does a skittish doe. In three long steps, he was at her side. He caught her upper arm in an unforgiving grip.

"Yes, it's the night we rut until sunrise," Luc's disembodied voice informed her bluntly and cruelly from the blackness where he stood beyond them. "And lucky us. Lost down here in this chamber of horrors—when who should appear but the last woman on this earth who I want to fuck." A stray flicker of light caught the glint of gold as he raised his goblet in a macabre sort of toast in her general direction, and then tossed back some of its contents.

"Shut up, brother." Sevin knew his brother's blood was running high. So was his own. Already he felt the faint cramping in his loins, felt his skin prickle along his thighs. A light down of hair would soon cover his haunches and extend lower along his legs. An outward indication of the insatiable beast he would become. The beast that would mate this woman.

No! She's human. Like Clara, a voice raged inside him.

He didn't want to harm her—to change her in any irreparable way. But maybe it would be different now, he reasoned desperately. He'd been young when he was with Clara, both of them had been. Among her kind, fornication had not been forbidden to those who were unwed. And marriage came about at an early age—she'd had a younger sister who was already engaged.

He'd come into her tribe at fifteen and turned eighteen only weeks before he'd left it. With that last birthday had come his first Calling. Because she had loved him, Clara had gone along with his depravity on that night. And in the nights that ensued, she'd accepted his casual inclusion of additional partners in their liaisons. Had claimed to understand his fierce need to test the boundaries of his sexuality, to explore every carnal pleasure available to them.

In those lost years, he'd been without his family. Absent their guidance—a guidance every Satyr male required at this juncture in life—he'd been reckless, too careless and unworldly to recognize that Clara had only pretended to accept his ways.

But all had been made horribly clear to him in the note she'd written before ending her own life. Reeling from her death and his part in it, he'd left her tribe immediately after her burial. He'd gone back to Rome to find that Bastian and Dane had returned during his three-year absence. Luc, however, had remained missing for another decade.

If Sevin followed through with his plans, Alexa would be forever bonded to him tonight. And he would in turn become responsible for her. This was an irrevocable repercussion of mating himself to a human.

After Clara, he'd sworn never again. He hadn't taken a second look at a human female for over a decade. Yet here he was, faced with an impossible choice. Let his brother die. Or mate them both to the reluctant woman in his hold. It was a choice, yet there was no choice at all.

He looked into her soft gray eyes, read her fear. He hardened himself against any sympathy for her. Luc had only recently returned to them from the very hell in which they now stood. A hell of her family's making. His brother had only just begun to learn what it was to live again.

Sevin would not let him die. No! Tonight boiled down to a single, crucial goal—keeping Luc alive. No matter what he had to do.

4

"Come. Both of you." At Sevin's steely command, Alexa stiffened, pulling at his hold on her. "No! Why?" she protested. Luc only glowered at him, unmoving.

Holding the lantern in one hand, Sevin kept a firm grip on her upper arm with his other. Though she struggled, he hardly seemed to notice as he led her through a portal in the wall. Once they passed through it, he released her. Too late, she could see he hadn't simply led her down another tunnel. They were in a room. A trap.

In here, the prospect Lucien had so crudely laid before her moments ago began to seem all too possible. She'd always been so curious about the Satyr. Had wondered how it might be to lie with one of them. But none of her daydreams had ever unfolded quite like this! What sort of beasts would they become tonight? What did they plan to do to her . . . exactly?

This unknown was sufficient to make her blood pound in her ears. Her eyes flew to the door. She took a step toward it, but at the same time Lucien stepped forward from the corridor, blocking it with his body. So instead, she slipped out of the pool of light again. With her back to the wall, she felt only marginally safer there shrouded in darkness.

Leaving his brother as de facto guard, Sevin set the lantern on a shelf so it bathed much of the room in its glow. By its light Alexa could see that there were treasures stacked here and there. They had the look of ancient things, yet their gold shone as if recently polished.

"What is this place? And these riches?" she asked, half hoping the question might distract Lucien so that she might escape.

Sevin glanced at her over his shoulder. "You don't know?"

She shook her head. "I've never been down this far."

Lucien snorted in disbelief. He took another swig from his goblet. Whatever was inside it was not improving his humor. He didn't want her here. If she tried to get past him, would he let her? She began sidling around the edge of the room, still hanging back under the cover of shadow.

Meanwhile, Sevin commenced arranging things to his satisfaction. Opening several trunks he pulled out various fabrics, none of them as dusty as they should've been if they'd been in storage down here for some time. Tossing them down to the stone floor he unfolded them to cover the entirety of a vacant area along the wall. Then he knelt and quickly created what looked to be a makeshift pallet. A bed.

Alexa began to panic in earnest. "What about the sycophants, the ones Eva told me of whose skin shimmers?" she asked desperately. "Can't you bring them—"

"Shimmerskins, you mean. We're unable to call them forth down here." Sevin gestured generally toward the walls. "Something about this rock or perhaps the depth we find ourselves in. I don't know. So, you see, we will need you."

"I won't," Lucien grumbled.

"You'll do as I say," Sevin growled, cutting him off. "Even if I have to force you. Both of you."

At that, Alexa made a wild break for the door. Unexpectedly, Lucien locked a linen-sleeved arm across the opening, blocking her exit. She pushed, but it was as unyielding as an iron bar. "Let me out," she hissed urgently, her voice lowered so only he would hear. "Don't you want to be rid of me?"

Lucien twisted her around, catching her silk-covered arms painfully high behind her back. "I'd like nothing better than to let you get yourself lost in these catacombs," he growled at her ear. "But my brother will need you soon."

"That's enough, Luc," Sevin warned.

"It will be interesting to see how you like captivity, now that the shoe's on the other foot," Lucien taunted at her ear.

And then she was free. Whirling around, she backed away from him, her eyes wide. Gazing into her face, something changed in his expression. Was that a hint of concern seeping into the vehement dislike she read there? Surely she must be mistaken.

He took a step toward her, but she leaped away with a tiny squeak. "Have you f—been with a man?" Lucien asked her, suddenly seeming less bent on scaring her to death.

Alexa knew what he was asking. But the fact that he felt at liberty to ask at all made all of this seem far, far too real. She slunk back into the shadows. Yes, she'd lain with a man, though the word Lucien had almost uttered more accurately described what had transpired in Venice. It had been only once. And it had been a cruel disappointment.

"Answer him," Sevin asked from somewhere behind her. "It will matter." She saw that he'd found some glass bottles, the colorful ones made in the north from the look of them. And for some reason he'd set them within easy reach of the bed he'd made. She pressed back into the corner again, wedging herself between some sort of throne and a collection of urns.

When she remained mute, he stood and went to an enormous golden fountain, washing his hands and face in its pool. Turning then, he planted one hand at his hip and sent her a level gaze. His white linen shirt gleamed in the dim light. Knowing he couldn't see her in her hiding place, she nevertheless shook her head as if that alone would keep him at bay.

"Come now, I know we are not an anathema to you. You were engaged to Dane at one point. Before he married Eva."

"That was my mother's doing," she said. "He and I hardly said three words to one another during our engagement, which lasted all of three minutes. He was handsome. I was far too young and stupidly infatuated with the idea of marriage. I'm older now and wiser."

"It was only four months ago!"

She laughed bitterly. "I've done a lot of growing up in the interim, I assure you."

He frowned, beckoning to her. "Come out of that corner, damn it."

But she only pressed back harder against the wall behind her. "No. Let's try to find our way out," she pleaded. "Now. We have hours before the lamplight burns away."

In a half dozen easy steps, Sevin was standing before her. "It's too late." He reached for her, but she ducked away. He stalked her, and easily cut her off when she tried to dart past again. And all the while Lucien only watched, as one predator watches another toy with its prey. At least that was how it seemed to her at the moment, with Venice fresh on her mind.

Sevin caught her in a corner. Bracing his hands on perpendicular walls to either side of her, his arms served as prison gates that entrapped her as he leaned closer and murmured in her ear. "Like me, maybe you didn't want this to happen between us in this way. Or under these circumstances. But I felt the desire in your kiss this afternoon in your carriage. The Satyr have a talent for reading what women want."

She averted her face. "Then you must know I don't want this."

He tilted her chin higher, brushed his lips over hers, coaxing.

"I'm afraid that's not an option. What happens between us tonight won't be a hardship, I promise you. There will be only pleasure. Fifty fulfillments, remember?"

Alexa gazed into those unfathomable silver eyes. The instinct to flee battled with the sudden strong spurt of forbidden attraction and feminine curiosity that his promise had inspired. Did she dare? No. She couldn't truly consider going along with his plans. Even if, ever since she'd first seen him and his brothers, she'd wondered how it might be to find herself the sole object of their passion. Even if, after her brief time in the carriage with him today, she'd dwelled upon his countenance, his heart, his nature, for the rest of the night. Had wondered how it might feel to be covered and dominated by a man such as he. To be the focus of his legendary lust.

Heretofore, such considerations had always been relegated to her unspoken daydreams. They weren't something she'd expected could ever really happen. Not to her, anyway. She didn't know Eva's brothers-in-law—not even Dane—except in passing. And in her fantasies she'd never pictured that there would be *two* of them with her in a setting such as this.

Still, she knew that Eva had certainly mated with her husband, even during nights when the moon was full. And not only had she lived through it, she appeared happier for the doing of it. Her face lit with pleasure whenever she spoke of Dane.

Sevin was silent as she debated the matter he'd put before her, turning it over and over in her mind until she thought she might faint. She was not meant to lead a passionless life. Nor to align herself with a docile man. Something in her yearned for a fierce sort of loving. But where did the cruelty of Venice end and the heady sort of passion she craved begin? And which might she find with this man? Or was it possible she would find something in between?

"I have some experience at this," Alexa admitted to him at

last, obliquely answering his brother's earlier question. She could see she'd surprised him. "But not enough for what you're asking," she added.

He brushed a lock of her blond hair behind her ear and studied her face. "I can make it so that you won't remember anything of what happens here when you wake tomorrow. Is that what you want?"

When she didn't reply, he slowly straightened and caught her face in his hands. His eyes held hers as the pads of his thumbs gently brushed over her cold cheeks. Instantly, she felt a strange sort of calm come over her. Her shoulders relaxed, and her body sagged bonelessly into his. She heard the drugged quality of her voice when she spoke again. "What are you doing to me?"

His hand slipped around her nape under her hair, stroking the tendons there. "Making you forget."

Forget? Against his chest, Alexa's brow knit. Tonight she could know pleasure. Fifty fulfillments, he'd said. Enough to last a lifetime. She had little doubt that he could provide them and make each one as perfect as the one before. If she was doomed to toss and turn in her lonely bed and live a respectable life for the remainder of her years, perhaps . . .

With the last vestige of her will, she put her hands on his chest and pushed, her gaze lifting to his.

"I don't want to forget," she whispered.

Sevin's blood heated. The woman in his arms had just given him permission to do as he planned.

"What I do want is your promise that you'll do nothing that will bring physical harm to me," she added.

"Agreed," he said slowly.

Her eyes flicked beyond him to his younger brother, where he still stood in the doorway.

"I speak for Luc as well," Sevin assured her. "We're made in such a way that our carnal efforts with you will not only bring you pleasure, but they will also ease any physical discomforts as matters progress. With each fulfillment, your desire to hunt the next will only increase, and your wish to continue on will be replenished."

Her brows rose, doubting him.

He put his hands on her shoulders, ran them down her arms to her elbows and higher again, gentling her to his touch. "Don't worry. I—we—know what we're about in all this. Just relax and . . . enjoy."

What he promised her was true, Sevin knew. Yet it was also true that he *would* bring about a change in her, though it would not be a real harm in the way she meant. He would act first with her tonight, before Luc. It was a crucial distinction, for it meant he was the one with whom she would become forever linked.

After this night, her body would crave his. She would suffer his loss in her bed, pine for want of him. But perhaps this would be a fitting punishment if she turned out to be as guilty as her family in their acts against his. By morning, he would know.

"And further, you will agree that in return for . . . what we do here tonight . . . you will cease harassing me," Alexa went on. "No more asking me to leave Rome."

"Done. Now—let us seal our bargain." He sleeked his hands underneath the fall of her long pale hair, slowly moving them over her back. At the feel of her cool silken gown gliding over her shape under his hands, sudden need slammed through him. He lowered his head, his mouth finding hers. After a brief hesitation, she put her arms around him. His head angled and he kissed her more deeply. This kiss, like those in her carriage, heightened his desire to mate her, but they told him nothing about the matter of her guilt.

That knowledge would come later.

Across the room, Luc had remained stubbornly silent throughout their negotiations, as if they had nothing to do with him. But there was already fever rising in Sevin's own blood, a blood that linked all four of the brothers. In spite of Luc's diffidence, his need had to be rising, too.

Although they couldn't see it down here belowground, Sevin could feel the moon coming. The steady thud of his heartbeat was stronger now and faster; the touch of Alexa's hands on him more keenly felt. Soon all would begin. And then, this female he held would present a temptation his brother would not be able to refuse, no matter how he fought it.

The same applied to him.

Lifting his head, Sevin gestured to Luc, indicating that he was to come closer. "Let her drink from your goblet," he said. With obvious reluctance, Luc did as asked. His face had a drawn look about it and there was a white line around his lips as if he were in pain. But it was a pleasurable pain that Sevin recognized—one he was feeling as well as their Calling drew ever nearer.

Keeping one arm around Alexa, Sevin murmured to Luc in the ElseWorld language. "It's almost my time."

Luc nodded. "Mine as well."

"Swear to me that you will lie with her tonight. That you won't run."

Luc looked away.

With a grimace of impatience, Sevin gripped his brother's arm and jerked him closer so they looked each other in the eye. "Swear to me as I ask, Luc. Now, on the blood of the ancients. If you will not—if you refuse the Calling against your own nature—I swear to *you* that I will as well. I'll send this woman to find her way home with her lamp, alone and untouched. And you and I will die here together in darkness."

Luc shook off his hold. "Will you be able to tell the extent of her involvement with the Bona Dea? After you've mated her?" he hedged with quiet anger.

"I believe so."

A long moment passed. And then, with a barely perceptible nod and softly sworn promise, Luc moved away to lean against the opposite wall, shrouding himself in shadow once more.

Alexa lifted her lashes, feeling pleasantly drugged from Sevin's kisses. Lucien had drawn near to them. The brothers were exchanging low, urgent words she didn't understand, spoken in some inscrutable language. It was reminiscent of an Italian dialect found only in the hill country, only more archaic and dark.

She watched as Sevin took the goblet from his brother and tilted it to her lips. "Drink," he told her. "It will make you want what is to come."

As Lucien left them, she hesitated, staring at the ruby liquid swirling like blood in the bottom of the goblet. She felt a strange sensation, as if Sevin's mind were pushing at hers.

Trust me. All will be well.

As if with a will of their own, her hands lifted, taking charge of the goblet and tilting it higher. She felt Lucien move away as she took one sip, then another—and still more, at Sevin's urging.

How very easily it slid down her throat, warming her, soothing away her every misgiving. It surged through her system, sending with it a blast of euphoria. She drank again, finishing it. The prurient desire in her strengthened, her flesh prickling.

Her fingers relaxed and the goblet fell from them to the cool stone at their feet.

With a flick of his hand, Sevin erected a barricade around the perimeter of the room, his magic rendering them secure here. Although air would continue to circulate, no one and nothing could come or go from this chamber now, except the three of them. They would be safe here until dawn.

Gently, he tugged Alexa from the corner into the pool of soft light. Turning her to face in the direction his brother had fled, he stood before her slightly to one side so that Luc would see her as well. Gaslight limned her in gold, casting shadows of dark bronze beneath her full breasts and along the press of her thighs through her gown. She had no idea how the sight of her like this affected him, how much he wanted to begin. But, no, they must wait for the moon, only minutes away.

For now, he would only tease her, a dangerous game that would test his restraint and that of his brother. He felt her watching him as his fingers traced the neckline of her bodice. Knew Luc watched her, too, since the lamp would reveal her to them both.

Dipping in the dusky hollow between her breasts, he opened the tie of her gown and carefully widened its bodice as if unwrapping a fine gift. She pressed a hand there, clutching the tie, clinging to her modesty by a thread.

He drew her hand upward and kissed its palm. *Let me,* his mind whispered to her.

When he let her go, her arm fell unresisting to her side. The gape at the front of her gown widened, until he brushed it from her shoulders. It drifted lower, then caught and clung at her elbows, forming a sort of skirt that draped her only from waist to floor.

The back of his fingers slid upward from her ribs to brush the undersides of pale, unclothed breasts, then rounded higher to gently catch and twist peach-colored nubs. She drew in a sharp breath, but didn't try to stop him again. Cupping the weight of her breasts in his palms, he rubbed his thumbs over her nipples, drawing on them in a way that made her moan.

At the sound, a low growl rumbled in his chest and his cock surged, wanting her.

He felt Luc's avid gaze, knew he was fighting his need to watch.

"She is beautiful, is she not, brother?"

Silence.

The woman in his arms caught his wrists and gazed at him through her lashes. "What will happen? How will things un-fold between us?" she murmured. Her gaze slipped past him to Luc. "All of us."

Sevin stroked his hand over her hair, enjoying its cool silk. "I will lie with you first," he told her. And then she would take his brother.

Matters had progressed in this way with every Shimmerskin or fleshly female they had shared between them under a full moon since Luc had been released from the catacombs. Because of the time his brother had spent in captivity, he could not be left alone on nights such as this when their blood called them to mate.

If they did not bed the same woman—sometimes the same women—Luc could not be trusted to fulfill the cravings of his own body. So Sevin had made sure to be there with him on each Calling night that had come and gone. He'd made sure that Luc did what was needed to sustain his life. This night would be no different, in that regard at least.

Suddenly, a hard shudder racked his entire body as a sensa-tion that was equal parts pleasure and pain bolted through him without warning. A ragged groan erupted from a place soul-deep inside him.

It was a cry echoed by Luc across the room. Somewhere outside, in the sky beyond the catacombs, the moon was within seconds of showing itself. The Change was coming. Soon all would begin.

Sevin wrenched open the buttons of his shirt. He heard Alexa's gasp as he crushed her to him, one hand on her back and one on her bottom. He relished the feel of her silken flesh against his naked chest. Of her soft woman's body conforming to his harder one.

He bent his head. Their lips touched; his parted hers. Their breath became one breath, their tongues slid together. The elixir that was blended from the grapes of two worlds was clean and sweet in their mouths. His hand drove into her hair, holding her as he kissed her as deeply as he'd wanted to hours before, in the carriage.

Would she prove to be as guilty as her family? His talent would reveal the truth, eventually. But for now, with the moon coming, he cared only that her skin tasted like heaven, her mouth like peppermints and wine.

Somewhere outside this ghoulish place, the full moon chose that very heartbeat of time to emerge from the horizon and observe the world with its brilliant unblinking eye. With the coming of its light, cramps seized him, turning his muscles to stone.

Somehow managing to keep a precarious hold on his wits, he held her fast with an iron-hard arm clamped around her. Moving his body at an angle to hers, he ripped at the fastenings of his trousers with one hand. A sublime and terrible agony struck him as the Change began. A harsh, inarticulate shout was wrung from him. It was the same cry his ancestors had given upon the commencement of every Moonful that had come their way over centuries past.

His abdomen knotted granite hard, then he felt the familiar knife-sharp twist. His face contorted into a mask of both anguish and joy.

Distantly he heard Alexa's soft confusion. "Lord Sevin? What's wrong? What's happening?"

He bit off a snarl, unable to form the words to explain. The snare of his arm around her tightened, some ancient instinct within reminding him it was paramount that he keep her—his mate—with him until this turmoil ceased. Until he was changed. Ready.

Her muffled protest seemed too remote to heed as he fought to stay on his feet. For now he could only endure, as the last physical change of the Calling night occurred in him.

This was a dangerous time for men of his kind. In these peculiar moments of weakness, their females could escape them or their enemies could do them harm. But from weakness, a new strength would be born. One that would sustain him through the long lusty hours that lay ahead.

At length, all was done. He straightened again. When his arm relaxed around her, Alexa breathed deeply, audibly pulling air into starved lungs. Only then did Sevin realize he'd had a stranglehold on her ribs.

He enfolded her in his arms more gently now and swept her hair aside, displaying the small inked flower she bore there on the side of her throat. At the sight of it, his heart stopped and then raced on, pounding in his ears.

Your beloved. You will know her by the iris.

This was the flower their wine god had favored. An aphrodisiac to males of his kind, it had been used in Calling rituals throughout the centuries. He bent her back over his arm, one palm cradling her head. His mouth found her skin, pressed itself hotly to the floral design, marking her there as his.

At length his gaze lifted. Beyond her, he met his brother's eyes across the room, saw them glitter through the darkness like those of a leopard in the night jungle. They were both changed now. Freakish creatures of the kind that might fuel a human's erotic nightmares. Bizarre anomalies, that in this century, dwellers in this world had brushed off as myth. Until recent months, when they'd found out otherwise.

"You're different," Alexa whispered, skimming a hand along his thigh. He took her curious fingers and drew them to his hardness, naked in the gape of his trousers. He needed to feel her touch there. Wanted her to acknowledge the changes in him. Wanted to watch her face as she stroked him.

Using her hands as if they were his own, Sevin touched himself, drawing her fists under his, upward along twin lengths from root to crown. The coming of the moon had wrought this change in him. Had gifted him with an additional phallus ripped from his own flesh. It strained from him, rooted only an inch or so above the traditional one branching from the dark thatch at his groin.

After a single ejaculation, this new, second shaft would be gone again, only to reappear a month from now in accordance with the visit of the next full moon.

His passions were on a tenuous leash, his body fully prepared now for all to begin. Both erections twitched under this woman's touch, hungry for a more intimate taste of her. Aching for the soft, slick haven her body could provide.

5

So the rumors were true! Alexa had seen the depictions of the Satyr in the museums, and had suspected as much, of course. But to see this for herself. To touch him like this. She gazed at the columns of hard masculine flesh under her stroking hands, mesmerized. It hardly seemed possible that a man—even one from another world—could change in such a way!

Sevin's linen shirt hung open, and the lantern flickered its golden light across the sleek, well-formed contours of his broad chest. She let her long hair fall forward to curtain her face from him as she studied the phalluses that jutted upward from his pelvis and groin, one set just above the other. They were barbaric in size and strength with blood-rich veins roping their lengths, and their fat, smooth crowns flushed a dusky red.

He helped her to stroke them, and she knew he was mimicking the way he wanted to move them inside her. They were hot and vibrant under her hands, heavy with erotic intent, iron encased in sleek velvet. When he taught her fingers what he liked, she felt his body quicken, saw the muscles of his belly go taut and corded.

Her pulse fluttered at the hollow of her throat and she swallowed a tremor of fear. Her single personal experience of carnal matters had been so painful and disappointing. She prayed this would be different.

"Don't hurt me." Though her demand came as a whisper, he heard it.

His hands left hers and he pulled her into the cave of his chest, his touch surprisingly gentle as he surrounded her with his body and scent. "I won't. I swear it," he promised. It was a low masculine growl, and one she somehow sensed she could trust. She nodded slowly, accepting his word. Her arms encircled him, her fingers tucking just inside the back of his loosened trousers.

"Luc." His head lifted toward his brother and he jerked his chin toward the pallet he'd made across the room. "I came across some bottles in a cabinet. Unguents and oils set out there on the blankets. Find something and bring it to me." Lifting her by the waist, Sevin crowded her backward a few steps until she came up against some leather-bound trunks along the wall. Stacked one atop another and two deep from the wall, they rose only as high as her waist.

In seconds, Lucien was beside them. As he handed something to his brother, his eyes flickered over her. Male hunger came and went in them, so fleeting she wasn't sure she'd truly seen it. Then he was gone again.

She heard the clink of glass as Sevin pulled the stopper from the decorative bottle he held now and poured something viscous from it into his palm. Tossing the bottle aside, his other hand ruched up the front of her gown—it barely clung to her now and sagged from her waist to the floor, secured to her only by the crook of her bent arms.

Beneath its skirt, his fingers found the apex of her thighs, threaded through the soft, feminine bristle there. A strangled moan escaped her as they pushed between her legs, palming and stroking her most private flesh.

Alexa clutched the chiseled muscles of his upper arms, needing an anchor as so many delicious, wondrous sensations assaulted her at once. His clean breath mingling with her own. A thumb oiling her clit. A tongue sliding along hers. Long fingers stroking the pink folds of her flesh with slow, easy, rhythmic movements. His kiss. Deep inside, her core began to melt for him, readying her with a natural feminine slickness meant to ease his way in the performance that lay ahead.

She wilted against the trunks at her back, the heels of her hands lifting to clutch the edge of the uppermost of them. Her head lolled back and her entire body swayed under his every voluptuous stroke. *Mmm.*

When his touch left her momentarily, it was to briskly smear the remainder of the oil on his erections. He was so close that she could feel the push-pull of his hands, the occasional nudge of knuckles at her belly. She heard the smacking sounds, and smelled the spicy scent of the oil as he worked himself.

His hands rose and cupped her breasts in an arousing, voluptuous massage. His mouth captured a peak and dragged on it in a sweet, sensual pull that had her moaning. Their eyes met and clung. Sevin brushed her lips with his a final time, and spoke to her in his language—a low sound of carnal intent.

Then he lifted her slightly and turned her to face the wall. She bowed forward over the uppermost trunk and the length of her hair slid smoothly across one shoulder to drape her forearms where they rested atop it. A small corner of her mind was aware that his brother watched them from the shadows, and the scandalous notion that they were not alone in this beat a terrible, forbidden excitement through her.

Behind her, she heard the rustle of Sevin's clothing, felt his trousers shoved low. All seemed so surreal here in this dark, cool room bathed in golden light. She could hardly credit that she was here with this man, a virtual stranger. That this was actually going to happen between them. That it wasn't simply an erotic dream. Why did it all feel so easy, so right?

The back of her gown lifted. Strong, furred thighs forced hers wider. She sensed the barely leashed urgency in him now, and matters proceeded with haste. Hands came, each fisted over a phallus. Plump, smooth crests nestled in place, one at the heart of her feminine folds, the other finding the divide of her bottom.

She drew herself up, stilling like a doe under threat from a predator.

Then came the sharp bite of a dual penetration. Her eyes went fixed and her hands fisted on the trunk. She gasped as she felt flesh give way to the masculine pressure. His groan of pleasure tangled with her sharp cry as the oiled heads of his erections breached her. Inside her, they were smooth, immense, slick, and scalding hot. She rose on her toes to ease the sensation, but he was already plumbing deeper.

A broad hand settled at the bone of her hip and tightened reflexively, sending an erotic thrill over her skin to throb at her feminine core. His other hand came around her, fingers bunching in the fabric of her gown at her belly to hold her ready for his lovemaking.

Her eyes stared unseeingly at the trunk upon which she rested, and she drew careful, shallow, silent breaths. Every fiber of her being was focused now on their connection, on his slick, ceaseless ingress. As his masculine flesh steadily advanced, so her feminine flesh succumbed. She wanted to urge him on, and yet at the same time, wanted to push him away.

In her many daydreams, she could never have imagined the incredible sensation of having this powerful man mating himself to her in this animalistic way. When uncertainty gripped her, and she was sure she could take no more, he seemed to sense it and he would slow himself. His lips would brush her nape, telling her how much her flesh pleased him, how good it felt to be inside her, coaxing her to relax for him, take more of him.

Finally, eventually, ultimately he slid home. He bent low, a guttural pagan groan of pure ecstasy escaping him. She cried out, her spine curling under him.

She was full, so impossibly full. It seemed impossible, incredible that he could be so deeply buried inside her. But she felt the truth of it in the hardness that stretched her tender openings, in the soft scratch of his groin against the delicate skin of her bottom, in the powerfully muscled thighs that pressed hers wide.

A strange sort of pride welled up in her—that of a female who has managed to provide succor to her mate. Amazingly, she felt no pain, only a thrilling anticipation. It was as if her flesh had been specifically designed to glove this particular man in this intimate, precious way. Surely, they must have been created by some greater hand to fit so perfectly together.

Arms surrounded her and Sevin enfolded her into his embrace as they half lay on the trunk. His broad palm took the weight of a feminine breast, squeezing sensuously and drawing its peak outward in a way that made her moan. In reaction, her tissues convulsed on his phalluses of their own accord.

His mouth found the side of her neck just below her ear. His voice came, strained and hot on her skin. "Gods, Alexa. If you keep that up . . ." He drew a shuddering breath, then his hips withdrew slightly and he commenced a slow, measured push-pull.

He braced himself wider, so her thighs draped his now. His fists slammed upon the trunk on either side of her, his fingers clenched tight. Yet still, his thrusts were tense, measured. "I promised to go easy with you," he muttered, as if trying to remind himself of this fact.

"I don't care," she whispered, shaking her head. "I just need . . . I want . . . more . . . oh, please."

"Yes. Gods, yes." He fucked her hard then, his body hunting its pleasure in hers in earnest. She could feel his crowns moving inside her, rubbing her in just the right way. Hot hands smoothed upward along the long muscles of her back, from her hips and over her ribs, then back again. They clenched on the globes of her bottom, held her hip bones.

She fit herself to his rocking rhythm, bowing for him when his inward push lifted her slightly, and arching when he suctioned away. The stark slap of their flesh was loud, their sharp cries and soft moans echoing in the quiet, a lecherous, seductive sound. He fucked her fiercely now, grunting his enjoyment and murmuring small encouragements. Telling her how well he liked the stroke of her flesh, how good it was, how soft, how wet, how slick.

His words slipped in and out of that other language she didn't comprehend as he seemed to lose himself in her and in this carnal dance they did. Her eyes fluttered open and she gazed at his shadow on the wall before her. It loomed large, his shoulders so wide and his frame so massive that she could see nothing of her own shadow. It seemed that he had overtaken her, dominated her, so that it was impossible to tell where one of them began and the other ended. She was one with him, connected in a way she'd never felt connected to another being.

He covered her back, his forearms braced on either side of her so that Alexa was forced to bend lower under him. She rested her forehead on her fists. Damp tendrils of hair framed her flushed face. Her eyes were closed, her mouth gasping. The leather-bound trunk grazed her soft skin, dragged lightly and thrillingly at her nipples as her breasts shuddered with each powerful buck of her lover's hips.

The passionate friction licked sensation at her nerve endings, curling, coiling, amplifying. She churned with it. Burned with it. Hurtling toward a fulfillment she'd never experienced, yet had yearned for—and already felt within her reach. She tilted her hips for him, panted, bowed, and arched. Begged, pleaded.

Reached for that wondrous feeling that was, as yet, just ... out ... of ... reach. ...

Across the room, Luc stood in shadow, watching them. Tension clenched his every muscle. His skin felt too tight, his blood's pump too hot.

With the moon's coming, his body had changed in the same way as his brother's. Like all the Satyr tonight, his carnal need was all encompassing, a taut blend of pleasure and pain. He would sicken soon, if he did not take this woman after Sevin had mated her. His gaze narrowed on her, revolted by the thought of fucking a Patrizzi.

But, gods, he was hurting, and dying to do just that. He'd loosened the fastenings of his trousers earlier, rather than find himself strangled within them when the Change occurred. And he'd brought one of the bottles of oil for himself when he'd fetched Sevin's. Now he opened it and spilled oil into his cupped palm. Then, with a hard toss, he sent it into a corner where it cracked on the stone floor, but did not shatter. The couple across the room took no notice.

His spine hit the wall behind him, and he took himself in his own oiled hands. His head fell back as he began long, slow, dual upward tugs. In the wake of his fists, labyrinths of purpled veins sprouted along his lengths. *Ahhh, gods.*

At the top of his strokes, the O of his fists met the jutted rims at the plinths of his crowns. He heard his brother's low growl; heard the Patrizzi woman's thready moans as he whispered to her in the ancient language.

His pricks surged and he groaned. How much more must he stand? How horribly ironic it was that he must change in this way once a month—that his body must be driven to crave for-nication—when all he wanted was to be left alone! To feel nothing.

His grips angled so the knuckles of his forefingers massaged the sensitive notches at the undersides of both crowns. Round-ing the plump heads, his thumbs found and smeared twin pearls of pre-cum in identical slits.

A hard shudder took him.

Slowly and with experienced hands, he set a familiar, arous-ing pump, masturbating himself. *Why could this not be enough?*

Why must the blood of his ancestors sing in his veins and call to him, demanding more? Why must it bid him to ignore his phobia of having another being touch him skin on skin, in order that he take a female under him and engage her in pas-sionate pursuits throughout this long, treacherous night?

In the distance, Sevin's voice turned rough, urgent. During passionate engagements, he and his brothers were all linked, causing him to share an echo of Sevin's pleasure.

Luc's erections strained, the knotted veins now standing from them in such stark relief that he could feel the difference under his hands. Even from across the room, he could sense his brother's desperate wanting of the woman he held. This was more than just fucking. Sevin *cared* for her. Why? She was no better than any other. Worse than most, by his estimation.

Luc gritted his teeth against the terrible lust that now racked his body. He would not be able to find relief by the use of his own hands no matter how he worked at it. Only the cradle of a woman would offer the sort of sensual oblivion that would keep him sane on a night such as this.

His eyes opened and found his brother's partner. The lamp-light burnished her pale hair to gold and glistened on her sleek, undulating back. Sevin was right. He would need her.

At least she didn't have the look of her brother, Gaetano. His torturer. At the thought of him a tremor of dread shook

Luc. His jaw hardened against it. No, he must not think of that now. Not here, of all places. That bastard was dead. He'd seen to that himself, using his talent to kill him on the same day his brothers had rescued him from these very tunnels.

Now he only needed to forget. To lose himself in this night. In a woman.

He smiled faintly, as a thought occurred. Gaetano would surely have hated the very idea of his former captive, Lord Lucien Satyr, fucking his pristine sister. Perhaps that in itself was reason enough to force himself to mate Alexa Patrizzi when Sevin was done.

Sevin's slitted gaze watched Alexa's smooth back, mesmerized by its sensuous bow and arch as she took him into her and then gave him up and then took him yet again. She stood between his legs, half lying upon the stack of trunks before them, her pale hair a silken swath in the darkness.

Her breathy moans rode the air, mingling with his low carnal groans. He murmured to her, dark sex words. Words his ancestors had whispered to their mates on nights such as these throughout centuries past. He wanted to come inside her, to feel her take his spend, to feel her cream for him, pulse for him.

His thighs went outside hers, pinning her even tighter for his push. She took him like two hot, slick fists, again and again. His white-knuckled hands gripped the sides of the leather trunk. The stack of them lurched against the wall under each of his powerful thrusts. Her gossamer gown was bunched high at the small of her back, its sleeves still precariously looped at her elbows. The perfect white globes of her bottom shuddered as he ground his flesh into hers like the aggressive, rutting animal he'd become.

She was panting now, emitting tiny whimpers each time he fucked her, urging him on with her dulcet moans and ecstatic cries. She was tight, buttery-slick, and hot. So fucking hot.

All thought had flown from his mind. There was nothing but this. The two of them together. Him holding her. Fucking her. Raw need spiraled in him, ever higher and darker. Harsh breath sawed in his lungs. His balls drew up painfully tight. He felt himself losing control. Felt himself hurtling toward the most monumental ejaculation of his life.

Alexa shrieked at the suddenness of her own climax, her body curling and going stiff under its force. Her tissues milked at him—enticing his cum, promising him ecstasy.

His hands flexed on her hips, and he groaned hoarsely, a low animal sound that was a harbinger of his finish. Then he drove himself deep, so impossibly deep in her. One . . . last . . . time. His teeth bared and the tendons in his neck went stark as every muscle in his body seized.

Then a triumphant, strangled shout tore from his throat as he found his release at last, at last. She cried out again under the force of it, and her nether flesh clenched on his cocks with a renewed, delicate strength. He came again, yet again, deep inside her, in hot rhythmic spurts that went on and on. . . .

Ahh, gods.

He reached for her and pulled her to stand with him, cradling her body to his. Crossing his arms over her, he crushed her breasts in his hands and twisted their sensitive peaks. She arched and covered his hands, moaning with pleasure. They stood there together, arching under each successive pulse of their flesh.

Then he pressed his mouth to the iris inked on her throat. Marking her. Binding her to him. Binding himself to her in the most elemental way possible.

She was his now.

And he, hers.

Alexa drew a sharp breath as yet another echo of the orgasm she'd just experienced shuddered through her. She felt Sevin's phallus pulse inside her in response. His body was warm at her back, his spill slick inside her. She sighed, replete, her body and mind more relaxed than she could ever recall.

He held her close now in the humid aftermath of passion, their breath still heaving as one. She'd felt his pelvic cock retract inside him earlier, once it had finished. But the cock rooted at his groin still filled her, lodged heavy and thick within the snug harbor of her vaginal walls.

It had all been so different, so wonderfully different than that horrible experience in Venice. Yet Sevin had been right in what he'd said before. Her desire for him—for more of this—hadn't waned. Already, she wanted him again. Wanted the ecstasy again. It was addictive. *He* was addictive. And he was hers, for the rest of the night.

Long seconds later, she stilled. Something intangible was there, brushing at the edges of her mind. It pushed, oh, so gently. Pricking at her memories. Invading them. Her eyes flew open. Her brow knit as the mental nudge came again, more insistently this time.

Stiffening, she turned her head toward her lover, the man whose body was still linked with hers. "No. I don't want to remember," she begged. "Please."

"*Shh,*" he whispered, his hand gently smoothing her hair. "Relax," he murmured. His body disengaged from hers, but still his mind probed hers, delving deeper, searching.

Alexa gasped and then whimpered and shook her head. "No! Don't make me think of them," she whispered. "They were monsters, best forgotten."

Sevin hardened his heart against her pleas. "*Shh.* Luc has to know." And then more quietly, he added, "*I* have to know."

Gods, please don't let her turn out to be a liar, he silently prayed.

He let his mind ease farther into hers and eventually she relaxed under him, unaware now that he was rifling through her memories. And then abruptly, he found what he was looking for.

In his own mind's eye, he saw Alexa standing in a room that was unfamiliar to him. But she knew it well and her mind informed his. It was a small but elegant library in the Patrizzi mansion on Capitoline. The date of the scene he would witness taking place here was roughly four months ago. It was a scene that was only a memory. Her memory. One he would coax her to share with him now.

He joined her there, stood alongside her in this remembrance. He was an unseen specter in her family home, there to watch a specific drama unfold.

Across the room from her stood her mother and brother—Serafina and Gaetano Patrizzi. The mother was in an argumentative mood, vastly irritated with Alexa. . . .

"What's going on?" asked Gaetano, looking from Alexa to Serafina.

"I'm glad you're here, Tano," his mother told him. "I've decided it's time your sister learned the truth about the workings of our little family business."

Gaetano's eyes sharpened, and his voice turned agitated. "Why?"

Serafina shrugged. "Because the other Daughters of Bona Dea and I have agreed it's time. Shall we go?" With that, she lead her two grown children toward the opposite side of the room, pausing beside a bookcase filled with jars and vials. The labels indicated they were products sold by Bona Dea Cosmetics, the Patrizzi business.

"You're coming down, too?" Gaetano asked, glancing back at his sister.

"Down where?" Alexa asked blankly. "What business?"

Serafina laughed lightly. "Our cosmetics, of course. Haven't you ever wondered how they are made, and where?"

"Well, yes, I've asked you many times, but you said young ladies were not to concern themselves with matters of finance and manufacture."

Serafina cupped her daughter's cheek fondly. "Ah, but you're grown-up now, and one day you and Tano must carry on for the family when I'm gone. It's time you learned." Along the wall, she pulled a lever that turned the bookcase.

Alexa gasped when an opening appeared behind it that lead to a tall, crude tunnel hewn from rock. A hidden entrance to the catacombs!

Serafina stepped inside and lit a decorative lantern with a matchstick.

"Why didn't I know about this?" said Alexa, moving to peer inside. "It's rather Gothic. Frightening, actually."

"You haven't seen anything yet," her brother murmured.

"Come along." Serafina nodded to Gaetano, who lit another lantern and gestured for Alexa to precede him through the labyrinth. "The first thing you must understand," Serafina went on to her daughter as she lead the pair inside the serpentine corridor, "is that there is a world beyond ours, accessed through a gate in Tuscany. Your friend Eva is from that world, as are the Satyr lords."

Alexa stopped short. "What?" she asked faintly.

"Why does she have to know?" Gaetano bit out. Alexa looked his way, her brow knit.

"But how adorable," Serafina cooed at him in delight. "You, playing the protective older brother. That will work nicely into my plans, for your sister is to be inducted into womanhood soon. And since your father is no longer with us, you have been chosen by the Daughters to stand in for him with her."

Gaetano looked stunned by this announcement.

"What are you talking about?" Alexa demanded, sounding wary now.

"She wants me to act as Faunus with you," her brother told

*her angrily. "A man who sought incest with his own daughter,
Bona Dea—as in our own Bona Dea Cosmetics. I'm to get you
drunk, then lie with you as a husband would. They'll likely
drug you so you won't remember afterward."*

"No! Stop it!" Alexa was pale now and she backed away.

*But Serafina grabbed her wrist, pulling her close again. "I
know it seems strange now, but you'll grow used to it. It's a tradition in our family." She smoothed back a strand of hair that
had fallen across Alexa's brow. "My father bedded me when I
was your age. But your father is dead, so Tano is my choice for
you. Better he than one of the bloated husbands of the other
Daughters. They take their pleasures in the bowels of the earth,
while the Daughters and I conduct other business here."*

*Alexa shook her head, and Sevin felt her horror. "You can't
mean it!"*

*"We're descended from gods, Alexa!" her mother exclaimed.
"Bona Dea and Faunus dictated long ago that a mating has to
occur among family before you can eventually wed. It's tradition. Be proud."*

*Alexa looked at her mother and brother as if she'd never seen
them before. "Proud? I've never been more ashamed!"*

With that, she turned and ran.

Thank the gods Alexa had escaped. It was Sevin's uppermost
thought as he released her mind from his thrall. And then came
the additional realization that she was innocent! She'd had no
part in her family's schemes. Euphoria filled him at the knowledge.

He'd already disengaged from her, and now he turned her
into his arms. Her face was dewy and still flushed from an earlier passion. Her gentle tears flowed, damp on his chest as she
stood unresisting in his embrace, her arms lax at her sides.

"Make me forget," she whispered, and his heart twisted
painfully for her.

"The memory will fade again into the recesses of your mind in the coming hours," he promised. "By dawn it will be as distant as it was before I resurrected it."

If he could, he would erase the pain of the scene he'd just witnessed from her mind forever. She'd been sickened to learn that her family—the very mother and brother who had nurtured her, and whose blood flowed in her veins—were monsters. He'd felt her reeling under the devastating impact of the discovery. And now he'd reopened the wound, rendered it as fresh and horrifying as that day, months ago.

He rubbed a soothing hand over her back, and kissed the top of her bowed head, murmuring to her. Giving her time to recover.

Beyond her, he felt Luc's need, but Sevin didn't acknowledge him. Not yet. This moment was for her. For healing.

Eventually, her tears died away, and Sevin lifted his gaze to meet his brother's. "She didn't know," he announced softly.

Luc's mirrored eyes glittered through the surrounding murk, suspicious. "Don't lie just to get your way."

"It's true, I swear it on the ancients," Sevin said with quiet assurance. He watched the lingering doubt slowly extinguish itself. Saw the precise instant his brother believed.

6

As Alexa swam back to consciousness, she snuggled into the lee of Sevin's broad chest. His attention had wandered from her briefly. The brothers were speaking to each other again in that foreign language—their native tongue.

Though she had struggled against the memory he'd brought to the forefront of her mind, she couldn't be angry with him. She understood his need to discover the truth and was glad she'd been vindicated. Still, she didn't want thoughts of her family to mar this time and sought to push them away.

With a sigh, she slid her arms around his waist. Through the veil of her nightgown, she felt the hardness of his phallus. Only one remained now, and it stood high and ready from the pelt at his groin.

She thrilled to the knowledge that they would mate again soon. Perhaps this time, she might gaze into his eyes and know his mouth on hers when a second fulfillment ripped through her.

As he'd promised, his taking had not harmed her. Instead, it had left her body humming with a desire for more of the same. Her flesh was highly sensitized to his every touch, and when he idly caressed her back as he spoke with his brother, she shifted in his arms at the pleasurable sensation, like a cat being stroked. A faint echo of her former orgasm gently quaked inside her, and her nether tissues pulsed, slick with his viscous spill.

Though he'd been forceful with her, it had been a passionate force, not the cruel handling she'd experienced in Venice. The latter had been an act of power and brutality, while this man's lovemaking had been born of a marrow-deep masculine desire. A desire to both give and receive pleasure.

Feeling a new tension seep into his body, she lifted her head, immediately sensing his anticipation. Then came the warmth of a second man at her back—one who'd come to stand mere feet away. She'd tried to forget him. But now she took a fortifying breath and then turned her head slightly in his direction.

It was Lord Lucien Satyr. A man who hated her.

His soulful eyes flickered over her and a muscle jerked in his cheek. Suddenly self-conscious, Alexa tugged her gown higher and shrugged into it. The two brothers who towered over her made no move to stop her. She linked the fingers of her hand with one of Sevin's, then glanced at Lucien again.

He was young, she realized, certainly no older than she was. And so very beautiful, like some wounded angel. His features were the stuff of romantic legend, his body strongly muscled. His shirt was unbuttoned, and the skin of his chest was smooth and paler than that of his brother. His was a body that had not known the sun for a dozen years. All because her family had drugged and imprisoned him, here in this cool, forgotten place.

Before any other human in Rome had known that Else-World existed, her family had known. They'd brought Lucien down here along with other creatures they'd captured from that adjacent world. They'd sold his sexual favors, and used him in other ways equally heinous.

"I'm sorry," she whispered. "Sorry for every hurt and every cruelty my family forced upon you." She reached a hand out to him.

But before she made contact, Lucien snatched her wrist in his fingers. "Don't touch me," he murmured. "Let me touch you instead, and all will be well."

Her eyes searched his, her heart weeping for him. The abuse he'd suffered had made him this way. Had made him shun the touch of others, and doomed him to loneliness. Although she didn't understand the whole of it, she only nodded and he let her go.

Sevin's arms came around her in a loose hold, and she relaxed into his support as she studied his brother. "I had no part in what happened to you," she told Lucien solemnly.

He nodded, a curt movement of his dark head, and a small silence fell. Alexa felt the brothers' watchfulness, sensed them waiting for her to make some move. Determination filled her, a need to set things right. A need to ease this man's pain. At length, she straightened away from Sevin.

Holding the eyes of his beautiful, wounded brother, who stood so still and distant before her, she spoke. "Let this night be my payment—freely offered to you—as a recompense for what my family did," she told him. As her words died away, she pushed her nightgown from her shoulders, letting her arms fall to her sides. The gown lost its moorings, and drifted lower, falling from her in a smooth silken swish to pool at her feet.

Lucien studied her for a long moment, the same lean, hungry look in his eyes that she'd seen before. Then his head lifted and he gazed over her to Sevin. Something passed between the brothers, some unseen signal, though neither moved.

And then Sevin took her shoulders and turned her to face him.

She rested her palms upon his chest and he covered them with his own. Behind her, she heard the shift of clothing. Fabric brushed her bottom as Lucien's trousers lowered, and she shivered, leaning into Sevin's embrace. Though she'd given permission and would willingly submit, this was all too new.

Her curiosity about the Satyr had long been a part of her, and she had a rich imagination when it came to her daydreams about them. But her imaginings had never taken her to a place where two brothers would lie with her; where one would hold her close, while a second joined his body to hers.

But within seconds, the pale damaged angel behind her would come inside her where his elder brother had so recently been. The smooth heads of his twin phalluses would find her feminine slit and the opening in the crease of her bottom, and push inside her there. His path would be easier than it might have been had another not paved his way. He would find her slick and ready and wanting. Made so by his sibling's prior lovemaking.

Behind her, masculine hands drifted lightly over her ribs, downward to hold her hips. Her eyes flew open and lifted to Sevin's. He was gazing down at her, his silver eyes full of an emotion she could not decipher. He took her hands and looped them around his neck, holding her as he angled his head closer.

"Thank you," he whispered.

Then he put his mouth on hers, swallowing her cry as his brother took her.

Just after dawn, Sevin washed up at the fountain's basin, wondering again at the source of its fresh waters as he pulled on his trousers and boots. Shrugging into his shirt he stood and stared down at Alexa where she lay sleeping on the makeshift bed he'd constructed the previous night.

She lay on her side, one leg cocked and a forearm pillowing her head. Blond silken waves of hair spilled out across the blanket around her like a halo. His eyes roved over her, noting the bruised shadows under the sweep of her lashes, the chafing his evening beard had left on her white throat, the voluptuous breasts marked by his passionate mouth.

He pulled a fresh blanket from one of the trunks and laid it over her so it covered her nakedness. She didn't stir. After a Calling night, males of ElseWorld blood were energized, but their women usually slept the day away.

Their women. Yes, she'd lain with both Luc and him last night. But she'd been *his* woman. And though this had gone unspoken, all of them had known it.

She'd shown herself to be innocent of her family's wrongdoing. And she was neither a harlot, nor a mistress a man paid to enjoy between the sheets. Therefore, he must repay her for what she'd done in the way any man of good breeding must. With marriage.

The thought was a new one, and one he'd never considered before with any woman. Not even Clara, for they'd been too young, and in her tribe marriage was not the expected result of a mating.

Yet the idea of wedding this woman did not terrify him, strangely enough. Rather it filled him with determination to see it come about. He could not regret all that passed between them and found that he relished the thought of having her beside him in the years to come. His soul and body recognized her as his, as what was meant to be.

After this night, a remembrance of their joining would remain with her, a new constant in her physical makeup. She would long to lie with him again, and if she proved stubborn and difficult to convince in the matter of a marriage to him, he would use her desire as leverage. As her husband, he would protect her, cherish her. He would not let her go the way that Clara had.

"Lantern's still got a few hours left in it." Luc's voice was pitched low so as to let Alexa sleep a few minutes longer. Already bathed and dressed, he stood across the room tinkering with the lamp.

Sevin slanted a glance in his direction as he began buttoning his shirt. "Are you all right?"

Luc shrugged, not meeting his eyes. "The headache's gone, if that's what you want to know. A Calling night always has the effect of relieving it. And I'm alive. Thanks to you."

"Thank her, not me." Sevin nodded toward Alexa.

"Maybe I will." A slight smile tugged at one corner of his brother's lips and then was gone. Luc gestured toward the riches stacked high in every corner. "That fountain and most of these artifacts were made in ElseWorld. Are they from the Forum digs? Stored here by smugglers, do you think? Or by the Patrizzis?"

"Bastian is the expert," said Sevin, shrugging. "He and I will come back later to examine everything. But first things first. I'll wake her. Then let's find our way out of here."

Luc nodded. "Any thoughts on which direction to choose? Toss a coin or . . . ?" He broke off mid-sentence.

Sevin glanced back to see him swaying on his feet.

Luc held out both his hands, staring at them as if he'd never seen them before. "It's happening again."

Alarmed, Sevin lunged for him just as his brother instinctively reached out for an anchor. His hand found Sevin, and clamped on his arm. The room around them began to waver and spin as it had the night before. Sevin felt disoriented and was hit with a sense of vertigo.

"Wait—Alexa!" He started to jerk away, but it was too late. He only had time for one last glimpse of her before she and the room were gone.

Or rather he and Luc were gone.

Seconds later, the two of them were back in the *Salone di Passione* again, far across Capitoline Hill from the sleeping woman they'd left behind. He prayed to the gods that she would not become lost before he found her again.

Hearing Sevin cry her name, Alexa was abruptly jolted from sleep. She sat up, remembering the entire night that had passed before with immediate clarity. Her eyes searched the room, lightning fast.

"Sevin? Lucien?" Gathering the topmost coverlet around her nakedness, she stood and went to the door. Interminable darkness stretched in both directions. "Sevin!"

Only her own voice echoed, mocking her. She was alone. In a very short time, she'd learned enough of Sevin's character to be certain he would not have intentionally deserted her. She could only assume the two brothers must have traveled elsewhere in the same unexpected, magical manner that he'd said had brought them here last night.

Though this place was incredibly eerie, she tried to stay calm. At least the lamp was still burning. She searched out her nightgown, dressing quickly. Assuming she would spend the evening alone last night, she'd donned these frilly feminine nightclothes that she so enjoyed. Her mother would have hated them, deeming them unfit for a lady. They were things Alexa had impulsively bought in Venice as she'd sought to cast off her former life and find a new one as quickly as possible. But now she wrapped a thin blanket around her shoulders to serve as a cape of sorts.

Moving about this morning was a test of her tired muscles.

Her body ached sweetly with every step, a pleasant reminder of the hours she'd spent with the brothers Satyr. A hundred fulfillments indeed. They'd been rough with her on occasion, but it was a thrilling sort of impassioned handling that had greatly appealed at the time.

Yet surprisingly, there was no pain this morning. Unlike the single other time she'd lain with a man a few months ago. The experience with him had lasted mere minutes but had pained her for a week.

Was that very man awaiting her even now in her home? she wondered as she lifted the gas lamp high and stepped into the corridor. She would strike out in the direction from which she'd come last night, hope to slip into the house unnoticed, and then dress in a more inconspicuous manner before she must confront her rapist.

As her bare feet flew through the serpentine tunnel, her mind was filled with thoughts of the night with Sevin. After their tenth mating, she'd lost count of how many times he and Lucien had joined with her and in how many ways.

She shook her head, remembering how she'd laughed with Eva only months ago about a statue that had been uncovered in the Forum. It had depicted a Satyr with not one but two male members at its groin. At the time, she'd thought it had been the product of an artist taking licentious license. She'd been wrong.

She marveled again over the fact that she was neither chafed nor terribly sore. As Sevin had promised, their gods had gifted them with an ability to soothe any physical stresses that their continued mating might otherwise have caused her. She had grown to greatly appreciate this ability in them as the night had worn on.

Their scent, their touch, their low-voiced words, and the pump of their seed into her had all been designed to keep her arousal at a fevered pitch, thus ensuring her willingness to mate with them for the length of time they required. She now felt thoroughly explored, and completely exhausted.

Unfortunately, she also felt ready for more.

This was not at all the outcome she'd hoped for. Instead, she had hoped that last night would quench both her curiosity about them and her fleshly passions, for a while at least. Instead, lying with Sevin was like partaking of expensive chocolate, or some other delicious confection. She could not forget the experience and feared she would want more after an all-too-brief interval of time had passed.

Though she had mated both men, there was no question that it was the elder Satyr who had taken charge of her. He was the one her body still craved. Her mind scrambled for a way that something more could be worked out between them, some sort of liaison in future.

No! She shook her head, trying to convince herself. This was the sort of dangerous thinking that had gotten her into trouble in Venice. She would hold the memory of last night dear, but a respectable woman did not carry on with a man she barely knew. Sevin had promised nothing, and she would ask for nothing.

Arriving at a crossroads in the tunnel, she stopped, holding the lantern high and looking both ways. She didn't remember such a crossing. She'd been so intent on her thoughts just now that she'd completely lost her bearings. Panic threatened, but she forced it down. She retraced her steps several times, trying to find her way. An hour later, she was drooping with tiredness and longing for sleep. How much longer would the lamp last?

Determined not to give up, she took a few more aimless steps down the corridor. And then, suddenly, she spied a long vertical crack of light just ahead. Relieved, she scurried toward it, then pushed at the door. It gave way easily, expelling her from the labyrinth into her mother's tastefully decorated private library.

But it seemed it was too soon to breathe a sigh of relief, for the room was not empty.

"What of the marble heads over there?" she heard a voice ask.

The room had been done in the Tuscan style, colored in ambers and peaches. It was appointed with at least two dozen busts and paintings culled from the ruins of the Forum—in the days before such treasure hunting had been banned.

The tall shelf she'd just moved had been hinged and built into one wall. At one time not so very long ago, its many shelves had been neatly stacked with smooth jars, vials, and small boxes, all similarly labeled. This library had been the nerve center of her mother's business empire, Bona Dea Cosmetics.

She stepped farther inside the library to find two men, both appallingly familiar to her. Dread curled in the pit of her stomach.

The younger of them sat on her mother's couch, perfectly turned out in attire that was the height of fashion. Laslo Tivoli, of Venice.

His father stood nearby, busily undraping a bust of Diana the Huntress in order to analyze its worth. "This one should fetch a hefty price," he muttered.

They'd apparently made themselves at home here last night. The bottle of her mother's expensive brandy was out on the side table, and two glasses sat beside it, one still full or else newly poured. The sight of it made her want to retch.

"Get out," she commanded, the words bursting from her.

At that, both men turned in surprise to look in her direction. It was difficult to discern that they were father and son. Both were handsome in their own way, she supposed objectively.

However, whereas the father was swarthy and muscular, with cunning eyes, Laslo was slender and handsome, with pretty manners. Manners that had hoodwinked her into trusting him.

She watched his father lift a cigar to his mouth. "Ah, here she is at last. My lovely runaway daughter-in-law."

She set the lamp down and drew her wrap more closely around herself. "Ex-daughter-in-law." Her entire body might be shaking with fear, but her voice did not.

Ignoring that, Signor Tivoli continued on. "Come back from the dungeons, it seems." His gimlet eyes slipped down her figure, reminding her she was in her nightgown.

Her eyes darted toward the door to the hall and she sidled in that direction, but Signor Tivoli moved to intercept her, and she stopped short. "You're looking somewhat bedraggled." He came closer and she shrank away, but he only studied her through the smoky haze from the cigar he'd stuck between his lips. "And smelling of sex."

"Father, please!" Laslo said in a long-suffering tone. He asked her no questions, however, apparently not caring if his ex-wife had just returned from an assignation, as his father had guessed.

Although she'd bathed her face and hands at the fountain, she hadn't taken time for a thorough wash, thinking it a waste of time she could ill afford when she so desperately needed to find her way home before the lamp burned out. Signor Tivoli looked toward the portal through which she'd just come, then he went to peer beyond it into the abyss. She moved to the safety of the library door, watching him. After a moment of consideration, he nudged the hinged shelf closed, flush against the wall.

Signor Tivoli was one of the most renowned architects in Italy, with offices in several cities. His son, Laslo, was a sought-after guest at dinner parties, a skilled flirt—and he was her husband. Correction—ex-husband.

Upon her arrival in Venice, fresh from learning that her mother was mentally unstable, Alexa had met Laslo at a social gathering. Immediately, he'd singled her out and his determined pursuit had begun. His devotion had been a healing balm to her after the shame and guilt she'd left behind here in Rome. She hadn't been herself then, hadn't realized she was still in shock. She'd let herself be blinded by his flattery and flowers, and wooed by his avowals of love. And very quickly, they had wound up married. She'd thought he would protect her from more hurt, but that had proven to be far from the case.

As she stared at him, the mantel clock suddenly seemed abnormally loud in the library. *Tick tock tick tock.* She shivered, remembering another clock, loud in the silence of her darkened bedroom on that horrible night in Venice. Her wedding night. A terrible pain, a dozen stabs, a burst of semen, male groans, withdrawal, a farewell slap on her bottom. The sound of a door closing. That had been the sum of it.

Then her tears had come, and along with them a determination to avoid a repeat performance at all costs. She was gone by morning to England for the two months it had taken to secure a divorce. And less than a week ago, she had come back to Rome.

Now these Tivoli men had caught up to her.

"What are you doing here?" she demanded of Laslo.

He sent her a helpless look. "I came at Father's suggestion. And he's right. It doesn't look seemly that you fled so quickly after the wedding. Everyone's been asking questions."

What she had once mistaken for polished manners was in truth only weakness. "Please, Laslo. Just go. Or I'll summon the *polizia*."

He made an affronted sound and got to his feet, straightening his jacket with a jerk. "You don't have to sound so peevish. You are the one who deserted me, not the other way around. Surely you must have come to regret your actions by now."

"You dare say such a thing, after what transpired between us?"

At this, Laslo's cheeks went pink. His eyes darted to his father, then fell to study his perfectly polished boots.

"I didn't *desert* you," she went on. "I divorced you. There's a defined difference in the eyes of the law. My attorney in England had the papers sent to you. You must have received them."

The elder Tivoli rocked on his heels, shifting his cigar from one side of his mouth to the other and looking unconcerned. "We did. They made for good kindling."

Her fist clenched tighter at the blanket she held around herself. "Burned or not, they are nevertheless still legal documents with copies registered with my attorney. Now you must excuse me. I'm going to my chamber—alone—to bathe. Please lock the front door on your way out and don't steal anything."

The amused voice of Signor Tivoli chased after her. "How can we possibly steal anything, *cara*, when everything here—including you—already belongs to my son?"

Alexa took the stairs as if the devil himself were pursuing her. She'd been afraid of something like this. She would have to summon her attorney from England. That meant more expense she could ill afford.

Her every instinct urged her not to retreat—to stay and sort this out now. But she was too exhausted—the kind of bone-deep exhaustion that a woman feels after spending the night in the arms of her lover. And his brother. Last night had been a vastly different experience from that time with her erstwhile husband. Too late, she'd realized that Laslo was a brute whose father ran his life.

And now it appeared that the elder Signor Tivoli also sought to run hers.

She yawned, shaking her head as she entered her room and locked the door behind her. She glanced longingly at her bed. But she couldn't find sleep yet, as much as she might have liked to. After her bath, she would return to this battle refreshed and more substantially clothed.

For she had little doubt that they would not be gone when she returned downstairs. She only hoped they didn't rob her blind in the interim.

7

"What the hells happened to you two last night?" Bastian demanded when Sevin and Luc appeared in the salon as suddenly and in the same strange manner as they'd departed it.

It was just minutes after dawn, and their eldest brother and Dane were already dressed, and looking much relieved to see the two of them appear out of nothingness.

"We were just about to go out combing the morgues," Dane told them.

Only ElseWorld males were up and about this early after a Calling night. Many were breaking their fast at the feast already laid out in the main bar. Their women would sleep far into the afternoon.

Would Alexa? Sevin wondered. He desperately hoped so. If she stayed put, they'd have a better chance of finding her again before she got lost. Those subterranean tunnels were said to extend for miles under Rome—a maze of corridors, niches, and bone-filled rooms. Even with her lantern she could easily become lost down there.

"Luc transported us to the catacombs for the night," he informed his brothers curtly. "Using some sort of newly discovered talent." His statement was greeted with a dumbfounded silence that gave him time to devour a croissant and wash it down with chilled water.

Watching him, Luc turned slightly green and looked away as if the thought of food was unpalatable after having undergone whatever physical trauma his talent had caused him in order to transport the two of them back here. "I don't know how it happens," he said, heading off questions. "I get headaches, especially in the days and hours leading up to the Calling. They began after I was released from the catacombs."

"And, of course you said nothing to us about it," Dane chided, shaking his head in bafflement.

"With proper training, your talent is something you could learn to control," Bastian told him. "The headaches as well. But you'll need help to recover."

"No doctors," Luc said emphatically.

Luc's refusal to seek treatment was a favorite subject of debate among them. It had been since he'd intentionally defeated all of the physicians assigned to his case when they'd sent him to ElseWorld for treatment immediately following his rescue. Now, as his brothers argued the matter in ways they'd all argued it many times before, Sevin summoned a servant. With terse instructions, he sent the man scurrying to the apartment he kept just off his office on the third floor of the salon, in search of a change of clothing for both him and Luc. Then he waved a guard over and sent him for ropes and lamps—supplies they would need to find Alexa.

When the guard left them, Sevin returned to the conversation in time to catch the tail end of Bastian's comment. ". . . I don't suppose that talent of yours could take you all the way to Tuscany and back," he was saying to Luc.

"Why do you ask that?" Sevin wanted to know.

In reply, Dane withdrew an official-looking document from

his pocket and slapped it on the table between them. "He asks because of this. It arrived by courier after you left last night."

Sevin picked up the proclamation, skimming it.

"What does it say?" Luc demanded, looking over his shoulder. He nudged him, wordlessly requesting that he read it aloud. Having spent so many years imprisoned in the catacombs, his reading skills were sorely lacking.

"It's from the Roman seat of government, but applies to all township and city borders in Italy. The substance of it is as we suspected," Bastian informed them both. "Anyone with Else-World blood in their veins is no longer allowed to travel outside the confines of their city of residence."

"Apparently, we are a danger to the human population and must be quarantined for the duration," Dane paraphrased, sarcasm tingeing every syllable.

"Damn. What's this here?" Sevin said, frowning as he noted a particular passage. "We are no longer permitted to purchase property in this world either!" He tossed the document back to the table in disgust. This put a decided wrinkle in his plans.

"We'll deal with all this later," he told his brothers. "We need to get back to the catacombs. While Luc and I were trapped there last night, we were unable to summon Shimmerskins. Something about the geology of the tunnels." He waved an impatient hand, brushing the likely reasons aside. "So we passed our Calling with Alexa Patrizzi, who ventured into the tunnels on her own and became lost. And she was left behind this morning when Luc transported us."

Bastian and Dane looked completely stunned now. "Gods, Luc," said Dane, sounding more concerned than ever. Luc had made no secret of his hatred for the Patrizzis.

"I don't want to talk about it," Luc told him tonelessly. "Now or ever."

"You damned well will—" Dane began.

Seeing the guard and servant returning with the requested

supplies, Sevin cut his brother off. "Later. I need you two with
me now," he told Dane and Bastian. "I'll answer any questions
on the way to the Patrizzi house."

He glanced at Luc. "You stay and watch over things at the
salon. Explain matters to Silvia and Eva when they wake, and
keep them here until their husbands return."

"No," said Luc, slowly shaking his head. "Dane can stay.
I'm coming with you. I know the catacombs by scent from my
time spent there. I'll be better able to find Alexa and the chamber of artifacts again."

That caught Bastian's attention. "Artifacts?" he echoed, immediately intrigued.

"Luc and I discovered a treasure trove in the catacombs last
night," Sevin told him. "Artifacts of ElseWorld make."

"Smugglers at work, we presumed," Luc put in.

"Let's get going," Sevin said impatiently. "The longer we
delay, the more likely it is that Alexa is getting herself lost."

"Luc's right. He and I should go with Sevin," Bastian told
Dane. "Don't worry. We'll watch out for him."

Luc rolled his eyes at their concern, looking as if he'd had
quite enough. Taking the rope coils from Sevin, he looped one
over each shoulder, and then struck out for the front exit. With
the bag of clothing in one hand and a lantern in his other, Sevin
followed. "Bring the other light," he called back to Bastian.

Behind them, he heard a frustrated Dane acknowledge the
wisdom of the plan and agree to remain behind and see that all
ran smoothly.

On their way out, Sevin, Luc, and Bastian passed a queue of
salon patrons—ElseWorld males, who'd been stopped at the
exits by guards. They were being searched and interrogated regarding last night's incident, as Sevin had requested. After all
that had happened, he'd almost forgotten about the explosion.
Giving a last instruction to the one-eyed sentry in charge of security, Sevin departed with his brothers.

"Without the use of Luc's talent, how are we going to find the entrance to the catacombs that's closest to this chamber of artifacts you spoke of?" asked Bastian once the three of them were in the carriage.

"We'll use the same entrance Alexa used to access them last night," Sevin explained. "It's inside her home—a secret door hidden behind a shelf in her mother's library."

He tossed a fresh set of clothes to Luc. The two of them began shucking off last night's garments and donning the fresh ones the servant had brought from Sevin's office, no mean feat for men of their height and brawn to accomplish inside a carriage.

"Will she cooperate?" Bastian asked.

Nodding, Sevin shrugged his broad shoulders into a crisp white linen shirt. "She was innocent in her family's wrong-doing."

Bastian lifted a brow in his direction. "You know this for a fact?"

Sevin nodded. "Through the use of my talent, I saw the very moment she learned the truth of what Bona Dea was. It came from her own mother's lips only a few months ago. Alexa's surprise was genuine."

Bastian's eyes narrowed, noting his brother's vehement defense of a woman he'd sworn to hate only yesterday. "And does she know she spent the Calling with you? Or did you cause her to forget?"

"She knows," Luc said before Sevin could answer. "Sevin bonded with her last night."

Sevin didn't need to ask how his brother knew. They'd all grown used to Luc's quirky, confounding abilities.

"Gods." Bastian ran a hand over his face, swearing under his breath. "This is surely more news than any man should have to digest before eight in the morning."

* * *

A doorknob twisted under the hand of Signorina Ella Carbone—the newest employee at the *Salone di Passione*. She slipped inside the small, well-appointed chamber allotted to her in the salon and slammed the door behind her with a strength born of misery. Only then did she allow her shoulders to bow under the burden of what she'd just learned.

We passed our Calling with Alexa Patrizzi.

Her dressing gown was a billow of silk and lace around her as she sank to the floor. She pressed a hand over her heart. She could almost feel it breaking. When she'd overheard Lord Sevin speak those very words to his brothers a few minutes ago, she had thought it surely would.

The very instant the sun had risen this morning, she'd ushered her male client out of the salon, and had then gone eagerly searching for news of Sevin. She'd passed no other women when she'd skulked to linger in the corridor off the main bar. They were all sleeping and would be until well into the afternoon.

Normally, she would be doing the same. But only because she was spent after seeing to the needs of her client throughout the night, not because she was like the other females employed here. For her blood was not ElseWorld blood like theirs. She was human, masquerading as fey. Her little secret.

It was a secret she kept through the use of a small bottle of fey scent hidden in her room—contraband from the Bona Dea Cosmetics empire, a family enterprise that rumor said had recently fallen into bankruptcy. She'd gone to great pains to obtain it. This scent was the only way she had managed to secure a place here within Lord Sevin's orbit. However, she would soon need another bottle of the stuff, and like a back-alley addict, she would seek out her clandestine supplier.

To gain and keep her employment here, it was necessary that she pass herself off as a creature of ElseWorld. After all, the salon did not employ humans. During her interview, she'd taken care that Sevin would not recognize her from their past acquaintance, for he might have turned her away.

Ella struck her fist on the rug by her knee. Oh! It wasn't fair. She'd so desperately hoped he would be lying here with her now. If her plans had come to fruition last night, they would have spent the Calling together in this very room. Perhaps at dawn, he might have even brought her some tea and croissants from the perfectly prepared victuals set out for patrons every morning in the main bar.

Instead, Lord Sevin had disappeared last night in the blink of an eye. She had waited for his return for some time—flirting with various patrons, but fending off all offers. Finally, she'd realized to her dismay that he must be going to spend his Calling elsewhere. And with little choice left to her, she had let herself be wooed by the stranger she'd just escorted out the salon's exit door.

She dashed away tears, her anger rising. Getting to her feet, she began to pace. Who was this Alexa Patrizzi? And why had Lord Sevin chosen her? Was she some uncouth harlot? A lady of refinement? Not a Shimmerskin certainly, for they were insentient and went unnamed.

Which meant that this Patrizzi wench must be flesh and blood. And Sevin had touched her, lain naked with her, pressed his lips to hers! And worst of all—fucked her. Hunted his pleasure within her body over and over last night. A wounded sound welled up from Ella's core, and she stifled it with a fist.

Sevin hadn't chosen a flesh-and-blood female in many months, not since she'd been employed here, certainly. The fact that he hadn't had seemed to her a good omen. It was almost as if he was saving himself for her, or so she'd fantasized.

Damnation! She'd been so certain she could coax him into her bed last night. If she could manage it with him just once, she was sure he would finally understand the truth. A truth she'd known herself for years.

That they were made for each other.

Ella flung herself onto her bed to lie amid sheets still scented with the semen and cologne of last night's client. His cock had not been generous, nor his stamina sufficient to suit her, but he'd showered her with compliments, coins, and a nice bit of jewelry. She'd already amassed a healthy cache of coins and baubles from similar clients. She'd only been here a few weeks, but she'd worked hard to please.

She'd thought Sevin might hear of how popular she was, become curious about her, and seek her out of his own accord. She knew what she was about between a man's legs. If only he would give her a chance!

Rolling onto her side, she lifted the gold necklace her client had gifted her with from the bedside table. Lying back again, she draped it over her throat, hoping the cold weight of its metal would make her feel better. More worthy.

But she was inconsolable and let out a small sob. Desolate tears leaked from her for several minutes more, trickling onto her pillow. This was all the fault of his youngest brother, that freak—Lucien. He'd transported Sevin away against his will last night. And then he'd introduced him to this other woman.

If not for him, Sevin might have stayed here and chosen her. Might have fallen in love with her as he was meant to.

It was well known among salon employees that Lucien selected the females that Sevin fucked, and then fucked those same women in his wake. Though this youngest Satyr lord was strange, he was handsome and she'd been willing to fuck him as well. Whatever it took to get closer to Sevin.

However, Lucien had spurned her and all others, only mating once a month when the fever in his blood forced him to. And even then, he always chose to lie with Shimmerskins.

Desperation and a sense of urgency seized her. She must think, and think well. What was her next move? She hadn't plotted and planned all this time only to see Sevin stolen out from under her very nose by another female! She'd done too much to lose him now, just when she'd finally found him again.

Jealousy soared in her, hot and destructive. When she found this Alexa Patrizzi, she would make her sorry.

Very sorry.

Sevin gazed impatiently from the carriage window as they approached the luxuriously appointed Patrizzi town house. In the cool mist of morning, the valley below looked otherworldly and desolate with its jumble of broken walls, odd lumps of stone, and occasional soaring column.

Within that valley lay the remains of the ancient Roman Forum. Its excavation was the sole reason his family had been brought here to Rome. He'd still been a young boy when they'd arrived in this world through the Tuscan gate, and Luc had not yet been born.

Much of the ancient Forum was still buried under sixteen feet of soil and refuse deposited by flooding from the Tiber River, war, and the passage of centuries. But large-scale excavations were underway now, and as lead archaeologist, Bastian had already uncovered the remains of the House of Vestals, as well as other of the Forum's buried secrets. And he was determined to discover them all.

Bastian was the only one of the brothers who'd found the same fascination in this valley as their father had before him. The ElseWorld Council had sent their family to this world with a mandate to uncover and hide any Forum artifacts that had been created by magical means by ElseWorld hands, lest they fall into the clutches of humans. Sevin had a few thoughts regarding that particular mandate, which he would share with his brothers as soon as he'd firmed up his plans.

Upon reaching the town house, he leaped from the carriage,

eager to find Alexa. His brothers followed him up the steps to the front door. When there was no answer to the bell, Sevin tried the door and found it unlocked.

Bastian raised his brows as they went inside. "No staff?"

Sevin frowned. A lone female was taking a dangerous risk in not locking her door or employing servants for protection. Anyone could wander in from the street. "Alexa! Alexa!" he called out. When there was no reply, his heart twisted with worry.

Stalking through the house, he poked his head around each door he passed. Luc checked the upstairs bedrooms and called down that she wasn't there either.

"She must still be in the catacombs," Sevin announced. "The entrance to them from this house is beyond a tall shelf in a library of some kind. From the vision she shared with me, I'll recognize it when I see it."

As they moved deeper into the house, he noticed a decided lack of furnishings. There was an expensive rug rolled up against one wall of a sitting room. That and a bare side table were all that occupied it. Paintings had been removed from some walls, and shelves were bare. It almost looked as if everything in the house was being packed up.

"Were you aware of any plans she had to move her household?" Luc asked him.

"She's not going anywhere, unless it's to my lodgings," Sevin asserted. But had she finally taken to heart his demand that she leave Rome? Now that he wanted the opposite? No, she couldn't have moved so quickly on the matter. Which meant this packing must have begun the minute she'd returned from Venice. What was going on here?

"You can't be thinking of installing her in your apartment in the *Salone di Passione*," Bastian said doubtfully. "Respectable women don't like to build their nests in their lovers' places of business. Especially within a business such as yours."

His eldest brother was right, Sevin realized. Perhaps he hadn't thought everything through as well as he'd believed. Just then he ducked his head into yet another room. A sense of *déjà vu* struck him as he beheld the chamber's coloring and the placement of its contents. There were the display shelves he'd seen in Alexa's vision, standing tall and empty against the far wall.

"This is it," he announced, bursting inside the room. Going over to the shelf, he gave it a test pull, then found a lever. Quickly discovering how it opened from the wall, he and his brothers shoved it wide, revealing the dark, endless tunnel of catacombs beyond.

Bastian gazed into the abyss, fascinated.

"Alexa!" Sevin shouted, and his voice echoed down the tunnel. "An hour has passed since we left her. She could be well lost by now. Keep calling for her, while I secure the ropes."

As he tied off the end of one of the ropes they'd brought to the leg of a couch, his brothers continued shouting for her. When he was done and they'd heard no reply, he handed the rest of the rope coil to Bastian, and spoke to Luc. "Do you think you can lead Bastian to the chamber we were in last night?"

"I think so. Last night she said she'd been in the tunnel less than ten minutes. I should be able to find my way from here," Luc began. "But—"

Sevin cut him off, explaining, "Let's try two different directions to cover more ground, just in case she has wandered off. And since we want Bastian to have a look at the artifacts, you should accompany him there, while I try a different path."

Luc nodded. Although his face was stoic, Sevin sensed the tension in him, and he took his arm, staying him. "Wait. Are you sure you're up to this?"

"Stop worrying. I'm fine." Shrugging him off, Luc took a lamp and lead Bastian inside. As the brothers' bobbing lantern swiftly disappeared into serpentine darkness, they let the coil unwind, so they'd be able to find their way back with no trouble.

Meanwhile, Sevin tied off the end of the other coil of rope. He had already gone a dozen steps into the tunnel and was about to veer off in a different direction from that his brothers had taken, when he heard voices behind him and the slam of the front door.

"No! I want you out!"

Recognizing that the shout had come from Alexa, Sevin retraced his steps. In a flash, he bolted toward the sound of her voice, following it to another sitting room at the front of the house. He stalked into the room, his eyes immediately finding and flicking over her.

Alexa. She'd found her way out of the tunnel on her own. She stood by the mantel now, removing her gloves. She looked beautiful. And exhausted.

He turned to the two well-dressed men in the room—a slender young one, and an older, swarthy, muscular one with a cigar in his mouth. He recognized neither. "You heard the lady. She doesn't want you here."

"Sevin?" Alexa gasped in surprise. When her wide gray eyes met his, an awareness of everything that had taken place the previous night flashed between them. Her face went pink.

"It's not *her* house, as it happens," the elder of the two men told him. "She has no right to order us out. And who are you to trespass anyway?"

Ignoring them for the moment, Sevin went to her. He needed to hold her, to reassure himself she was safe. With an arm about her shoulders, he tugged her toward the sofa, his head bent to hers. "Sit, before you fall down. Why aren't you in bed?"

Alexa gestured toward the two men. "I have unwelcome visitors, as you see. They escorted me to the telegraph office, where I sent a message to my attorney in hopes of seeing them and their claim removed from my property."

"Signor! I ask you again. Who are you to trespass?" the elder man demanded.

Sevin stood to face them, his expression menacing. He'd planned to broach the subject of marriage when he found Alexa. He'd worked out all the details in his mind, closed all the loopholes, prepared answers for all the questions and road-blocks she might raise. But there were two unexpected road-blocks in the room, and they greatly annoyed him. He wanted privacy.

"I'm Lord Sevin Satyr. Now get the hells out." He saw the fleeting distaste in the elder man's face when he realized Sevin was a creature of ElseWorld blood. Another damn ethnic purist, or a segregationist at the very least. Thoroughly irritated now, Sevin stalked toward the men, taking the younger one's arm and preparing to bodily toss them both out on the street.

"Wait! I have a right to be here!" the younger one protested, struggling. "I'm her husband! We married in Venice only two months ago."

Sevin's heart faltered as he read the truth of this statement in the man's face. *No!* He and Alexa were bound to one another. After last night, she was his. He'd have sensed if her heart was already bound to another man when he mated her.

"Ex-husband," Alexa corrected testily, and his heart picked up speed again. "We are divorced, as you and your father well know, Laslo. I have my copies of the official papers upstairs. Signed only last week."

Sevin's brows raised at this, and no wonder. Few women in all of Europe could claim such a status. And probably none as young as twenty-two years of age.

The elder man snorted. "You are Italian, signora," he scoffed. "There is no divorce here."

"It so happens that I was born in England twenty-two years ago, while my mother was traveling there," Alexa told him levelly. "Though I was there as a babe for no more than a few months, I remain an English citizen. Their Matrimonial Causes Act allows women to apply for divorce. We are no longer second-class citizens there, as we remain here in Italy."

Though she presented an unflappable front, Alexa was far from calm. Her attorney had told her there was a very real possibility that her claim could be revoked if contested. Divorce was frowned upon, even in England where it had been legitimized. She'd counted on Laslo putting up less of a fight about it.

"Nevertheless, you and my son were wed in Venice and you are both Italian residents," Laslo's father contended. "And in this country, the laws say that my son now owns you, your home, and its contents. Though from the looks of things, you've been selling off some of what's his." He gestured around the room, which was partially empty of furnishings as was the rest of the house.

Alexa's hands fisted on her lap. She'd found time to bathe, but she still hadn't slept and was far too tired to deal with this. "We're divorced. Married only briefly. Your family has no moral or legal right to my property."

Laslo's father folded his arms. "Yes, yes, so you claim. But I've yet to hear on what grounds you acquired this supposed divorce?"

Alexa glanced at all the men in turn, then her gaze focused on the senior Tivoli. "Concupiscent incompatibility with your son."

All eyes went to her ex-husband.

"Laslo? I understood all went as it should in your marriage bed," said Signor Tivoli. Then, not giving his son a chance to respond, he looked at Alexa. "Are you implying that my son was incapable of performing his husbandly duty?"

Alexa sent Sevin a mortified look. Then she shied away from looking his way again, unwilling to be reminded of what had passed between them only hours earlier. It was likely nothing to him. With those handsome features and muscles . . . and that appendage of his . . . he had likely pleased legions of adoring females.

She rubbed her throbbing temples with the tips of her fingers. "Surely this is a private matter for discussion only between my ex-husband and me."

"Damnation! Laslo! Did it go well or not?" his father demanded.

Laslo shrugged, his eyes studying the pattern of the carpet under his boots. "Of course."

"And have you bedded any other women since your marriage?" his father inquired.

Laslo looked pained. "No."

The elder Tivoli turned toward Alexa and Sevin and spread his arms wide. "There you have it then! Even in England, only non-consummation or adultery is recognized as cause for divorce."

"Laslo," Alexa chided softly. "You know all did not go well between us. It was a mistake best undone."

Her former husband looked her way, suddenly contrite. "I'm sorry, Alexa. I—"

"Shut up, son," growled Signor Tivoli.

With a frustrated glance at his father and an apologetic one at her, Laslo Tivoli wordlessly turned on his heel and left the house.

"I suggest you follow your son's example," Sevin told the elder man. "And if you return again, you'll find your way blocked."

"By magic?"

Sevin folded his arms, his silence a confirmation in itself.

"One day soon—very soon, I hope—its use will be outlawed and your ability to access it cut off," Tivoli vowed. "I look forward to that day."

"You'll have a long wait," said Sevin, unfazed. If all went as he planned, Roman lawmakers would soon begin to side with his family.

Signor Tivoli chomped on his cigar for a few seconds, observing Sevin with narrowed eyes. Then, with a scathing glance, he departed after his son.

After he'd gone, Sevin locked the front door behind him, secured other exits, and cast out a protective bespelling around the perimeter that would repel any non-ElseWorld intruders for the next day or so. Returning to the sitting room, he found Alexa exactly as he'd left her, looking pensive and distraught.

Going to her, he sank onto the couch beside her. When he took her hand in his, she looked up at him in dull surprise. "Oh. I thought you'd gone as well." She yawned delicately behind one hand.

"Where are your servants?" he demanded, irritated at her impersonal tone and her casual assumption that he would desert her.

"Dismissed," she replied, yawning again.

His brows slammed together. "So if I hadn't come, you would have found yourself here alone with those two?"

She only shrugged. "I can take care of myself. I don't need you to protect me."

At that, he grunted, a masculine sound of complete disagreement. "Why are your furnishings dwindling?"

"Your family ruined mine, have you forgotten? Our cosmetics business no longer thrives, and therefore my income is nonexistent. I'm not complaining. We deserved it. Just stating a fact."

"Are you planning to sell the house?" he asked.

She sighed, looking around. "I hadn't really gotten that far, but if there are to be more attorney fees, I suppose I will have to, won't I?" She gave a sad little laugh. "So I imagine you'll get your way in the end after all. I'll be forced out of Rome."

"You're not going anywhere. You're marrying me."

8

Alexa straightened, blinking at him in astonishment. "What? No!"

Sevin considered her, trying to determine the best way to get what he wanted. She looked like a beautiful, wilted flower this morning, one that required nurturing, not a tongue-lashing.

He sat and lifted her, unresisting, on to his lap. Leaning comfortably back against the cushions with her in his arms, he inquired mildly, "Why the devil not? They'll be back, you know. And you can't fend them off here alone."

She relaxed into him, laying her head on his shoulder. "You know that's not reason enough to wed. Besides, my attorney in the divorce advised me to live a respectable life from here on out so as not to draw any suspicion to the matter of my divorce. And I hardly think that a marriage to you will win me any friends *or* respectability here in Rome. Rather, I'd be made notorious."

Her fingers plucked idly at a button on his tailored shirt. "I'm not sure a marriage between us would even be legal in view of my former ties with Laslo. They will fight me on the divorce." She sighed again. "I'm afraid the Tivoli family is powerful and well established throughout Italy and has great wealth to draw on."

"So do I," Sevin countered, running a comforting hand along her arm.

Under her, his body was a strong, vibrant, masculine support. One she could not afford to lean on indefinitely. "I don't want to cling to you," she informed him. "I want to stand on my own for once."

"Then stand on your own. But let me stand behind you, a bulwark in this storm."

She looked up at him then, perplexed. After a moment, she put a hand to his cheek, caressing it lightly. "You haven't shaved."

His dimples made a brief appearance. "I was in a hurry to get back to you."

Seeing his smile, Alexa had to fight the instant dart of attraction that burst through her. Then he tilted her face higher, kissing her gently, and she was lost.

As her lips parted for him, a flood of memories from last night washed over her. Her wedding night with Laslo had been about brutality, not passion. And though she'd been bruised by the former, her lonely heart still yearned for the latter. Sevin had been forceful with her last night, true, but it had been a thrilling sort of handling rather than a cruel one. And all the while, she'd sensed an underlying restraint, and had somehow known that he would not hurt her. Not physically. But he could wound her heart, this man.

"You're a good man," she murmured. "A strong one."

He smiled in a self-effacing way, appearing bemused by the turn in the conversation. "Why, thank you."

She traced the crease of one of his dimples with the tip of her finger. "And admirable in your loyalty to your family."

"I begin to sound like a basset hound in your description. Cease, please, before I am further reduced."

"I miss that sort of familial connection."

"Then wed me, and join my family," he urged.

"This from the man who considered me the worst sort of anathema only yesterday? One who was set to banish me?"

"Things changed between us last night."

"Last night was last night," she said, shrugging slightly. "A fantasy, not real life."

His broad hand stroked her hair. "Marry me and your life could be full of such nights. We are bound to one another now." He twisted a pale lock of her hair around one finger as if to tether her to him. "If you leave me, you will suffer a withdrawal."

She laughed, trying to lighten the mood. "Someone is rather full of himself this morning."

"It's no idle boast. You're human. I have mated you during my Calling, given you my seed. Next Moonful, a month from now, you will pine and sicken for want of me, and I for want of you. So, you see, we'll ultimately be drawn together. You'll either become my mistress, or you'll wed me. I'd prefer the latter, but I'm adaptable."

Alexa tried to focus well enough to think things through. Though his proposal was certainly unconventional, it was appealing in its honesty. And he was appealing in every way to her. He was offering her admission into his inner circle. A place in his family. In his arms, in his life. Protection. Did she dare trust this turn in her fortunes?

She shook her head, mussing her hair against his chest. "I've been too impulsive of late and have learned to think before I act. And right now I'm too tired to think straight."

She felt his kiss brush the crown of her head. "Then sleep."

"What will you do?"

"Be here when you wake," he said simply.

"No, I need some time to myself. Can't you somehow cast your magic around my home, so that I'm protected inside it?"

He nodded, having already done so. "I'll stay then, only to see you asleep. But before leaving the salon, I will summon guards to patrol the exits to this house. They'll take you to the salon when you wake this evening. Agreed?"

She smiled at that, snuggling comfortably and fitting her body into the lee of his. Feeling safer than she had in some time, she was asleep within seconds.

Gazing down upon her, Sevin felt a tug at his heart. He smoothed a hand over her hair again and tucked a pale, errant curl behind her ear. Soon, he would take her to her bed-chamber, somewhere upstairs. He would undress her and leave her to a much-needed slumber in her solitary bed. He would find his brothers and learn what they'd discovered.

But for now, he only held her to him, enjoying her sweet weight against him, and the newness of their connection. The bond that had formed between them last night would only grow stronger over time. He had heard his brothers speak of this bonding when it happened to them, but he hadn't under-stood how strongly he would be affected by it until now.

Sevin shifted, securing Alexa more comfortably against him, as if his hold might guard her from every danger. Because of this woman and his need to protect her, finding a solution that would reverse the trend of hatred and fear toward his kind in this world had become that much more crucial.

Men like the Tivolis were determined to limit the rights of the Satyr and those of all ElseWorld immigrants. Soon they would seek even greater limitations and likely even try to push them back through the gate. Back to a world he didn't even know. A world that would be lethal to this woman.

She could not survive in ElseWorld; no human could. And although he and his brothers had all been born there, they had no ties to that world. Since they'd left, it had become a war-torn land ravaged by sickness and hopelessness. It was no longer a suitable place for raising a family or for building a thriving business.

He and his brothers must act now to win this fight. They must retain what was rightfully theirs in this world, or lose it all forever.

Growing pensive, Sevin scanned the room. Absently, he traced the slope of Alexa's waist with one hand, enjoying its feminine curve. Along with marriage to her would come the acquisition of this property. With that realization, a germ of an idea occurred to him and quickly took root. His entrepreneurial mind began churning with possibilities.

"Sevin!"

Hearing his brothers calling him, Sevin loped down the last of the stairs. He'd just deposited Alexa comfortably in her bedchamber and was returning to the main floor of her house when Bastian and Luc appeared from the direction of the library. Both looked somewhat more disheveled and dusty than when he'd last seen them almost an hour ago.

Luc glanced past him toward the top of the stairs. "You found her?"

"She found her way out earlier," Sevin explained. "She's resting."

Gazing at Luc now, he wondered if he would readily accept Alexa when she became a permanent fixture in their lives. And would she be able to reconcile herself to Luc's place in things? She might assume that last night had been an aberration, but this was not the case. Until he was fully healed, Luc would continue to require fraternal guidance with the coming of each and every Moonful in the future. Sevin would not turn his back on Luc in order to have Alexa in his bed on such nights, nor did he wish to leave her out of things in order to foster his youngest brother.

Sevin shrugged mentally as he joined his brothers, deciding that all would somehow work itself out in good time. Because, for him, things nearly always did.

"What did you discover in the catacombs?" he asked, moving beyond them.

"You and Luc were right," Bastian said, excitement lighting his eyes as they followed in Sevin's wake. "Those artifacts down there are of ElseWorld origin. They likely came from the Forum, culled by smugglers or illicit collectors over the years."

"Smugglers? Modern ones?"

Bastian nodded. "Possibly the Patrizzis. All the artifacts have been well tended, but it's hard to know how recently. The magic in them keeps them in pristine condition. We'll need to move everything and find a safe place for it so that I can make a closer study. Although where the hells we'll stow it all and how we'll move it will take substantial—"

"I know the perfect location," Sevin informed him.

"Oh really?" Bastian arched a brow, brushing a cobweb from his shoulder with a flick of his fingers.

"Where do you suggest we take them?" Luc asked doubtfully.

"We don't. We'll leave them right where they are," said Sevin. "In the catacombs under my wife's home. Although some will fit nicely into my new *Salone di Passione*. That Bacchus fountain, for instance." Entering the library, he crossed over to the shelf that served as a door to the catacombs.

"Did you acquire a new wife and a second salon while we weren't looking?" Bastian asked, offering assistance.

With a forceful nudge of their shoulders, they closed it. "The formalities will take place as soon as Alexa agrees," Sevin declared. "And the catacombs below us can continue on as a hiding place thereafter. They can even serve as storage for any new discoveries you make."

Assuring himself that the shelf-door was flush with the wall once more, he dusted off his hands and eyed his brothers, willing them to share his enthusiasm for his plan. "Think of it—until now, you've been relocating any artifacts with magical properties to your home and various other locations that are not as secure as we might wish. Now they can come together here, where we can keep a close eye on them, and where they'll be readily accessible to you for study. It's the perfect solution—one handed to us on a platter by the smugglers."

"You've forgotten something," said Luc. "Those very smugglers will return for their booty at some point." Sevin noted that their youngest brother had leaned his tall frame against the far wall, instinctively choosing a strategic position that offered a good vantage point from which to observe all angles of the room and which would allow him equidistant access to both door and window exits.

"Our magic and a half-dozen guards will be enough to keep such a cache safe," Bastian mused. "I think Sevin's onto something here."

Luc shrugged. "Regardless, the way the government is eroding our rights, we'll find ourselves incarcerated or forced back to ElseWorld before any of your plans can come to pass."

Sevin threw himself onto the sofa and gave a mighty stretch of his well-muscled arms and back. "I think I have a cure for that as well."

Both brothers stared at him. "And that would be?" Bastian prompted.

"While we've flourished in this world, ElseWorld has meanwhile deteriorated," he replied. "Infighting, war, the Sickness—a veritable dark ages has begun there. There's no question of us going back. Agreed?"

Bastian nodded. "I've come to believe that it's no coincidence that our parents came here when they did. I don't think it was only because our father was attracted to the Forum excavations." Taking a glass from the drink cart, he searched out something that looked like water and began pouring. "No, I think they saw what was coming. They wanted us all out of ElseWorld."

"So what do you propose?" Luc asked Sevin.

"That we put an irresistible temptation before these Romans. A new *Salone di Passione*. One that will employ Else-World staff, but will cater exclusively to human clientele. One that will woo them to our way of thinking."

"And you think it will be so easy?" Luc countered. "That this new salon will somehow magically render us safe here? That it will make the Roman government decide we are an asset instead of disciples of the very devil himself?"

"I do. Sex is the great leveler." Sevin leaned forward, his enthusiasm for his plans increasing with every word. He was confident of his ability to convince even the most doubtful. After all, at the age of eighteen, with no business experience under his belt, he'd convinced the Council to finance his first salon. "The passions of government officials run particularly high, and they are always eager for new diversions. They'll be susceptible to the lure, if we offer it."

While his brothers digested this, there came a knock on the front door. The one-eyed sentry from the salon appeared moments later along with two other guards under his command. He nodded to Sevin. "Following up, as ordered, signor."

Further discussion was put on hold as Sevin made arrangements for the safekeeping of the sole occupant of the house and for her delivery to him later that day. Afterward, as the three brothers locked up in preparation for departure, he took up their earlier conversation again.

"We'll make the new club an exclusive one, with memberships by invitation only," he went on. "Word will spread. And curiosity. Demand will build exponentially. And very quickly, this world will decide that our kind has much to offer."

"An interesting proposition," Bastian put in. "However,

there's the edict, remember? We cannot purchase property in Rome any longer. So where do you plan to build this diversion?"

As the three brothers stepped outside on the porch of the Patrizzi mansion, Sevin smiled, his silver eyes alight. "Right here," he proclaimed, spreading both arms wide to encompass the entire town house.

"So *that's* it," said Luc, crossing his arms. "You plan to wed Signorina Patrizzi simply to get the use of her home."

"That's a high price to pay even to safeguard our family, isn't it, brother?" Bastian asked.

As Bastian and Luc took the steps to the street, Sevin only smiled to himself, locking up with the spare house key he'd procured from the kitchen. Afterward, he cast out a reinforcement of the bespelling that encircled the entire perimeter of the house—one that would keep its single, precious occupant safe there until nightfall when he had instructed that she be delivered to him at the salon.

The slam of the carriage door behind the three Satyr lords and the clatter of its wheels as they departed was loud in the fashionable street a short time later. As it faded, there came a voice from the second-floor balcony off Alexa's bedchamber. She stood there even now in her nightgown, with her arms wrapped around herself as if she sought to contain her tumultuous emotions within them.

"I quite agree," she said, in belated reply to Bastian's departing comment. Noting the sentries Sevin had posted outside her home, she stepped back inside and *snick*ed the balcony door closed. "And it's a price I will never pay."

She'd woken from her troubled sleep to the sound of male voices and had ventured onto the balcony to eavesdrop. Having overheard their plans, she was too keyed up to sleep now. Yet she was too tired to think and desperately craved the release slumber would provide. Wandering into her mother's bedchamber, she located a sedative there in the drawer of her dressing table. Taking it, she then crept back into her lonely bed and fell into an uninterrupted, dreamless sleep.

But when she awoke again early that evening, Alexa found that she was no longer alone. There was a man lying in the middle of her floor, his head bleeding out on the tasteful carpet her mother had chosen, and a bloody poker beside him.

It was none other than her ex-husband, Laslo. Dead.

9

Sevin looked up from his desk on the third floor of the salon to see a woman standing in the doorway of his office, her expression condemning. Ella Carbone.

"There's news floating around that you plan to wed," she accused.

He tossed down his pen, having finished the last of the letters to officials in this world as well as the one beyond the gate. They would all be posted tonight, putting his plan in motion. As evening approached, budgets, columns of figures, and other salon business still sat on his desk, awaiting his attention. However, even an angry woman was preferable to more paperwork at the moment.

He eyed her. "The salon rumor mill is alive and well, I see. However, I *don't* see how that's your business, Signorina Carbone."

A variety of conflicting emotions flitted over his employee's pretty face, then she seemed to forcibly corral them and calm herself. "So formal." Adopting a teasing smile, she slipped inside uninvited, nudging the door closed behind her.

Sevin glanced at the clock on the wall beyond her. The guards who watched over Alexa had not yet brought word of her awakening, but he planned to visit her home again himself within the hour if she did not arrive here first.

Coming nearer, Ella straddled his lap, stroking his nape with long fingertips. He allowed her to do so only because something about her had suddenly captured his notice. For just an instant, she had reminded him of someone else.

He sat back in his chair to study her, trying to hold on to the fleeting sense of recognition. "You seem different somehow," he murmured.

She preened, taking his interest as a compliment. "Maybe you never really looked closely enough at me before," she purred.

He did now, trying to shake years of cobwebs from his mind. Then, abruptly, he lifted her away and stood towering over her.

"You're human," he accused. "Or at least partly so." He could see that his words startled her. She looked secretive and caught off guard, but quickly recovered.

Canting her head, she attempted to appear charmingly confused. "What? Don't be ridiculous, Lord Sevin. My blood is fey."

"You lie. There's human in your recent lineage. A grandparent, at least. It goes no farther back."

Panicking, Ella lowered her lashes, hoping she looked coy. She'd made a disastrous miscalculation coming here before she'd bathed. But she'd heard the rumors just now upon her return from a furtive assignation on Aventine Hill, and hadn't been able to wait before ferreting out the truth of them.

Although the rules of the salon forbade it, she entertained men on the sly. Often, as on this afternoon, they were human. There was a brisk trade in catering to such men. They paid exorbitant fees to lie with an ElseWorld creature. Little did they know that she was *not* one, but only acted the part with great conviction.

It was unfortunate that Lord Sevin had just discovered her most closely guarded secret. She had a story ready, of course, one prepared in anticipation of such a discovery coming to pass. It hovered on her lips, ready to spill.

Yet, looking up into his beautiful face, she found herself wanting him to finally know the truth. So she leaned into him, her hands flat upon the strong warmth of his chest. "Don't you remember me, *ves'tacha?*"

At her use of the Romani word for "beloved," Sevin was abruptly wrenched back in time. He took her upper arms in his hands and snatched her higher, seeing another face, one years younger. That of a girl only twelve years old. In an abrupt move, he tucked his face into the crook of her neck, sorting out the nuances of her scent. He drew back before she could mold herself to him again.

"You're Clara's little sister! The one who was to marry." He searched for her name, then found it. "Carmella." When he'd last seen her he'd been eighteen and leaving the gypsy camp that had taken him in for three years. She'd been in her early teens, already promiscuous, and engaged to wed a man much older.

Ella's face creased in a beatific smile. "Not so little anymore. And no longer engaged." She sent him a flirtatious glance and trailed her fingers at the neckline of her bodice, attempting to lure his gaze to her feminine contours. His eyes stayed on her face, searching it intently.

She frowned. Was he thinking of her sister? Looking for reminders of Clara in her own features?

He paced a few steps away, putting the desk between them before speaking again in a low voice. "I'm sorry, Carmella . . . Ella. So sorry. You must hate me for my part in what happened to Clara. I—"

"No! No, you stupid man." She slammed her small fist on the desktop, then leaned forward over it, displaying her cleavage to full advantage. "Have you been feeling guilty all this time? You didn't kill her. Her death was only meant to bring us closer."

"What?"

Ella straightened, realizing she'd said too much. But his guilt *was* misplaced. Clara hadn't meant to kill herself over him. Not in the beginning at least. Not until Ella had fueled her fears and eroded her confidence with half-truths and outright lies about Sevin's supposed dalliances with other women in the towns their caravan visited from time to time.

Finally, on one low night, Ella had lured her sister to the brink of suicide, and then she'd given her the nudge that had tipped her over. It had been a masterful performance on Ella's part, a falsified confession that she'd made Clara painstakingly draw from her. How she'd secretly smiled to herself, as she'd fabricated her tearful tale. It had been something to the effect that she'd witnessed Sevin fornicating with one of Clara's rivals in the woods that afternoon. In fact, he'd only gone out hunting with the other men of the tribe.

"I only meant that I—we all missed you when you left. Why did you go without saying anything?" she hedged.

After her sister had died, Ella had naively assumed that Sevin would wait until she grew up to take her sister's place in his bed and in his life. Instead, he'd disappeared. She'd only recently found him again. And now these rumors that he planned to wed. Had he chosen a partner? If only she could convince him to let it be her.

"It seemed for the best," Sevin replied.

Ella chose her next words to him with care. "I was only a girl back then, not filled out yet." She ran her hands down her figure, this time drawing his eyes. But there was no passion in his gaze. The fact that he was unaffected sent a spear of panic through her. "I'm grown now. Experienced. Your equal."

He shook his head. "You're human."

"You're wrong if you think that was the reason Clara couldn't handle you. She wasn't right for you. I saw that. Everyone did."

"You're right that we weren't meant for one another. We were too damn young. But I loved her in my own way," said Sevin.

"But not in a lasting way. And she knew. She was so afraid of losing you. Whatever you wanted she would have done in order to keep you. But your sybaritic ways were not hers. You need a woman with passions to match your own," Ella said with the width of his massive desk now separating them. "A woman like me."

"Ella . . ." He combed his fingers through his hair, looking uncomfortable.

Her eyes filled with tears. For once they weren't feigned. She could feel him slipping away and was terrified he would banish her from his side. No! She needed more time to woo him. To make him understand that he needed her. When she thought of the things she'd done—the terrible things. They'd all been in an effort to have this man love her. He *had* to love her!

She went to him and trailed a bright red fingernail down the center of his chest. He caught her hand in one fist. His touch, even one of rejection, sent a thrill over her. However, this wasn't going at all as she'd imagined in her fantasies.

"How is it that your scent is a mix of human and fey?" he asked suspiciously.

She shrugged, knowing he wouldn't like the truth. That she'd been dosing her skin daily with extracts that had been forcibly taken from a variety of ElseWorld creatures while they'd suffered imprisonment. The brother he so doted on had been among them, after all. And it had been his ruin.

"Clara and I had different fathers. Mine was human, and his taint has strengthened in me over time," she said, using the lie she'd rehearsed. "So you see there is no real barrier to—"

"Why the masquerade?" he interrupted.

"If I'd told you in my interview, would you have hired me? A half blood?"

Before he could answer, a knock sounded on the door behind her. It opened to admit one of the black-coated sentries. The big, annoying one that sported only a single eye in his forehead.

For some inexplicable reason, Sevin looked exceptionally pleased to see him. "You're back?" he asked, a question in his voice.

"*Sì,* and I brought you a visitor, Lord Sevin." Ignoring Ella, the sentry came inside and handed a plain white card to his employer. "Awaiting you in the anteroom, she is," he added.

Sevin read the card and tossed it down. Immediately, he sprang into action, snatching his jacket from the coat hook on his way out. "We'll discuss this later. You may stay on for now," he told Ella. Then he strode from the room.

The guard lingered, however, his unblinking eye pinned on her as if he expected her to thieve if he looked away. She perched on Sevin's desktop behind her, just to annoy him.

"Come along, signorina. I should lock up. Lord Sevin don't like his office left open for all comers."

"Oh! Of course." She smiled at him sweetly, pretending she hadn't just surreptitiously slipped one of the official-looking letters atop Sevin's desk into her pocket. Information was money. After she read it, she'd make sure it found its way back to his desk or into the mail tray. No one here would ever be the wiser.

As she slid off the desk, her hand swept something. Curious, she lifted the card Sevin had just received. Written upon it in a feminine hand were the words: *My home is for sale.*

Frowning, she flipped the card over, too anxious to care that the guard saw her do it. Two words were discreetly embossed in black upon its opposite side: *Signorina Patrizzi.*

Ella crumpled the card in her fist, anger boiling up in her. Then her lips curved into a spiteful smile. She'd left lip rouge on Lord Sevin's collar, purposely marking him for all the other employees to see. *What would this Signorina Patrizzi make of that?* she wondered.

Quickly, she went to her personal chamber to bathe and dress. Afterward, she would spy upon them and learn what she could until it was time for her next appointment.

Moments later, Sevin threw open the velvet drape that hung at the entrance to the salon's main arena. He scanned the anteroom beyond it, relieved to find that Alexa still awaited him there. Seated among the patrons and salon employees who mingled around her, she looked elegant, fashionable, and very human.

Upon seeing him, she leaped to her feet, looking relieved as well. But when he came close, she stepped back warily. "You got my message? What do you think?"

His eyes narrowed. "I think I'm pleased to see you." He bussed her lips with his and watched pink bloom in her cheeks. He'd questioned one of the sentries who'd brought her here just now and had been informed that just after she'd awakened, she had rushed the trio of guards posted outside her house here to the salon with suspicious haste.

"And I wonder that you are in such a fidget to sell your home all of a sudden," he told her. "Why?"

Because there's a dead body in my bedchamber, and I will likely be accused of murder when it is found. "I don't want to drag you into this," she said, shaking her head.

"Into what?"

"Nothing," she said, too quickly. His eyes fell to her hands, which were twisting her handbag into a tangle between them. Noting his study, she forced them to stillness.

"I'll be frank," she went on. "I know you want my house. I overheard you and your brothers speaking about your plans for it as you were leaving this morning."

His mind raced, wondering exactly what she'd overheard. "And you agree to those plans so easily?"

She nodded. "If you're willing to engage in the fight ahead with my husband's family for ownership of the property, I will sell it to you. And you are free to re-create your salon there. I have no quarrel with that. But I want a deal made immediately."

"Tonight?" he asked.

"Yes. I'm leaving Rome as soon as it's done. Don't try to change my mind."

"All right," he said smoothly, knowing all the while that he most certainly did intend to change her mind. "Wait for me here. I'll have a runner sent for my attorney."

Turning on his heel, he made for the doorway through which he'd just come. Stepping through, he held the velvet drape wide, watching her as he murmured privately to a sentry on duty there. He was taking no chances that she'd change her mind and disappear while his back was turned. This woman was proving far too slippery of late.

"Find out what news you can of the elder Signor Tivoli and his son, Laslo, both lately of Venice, and now in Rome," he told the sentry. "And have my attorney summoned. Immediately."

As the guard waved over a runner, Sevin turned back to Alexa, who was gazing around the room in fascination. He wondered what she thought of his creation.

"How long until they arrive?" she asked anxiously as he approached her.

"An hour perhaps. Then papers must be drawn up. You'll be here a while, possibly all night."

"Oh dear." She fully intended to flee the moment she had the funds from him, no matter how late the hour, but every second that passed in the interim heightened the danger that Laslo might be discovered. When she'd awakened this evening and found his body, she'd gone to her mother's room to hurriedly bathe and dress. Afterward, she'd urged the guards Sevin had posted outside the house to bring her here, leaving them none the wiser regarding the corpse in her bedroom. She shuddered, horrified by the remembrance of it.

Had Laslo killed himself? With a poker? But how would he have gotten past the guards in order to do so in her home? The door to the catacombs in the library had been securely locked, so he had not come that way either. However, she hadn't actually seen him leave the house that morning, now that she thought about it. Had he stayed on in hiding, with plans to do himself in on her carpet? It made no sense.

Whatever the case, she harbored little doubt that she would be blamed for his death. The divorce papers were undeniable evidence that she wished to be rid of him, and many in Italy would leap at the chance to chastise a woman for having sought divorce in the first place. Sentiment in Rome already ran against her family, and she couldn't take the chance of a trial. Though her mind had twisted the matter around and around, she always came to the same conclusion in the end. She had to flee.

"So this is your salon," she said, trying to turn the conversation. "It's beautiful. Quite grand."

Sevin smiled slightly, allowing her to change the subject. "I'm glad you approve. However, this is merely an anteroom, a meeting place for patrons to engage in verbal foreplay. Some of them never move beyond it. For them, a little flirtation with members of their species is enough. If one is looking for more, the main salon lies through that drape."

More? Alexa craned her neck toward the mysterious drape, wondering precisely what that entailed.

"Come. Have a look at what I intend that your family home will become."

She gazed at what little she could see beyond the gap in the curtain, intrigued in spite of herself. "Well, I don't actually have time for a tour. I was hoping we could iron out the details of the sale now, as I said."

"I usually transact business in my offices, not in the hallways," he said, slipping an arm about her waist. "And those offices are above stairs on the third level. My attorney will be taken there directly, I assure you." When her footsteps dragged, he added, "Or you could wait here, maybe do a little mingling on your own while I'm at work upstairs."

She glanced around at the strange creatures that surrounded them in the anteroom, some scantily clad, some with green skin, others with small horns, and still others with even more unusual physical characteristics. They were studiously ignoring her, but she sensed that her presence made them uncomfortable. She also sensed that Sevin had made his suggestion because he knew she would feel awkward remaining here among them.

"To your offices, then," she said, allowing him to lead her onward. She was curious about the salon, after all, and they must pass the time somehow until his legal man came.

The main salon was enormous, she discovered, as they stepped through the drape, boasting a gilded, coffered ceiling that reached three stories high. At the center of its floor, a carousel turned at a leisurely, mesmerizing pace. Wildly painted and lacquered dragons, unicorns, and other fantastic creatures pumped up and down on poles, their backs eerily bare of passengers for now. With furnishings and wall coverings done up in jeweled tones, and the soft strains of music in the air, the room was a feast for the senses.

Placing a proprietary hand at her back, Sevin began a stroll that would take them around its circular perimeter. He was silent, allowing her to absorb the sights at her own pace.

"What is that beguiling fragrance?" she couldn't help asking. The complex, evocative scent that permeated the massive room was one of the first things that had struck her as they'd entered.

"Magic," he told her simply.

"Oh," she said with a careless flick of her hand. "Of course. Magic." She rolled her eyes at the casual nature of his offhand announcement, and he gazed at her quizzically. This was all commonplace for him, she realized. "That is the sort of statement that underscores the vast differences between us and our worlds, signor."

"Differences are what keep life interesting, I've found." He smiled serenely as they passed two men lying together in a voluptuous embrace on a leather-upholstered couch. Both had scaled skin, and slender undulating tails extending from their tailbones.

Alexa dragged her eyes away from the intriguing couple to study the salon, entirely fascinated. It was hard to be circumspect when everywhere she looked, there was something at which she wanted to openly gape.

The expansive room was mildly chaotic and already full of patrons mingling with what she assumed to be his employees. ElseWorld species of all kinds milled about, some in translucent veils, others in elaborate costume or in fashionable street clothes, and still others like the two men on the couch—virtually naked.

Standing atop pedestals set around the room there were life-sized statues in various stages of undress. Although they appeared to be stone, she noticed that they occasionally moved in time to the soft, tantalizing music that emanated from the carousel. They were alive, she realized, but their flesh and clothing had been painted to give the illusion that they were sculpted of marble. Their poses were overtly sensual, meant to titillate. Some were paired in erotic embraces, while others posed alone.

So this was what he intended her family's home to become! Her mother would surely have turned over in her grave. It was a notion that made her smile.

Unoccupied platforms also dotted the floor space here and there, and a series of doors ringed the room at intervals. "For public engagements and private ones," Sevin obliquely informed her in answer to her question about them.

Just then, two tall, dark-haired men—one with a struggling woman slung over his brawny shoulder—passed them. Alexa stared back at them in outrage, then looked at Sevin. "Aren't you going to stop them?" she demanded.

But he only pressed a hand low at her back again, moving her onward. "Some things you see here might seem . . . brutal. Some are actually intended to shock an audience. But without exception, all are of a consensual nature. House rules."

Uncertain, she glanced over her shoulder after the trio, which had paused outside one of the doors along the room's perimeter. While the first man opened it, the woman hoisted over the second man's shoulder lifted her face and happened to catch Alexa's eye. Smiling faintly at her, the woman winked. Then she let out a pitiful, but obviously feigned, plea for help and pounded her captor on his back.

This time, Alexa could not help but openly stare, recalling herself only when the door closed behind the trio, secluding them inside one of the mysterious chambers. Sevin didn't notice, for he had paused to speak to a man in severe, tailored black. There were numerous such men in the salon, each of whom had carefully ignored them as they passed. They were stationed in unobtrusive locations, their sharp eyes alert and seeming to make sure all ran smoothly. While everyone else frolicked here in this hedonistic paradise, Sevin and his guards seemed to be all business.

"This way," he said at length, directing her up a staircase. As they took the marble steps up toward what she assumed were his offices, she scanned the panoramic scene below. "You could sell tickets to this," she said, shaking her head in bemusement, and he laughed, following her gaze.

"We attract a broad spectrum culled from Rome and beyond," he told her. "The salon boasts over a thousand members."

"Why did you build it?" she asked curiously. "I think everyone in my world assumes it serves as a sort of harem for you and your brothers, but that isn't it at all, is it?"

He laughed again, flashing white teeth and dimples that reminded her how handsome he was. Hearing him, other women in the salon below glanced up at him, their glances longing, lingering. He could have any of them. Most likely had already done so. Why choose her?

"I'm a businessman. I saw a need for a private location in which ElseWorld kind could safely congregate for conversation and concupiscent engagements with like-minded partners. And I sought to fill it. For the past decade, the salon has helped limit the potential for inadvertent exposure were such engagements to take place outside these environs."

"And now that your kind has been found out?"

He shrugged. "There's a greater need than ever. These people—these beings—and my brothers and I—this is a vital haven for all of us during our Calling, when we're dangerously vulnerable."

"So all this"—she gestured toward the scene below—"is an act of benevolence on your part?"

"I'm a man of business, not benevolence."

"But you'll concede that it's more than just random good fortune that the two overlap here in this venture of yours." Although he seemed unwilling to be considered altruistic, the label seemed to fit.

They were on the third floor now and he paused before a door, opening it. "My goals are centered around family, profit, and public benevolence. In that order of importance," he told her. "And as of last night, you became a part of my family. An important one."

Beside him, Alexa came to a dead stop in the doorway. The chamber he'd brought her to boasted sumptuous couches, low lighting, and a large bed.

She shot him a skeptical look. "*This* is your office?"

10

"That's next door. First, I wanted you to see where I live."
Sevin went farther inside, switching on another lamp.

"You mean that you reside here? In the salon?" Alexa asked,
taking a wary step inside. She was curious to know more of
how he lived, and they had time on their hands. But this was a
dangerous game.

"I sleep here." He went to another door on the adjacent wall
and opened it so that she could see that it led to a small hallway,
which in turn ended at another door. "But my real home is
through that door. My office."

Turning, he set his hands at his hips and glanced around his
bedchamber as if trying to see it through her eyes. "What do
you think of it?"

She thought it was aesthetically pleasing, she thought it was
lush, and she thought she wanted nothing more than to lie in
that enormous bed with him and forget her troubles in his
arms. Of course she said none of that to him. The things she'd
witnessed in the salon had primed her for something decadent,
and his proximity was having the usual effect on her. She won-

dered when the attorney would arrive. Hoped he would come before the two of them found a completely inappropriate way to pass the time.

"You can change anything you like here," he told her, when she didn't speak. "Wives often do, I'm told."

"I'm not going to wed you," she insisted, relieved at the turn in the conversation and hoping it would dispel the sense of intimacy between them. "I've tried marriage—"

"But not with me," he noted.

Spreading her arms, she made an exasperated sound. "You've known me less than two days."

"I've been aware of you for far longer."

He must have read the doubt in her face for he lounged against the door frame and folded his arms, then calmly reviewed the facts. "Blue dress. Blue hat. It was one afternoon early last February in the Forum. You were strolling with Eva through the excavation site. Before you became engaged to Dane. Before she became Dane's wife."

Alexa stared at him, surprised. Abruptly, a conversation from that day insidiously worked its way to the forefront of her mind:

"Can you imagine a wedding night with one of the Satyr lords?" she'd asked Eva. "I'd be frightened out of my wits!" She'd leaned in then, whispering so no passersby would overhear. "I've heard they sport a second member in their trousers. I've also heard they know well what to do with both of them. I was told by a reliable source that there's a particular statue of a Satyr enjoying a Bacchanalia in one of the temples. It holds a wine goblet, has furred haunches, a tail, and its male—parts— are high and at the ready for entertainment."

Although Eva had acted convincingly shocked, Alexa now wondered just how much of the truth she'd already known. As for herself, it made her blush to think how silly and naive she'd been back then. That innocent girl was gone now.

138 / *Elizabeth Amber*

"Shall we?" She moved briskly toward him and the short corridor that led from his private apartments to what she hoped would prove to be the relative safety of his more public office. As she stepped past, he took her arm, staying her.

With one shoulder against the wall, he studied her, his hand on her a scalding, possessive weight. "That day was the first of many times that I noticed you. Then that nasty business with your family and Luc intruded. I knew there was no possibility of anything between us. Yet each time I saw you I was reminded again. And my *interest*, however inappropriate, was revived. Strengthened. It has not been easy to keep my distance."

She knew exactly what he meant, for his nearness was affecting her. Making her want him. Want more of what she'd enjoyed with him last night. Did he really wish to wed *her*?

She shook her head, not realizing she was doing so and that he wondered at it. No, she'd made enough mistakes recently. He would leave her heart damaged, and they had both been hurt enough.

His head lowered, but she averted her face. "Please don't," she whispered. "Don't continue with this . . . lark. Your family has already suffered through its association with mine. And there are things you don't know about me. . . ."

With an easy shift of muscle, Sevin leaned with his back against the corridor wall, drawing her to him. "What things?"

"Private things." *A dead ex-husband bleeding out in my bedroom.*

At her reluctance, he growled low in his throat and pulled her closer until she was standing between his powerful outspread thighs. "Don't shut me out, Alexa. Give me the right to protect you. To love you."

Love? Did he mean in the physical sense, or . . . She gazed at him then, losing her heart somewhere in his molten silver eyes. Had she really thought them hard and reflective only two days ago? "You can't protect me."

"I assure you that I can," he promised with quiet confidence. "If you'll confess what's got you in such a rush to sell out and leave."

Lifting her hands to his shoulders, she shook her head. Her eyes were on his mouth. Her body remembered the pleasure it could give. Maybe just one last taste, tonight before she left Rome. What could it hurt? "I see the way women gaze at you. You've rarely had one refuse you anything. If I stopped running . . ."

He gaped at her. "You think that if all of this between us ends in marriage—that I'll lose interest?"

She lifted on tiptoe, her mouth pressing to the hollow of his throat, and she felt every muscle in his body tighten. "I'm not here to acquire another husband, only to tell you that you may buy my house. For a price. I know you want it for a new salon and a storage place for artifacts in the catacombs below. I wish you well."

"And you?" His hands moved up her back. She sensed that he wanted to kiss her, yet he made no move to do so.

"What about me?" she replied, her desperation for him spiking. "I'm sure you're not the only male capable of providing protection—or pleasure—to a woman."

He drew his head back, frowning down at her. "More capable than a human man. What exactly went wrong between you and your Laslo?"

She gave a sad little laugh. "I willingly allowed him in my bed, hoping to have the mysteries of the flesh revealed to me. Unfortunately, I've always had a curious nature regarding such matters."

"There's no wrong in that. What happened?" His warm hand stroked her nape and she relaxed against him, sighing. "Nothing good."

At the thought of another man hurting her, Sevin wanted to

punch something. Or someone. And then she murmured into his shirtfront, "Nothing like it was with you."

Desire speared him, need for her racing through his blood to heat his entire body. The need to take care of her, to love her, to mate her. "Ah, gods, Alexa." In a lithe move he swept her up into his arms. He'd been holding back, hoping to bargain with sex to get what he wanted. But to hells with holding back. He would argue the matter of marriage later with a cooler head, and he would win her assent.

Turning, he pushed her against the wall, taking her mouth with his. She welcomed him and their kisses were hot, their breath urgent and rough. He went lower, kissing her throat, the tops of her breasts. Wanting more. "Open this damned thing for me," he demanded.

He watched her unfasten her bodice for him, then her corset. Beneath them, she was warm, soft. His mouth covered the peak of one breast and then another, drawing on them until she moaned. The sight of them, reddened, wet, and erect from his attentions, affected him like an aphrodisiac.

A variety of debaucheries in which he wished to engage this woman—this *particular* woman—heated his mind. He lifted her thighs higher around him, rocking his sex at her gate, wrenching fabric aside. His voice rasped at her ear, telling her what he would do to her, here against this wall and later in his bed.

She moaned again and her slender, stockinged legs tightened around him. "Yes. Hurry," she whispered, her hands tugging his shirttails from the waistband of his trousers. His hands worked between them, ripping at the fastenings of his trousers.

Then suddenly, Alexa faltered. Her head lifted and she peered over his shoulder, frowning slightly. Had she just heard voices?

Oh no! There was movement in the public corridor just outside. Voices. Footsteps. Sevin didn't seem to notice, or perhaps he just didn't care that they might be discovered. Holding him at bay with one hand, she clutched the sides of her corset and bodice together with her other.

"Wait. No," she whispered. "Someone's coming."

He looked at her then, his expression clouded with a blend of desire and confusion. "What?" His eyes were heavy-lidded, staring greedily at her mouth.

She turned her head as he leaned in to kiss her again, batting at his roving hands. "No. There's someone out there."

"Who the fuck cares?" he murmured against her throat. "I own this place. They won't bother us." He shifted his weight, his hands going under her bottom, tilting her to better cradle his erection.

Mmm. Only her pantalets remained between them, and through this fragile barrier, his male member burned her, making her nether heart pulse for want of it. Her body was open for him, wet for him, dying for him.

He was a temptation she couldn't resist, and for these stolen moments, she would not try. "Be quick then," she urged softly.

His hand found the slit in her pantalets. She felt the nudge of his smooth, hot cock head. She tightened her thighs, slowing him.

"Once more. That's all this is," she whispered. He only grunted. Her fingers threaded his hair and she kissed him deeply, as he'd taught her last night. His thighs braced her weight, his hips pushed . . .

Then there came the sound of a door, the one leading from the outside hallway to his adjacent office.

"Sevin!" Dane's voice called from the office just beyond them.

"Five thousand hells!" Sevin groaned. Angling his head, he threw a reply over his shoulder. "Not now!" he snarled.

"Apologies, brother. It's an urgent matter." There was amusement in Dane's voice now.

"Go." Alexa pushed at him, wriggling and trying to straighten her clothing and hair.

Sevin stared down at her, still passionate and hungry. Briefly, he rested his forehead against hers. "This isn't over," he murmured. Then he was letting her go, and they were fumbling to right themselves. A moment later he opened the door to the office, one hand at her back.

"Your timing leaves something to be desired, brother," he growled. He was just about to continue berating Dane when he noticed that he held a baby in his arms. And his wife stood just beyond him.

"*Buona sera*, Sevin," Eva told him. "We apologize for barging in."

Alexa's eyes widened when she saw the child. Her hand fluttered down to her own belly, then she let it drop to her side. What had she been thinking just now? Her foolish behavior could have resulted in a child. *And what about last night?* she suddenly worried. The years ahead on her own would be difficult enough without a child to care for.

She said nothing of her fears, of course, and only nodded to Dane before slipping beyond him to greet Eva.

"Dane and I have business downstairs," Sevin told her after a brief word with his brother. The two men headed for the outer door.

"You'll check on the whereabouts of that attorney?" Alexa asked.

Sevin nodded, watching as Dane handed the baby he held over to Eva before their departure. He'd never considered himself father material, but suddenly the notion did not strike him as something so foreign. His eyes pinned the woman for whom his body still ached.

"You'll stay put here with Eva till I return. Promise me."

She folded her arms, not appreciating his tone.

"I'll post guards if I must. Please, Alexa. I'll worry."

She sighed, her tone distant. "Very well. But make haste."

At that, Sevin went back to her. Wrapping a hand at her nape, he gave her a brief, all-too-public kiss on the mouth. She blushed, looking flustered.

"Branded," he teased softly. "Now they know you're mine."

Releasing her, he smiled over at Eva. "While I'm gone, maybe you can convince her to wed me. So far, I've not had much luck in the effort." Then he and Dane left the two women together.

Eva's eyes lighted at the mention of a marriage in the offing. "Is he sincere? Oh, it would be so wonderful if you were to wed Sevin!" she enthused. "You would be part of the family and all this hatred between you would end. He's a good man. They're all four good men," she said, nodding toward the salon as if to encompass all the Satyr brothers.

Alexa raised a brow. "Is this the beginning of your campaign to convince me?"

Eva laughed. "Just my own observation. I trust and love Dane with all my heart. And he has only good things to say about the loyalty and heart of his brothers."

"What does he say of Sevin in particular?"

Eva positioned the child she held over one shoulder, swaying from side to side to comfort her. "That he has always been a charmer. Good at cards, good at business, good at conversation. Resourceful. That sort of thing."

Alexa folded her arms. "There was lip rouge on his collar, did you notice? It wasn't mine."

"Oh," said Eva, her brow wrinkling. "Well, he does work among dozens of beautiful women. But I assure you that these Satyr men are constant, once they choose a wife. Now tell me. How did this all come about? Do you love him?"

"I only met him two days ago." Alexa paced a few steps away, pausing to stare at a book that lay open on Sevin's desk. It was a discussion of ancient fountains, some resembling the one from the catacombs. She winced, her thoughts returning to the previous night. Not looking at Eva, she murmured, "You know I was with him during his Calling? And also with . . ."

"Luc. Yes, Dane told me," Eva admitted, her matter-of-fact tone putting Alexa at ease regarding the previous night. "It made me hopeful that I might acquire you as a new sister-in-law. I—"

Alexa turned, cutting her off. "There's something more I haven't told you. I was married in Venice."

"Oh, dear. Does Sevin know? Come, sit and tell me. My daughter is wriggling," Eva told her, taking one of the two matching visitors' chairs along the wall.

"There's little to tell," said Alexa, dropping on to the seat beside her. "My marriage was a mistake. I secured a divorce in England."

Eva's eyes widened, then she reached over and squeezed Alexa's hand briefly. "Well, good for you. And so you're free to wed Sevin?"

No, she wasn't free. In fact, she might wind up incarcerated if she didn't leave Rome soon. "I'm only here on business tonight. Despite what he said, there's no question of marriage."

Eva sat back, rocking her daughter. How Alexa envied her! She knew exactly where and with whom she *belonged*. She had a loving husband, a secure place in his family.

"Their parents died when they were boys, did you know?" Eva told her.

Alexa shook her head, wordlessly inviting her to continue.

Absently cuddling her daughter, Eva looked thoughtful. "Let's see, Sevin was fifteen or so at the time, I suppose. Dane and Luc had disappeared to the catacombs, and then Bastian became caught in the grip of an alcohol addiction that led him on a trek to remote parts of Europe. In their absence, Sevin was turned out of his home, destitute and left to fend for himself for several years. However, not only did he manage to survive, he even singlehandedly convinced the ElseWorld Council to allow him to build this place, and then saw it all get done. No mean feat for an inexperienced young man in his teens."

"I'd assumed he'd always lived in luxury," said Alexa, stunned at this revelation. "After all that, it's little wonder he works so diligently to keep his family intact."

"You and he have both suffered abandonment by your families. It gives you a common experience. That can be the basis for a strong bond."

Alexa shook her head. "I admit that the lure of joining his family is a strong one for me, but . . ."

"Don't forget that there would be other benefits to wedding him besides the family you would acquire," said Eva, giving her a significant look. "Nightly benefits. Of the kind which greatly soothe and outweigh most other difficulties."

"Ah, yes," said Alexa. "I take your meaning."

At that, the two women shared a smile, both well aware of how very delicious those nightly benefits could be when it came to Satyr men.

Eva departed a minute later to see to her daughter's feeding, promising to return shortly. In her absence, Alexa wandered over to Sevin's chair. Plopping down on it, she imagined him sitting there and working. Idly she studied the columns of figures on the ledger left open on his desk. Noticing an error in his calculations, she corrected it.

With little else to occupy her then except her worries, she took up the book of fountains again, flipping through it. Studying one of the illustrations in particular, she bracketed her hands around a portion of it as if to make a frame. Her heart picked up speed. When taken alone, that part of the overall fountain seemed very familiar.

In fact, it bore a striking similarity to the entirety of the fountain that stood in the catacombs. She'd had ample enough time to study it that last evening—hours, in fact. When she tried to recall the details of it now, a particular scene from last night sprang up in her mind's eye.

She remembered that Sevin and Luc had drawn water from the fountain. It made her blush now to recall how they'd proceeded to wash her intimately, their big hands slicking over her flesh, until they'd all wound up in a breathless, sybaritic tangle. The feel of Sevin's body against hers was so fresh in her mind.

A shiver prickled her now at the remembrance, and she shifted in his chair. His weight had pressed hers to the fountain's cold, slick stone. How hot her skin had been from her lovers' use of it, and how soothing the overspray from the fountain's waters had been as—

Hearing a sudden noise in the adjoining apartment, she started guiltily. She half rose from her seat, looking toward it. "Sevin?" When there was no reply, she went across the adjoining hallway to his bedchamber and peeked inside. "Sevin?" she called again.

A voice from the closet called out at the same time. A woman's voice. "Sevin? Is that you, *caro*? I'm sorry I'm late. Did you miss me?"

Alexa gasped. "Who's there?"

When the woman stepped out of the closet and into the room, Alexa found herself staring at an exquisitely beautiful creature with red hair. "Who are you?" the woman demanded, her delicate brows drawing together.

"Signorina Patrizzi," Alexa admitted. "And you?"

"Signorina Carmella Carbone. Sevin has spoken of you." The woman's gaze swept Alexa, obviously finding her wanting. "You're the one he fucked last night, aren't you?"

Heedless of Alexa's second gasp in as many minutes, the woman continued. "Are you the one he plans to wed? Because of the proclamation?"

"What proclamation?" Alexa asked blankly.

The woman gave her an impatient look. "The one that prohibits any ElseWorld creature from purchasing property in this world. Clever of him to marry into property instead. A trifle annoying, however." She pouted prettily, drawing Alexa's notice to her mouth. Her lip rouge was an unusual orange tint. *The very same color I saw on Sevin's collar earlier!*

"We were supposed to lie together for the Calling, did you know? But I'm sure he'll make it up to me tonight." Signorina Carbone grinned wickedly. Alexa stepped back as if from a blow, putting a hand over her heart.

Ignoring her, the signorina proceeded to make free with Sevin's room. Going to a cabinet, she took something from it, then plunked it on the bedside table. It was an artificial phallus made of lacquered wood! A device for giving pleasure. One that Sevin used in engagements with this woman, apparently. Alongside it, Signorina Carbone had set a flagon, likely filled with lubricant.

Feeling all the blood drain from her face, Alexa made for the door.

"You must ask him to make use of these with you sometime. He's really quite talented," Ella suggested casually. She pulled back the coverlet on the bed. Her back to Alexa, she began removing her robe. "Oh! I didn't think to ask. Has he arranged for you to join us tonight?"

Hearing footsteps out in the hall, Ella looked over her shoulder to see that the Patrizzi wench had fled. She closed her robe again, smiling to herself. "That's it. Run, *puta*," she murmured.

Then she slipped from Sevin's apartments and made her way to her own chamber, where she quickly readied herself. Now that that was taken care of, she had another appointment that would take her away from the salon for the next few hours.

If all went well tonight, things might take a more desirable turn with Sevin afterward. Or so her upcoming client had promised.

Upon returning to his office three-quarters of an hour later only to find Alexa gone, Sevin let out a roar that echoed throughout the entire salon. "Damnation!"

Dane had brought disturbing news from Bastian regarding the explosive that they'd found in the bar yesterday. Thinking her safe with Eva, he'd tarried with his brothers over the matter.

Summoning every guard in the salon now, he initiated a search for her. When she was nowhere to be found, he struck out for her home, praying to the gods that he hadn't lost her.

11

Signorina Ella Carbone stepped into the hotel room, enjoying the sophisticated stylishness of its furnishings. They were expensive, just like the man waiting for her here. She didn't know his name, but he was human like her. Unlike her, he came from money.

She wanted to come from money. And even more, she wanted to *come* under Lord Sevin. She smiled inwardly at her private little joke. If was the first genuine smile she'd managed in a while, for she'd begun to fear that any hope of having him was slipping away.

But she was resourceful and not the sort to give up. Out of desperation, she'd contacted this man. He had assured her he would help her achieve the outcome she desired with Lord Sevin. Or remove the major roadblock to her happiness, at any rate. He'd made good on his promises before, so she trusted him. Of course, he always wanted something in return, but she was accustomed to bargaining with her body.

Hands in his pockets, he studied her now with his hard eyes. She went to him and smiled flirtatiously, pressing her body against him. "*Buona sera,* signor. Your message to me indicated that we have a deal?" Her hand brushed his cock lightly. He wasn't hard yet, but she knew how to change that. She gave him a few practiced strokes. When she felt him lengthen in his trousers, she stopped.

"I take care of your needs," she purred. "And in return, you'll take care of that little bit of business I mentioned?"

He nodded, then pushed her away. "Yes, yes. We have a deal. Now wash that fey stink off, and we'll get started in earnest on your part of the bargain."

She paused, angling her head. "You brought another bottle of the same scent? I've run out and can't go back to the salon smelling like a human."

"I brought more for you to douse yourself with when you go, don't worry on that score." In fact, he hadn't, but she wouldn't be needing it anyway.

Ella rolled her eyes, but began removing her clothing and washing herself at the basin. "Most clients like that 'stink,' as you call it, you know. In fact, Lord Sevin is planning to start a club in which humans like you can wallow up to their balls in 'fey stink.' Or in the scent of an assortment of other ElseWorld creatures, if they're willing."

The signor took in that information with great interest, though she didn't realize it. Stupid girl probably planned to sell the news, but that wasn't going to happen. It was his news now.

"That a fact?" was all he said.

She nodded. "Bet you won't be dipping your cock inside the snatches of any true ElseWorld creatures though, will you?" she teased.

He smirked. "You might be surprised."

"I would be, after all your talk against them."

Although she tried to be coy at her bath, he only watched her dispassionately. This sort of flirtation didn't sufficiently move him. He needed more from a woman. Ella had been a pleasant enough companion over the past few weeks. She'd gladly repaid him for the fey tincture he supplied to her, with sex—and more importantly, with information. He'd culled her out to work for him because of her employment in the *Salone di Passione* and because she listened well, both to his instruction and to gossip.

He hadn't heard that the Satyr were planning a club in which humans and ElseWorld savages would mingle. However, such news would buy him favors in the Italian ministry. And he'd gotten the information for free this time. It put him in a good mood.

He leaned against the wall opposite the end of the four-poster bed and watched her dry her skin. Poor little chit thought Sevin Satyr was going to wed her. Fool. But far be it from him to disabuse her of that little fantasy in her last hours.

"You always look so refined. It's what I love about you," she said, gazing at him as she smoothed a cloth over her light olive skin. Her flattery was often a pretense, but he could tell this was genuine. She coveted refinement and emulated it well. But she was trash. Gypsy trash. Always would be.

When she finished her toweling, she put on her shift again. It was a wisp of a thing, translucent red, with velvet bows and lots of lace. It barely covered her ass cheeks and she wore nothing beneath it. It was an expensive whore's garment worn by an expensive whore.

Going to the end of the bed, she bent to stroke one of the straps of leather he'd placed there, knowing he liked to see her do it. Knowing he liked to see her bare ass when she did it.

Standing at the foot of the bed, she placed her hands flat on its mattress before her and arched her slender back. Head and ass up, just as he enjoyed. His breath came faster, and his eyes sharpened on her, waiting.

Reaching around with a graceful hand, she slowly tugged up the hem of her gauzy shift. Spreading her legs slightly, she tilted her ass higher still. Her fingers came over her bottom, finding her feminine folds. She forked them wide, opening her slick, pink nakedness. Inviting him to look. Inviting him in.

She looked at him over her shoulder, eyes glittering. "See anything you like?"

He straightened slowly and went to her, watching her stroke herself for a long moment. Lightly, he ran a hand over the dimpled rump on display, rubbed his thumb over the pruney moue between her cheeks. He was going to miss this ass of hers.

"Have you fucked him?" he asked idly, pulling the tails of his shirt from his trousers. "Your Satyr lord?"

She frowned.

He laughed, and slapped her ass, moving away to study the selection of leathers he'd carefully displayed on the mattress beside her. "Not yet, eh? You think you're going to get him by playing fast and loose with other men like me?"

She straightened from the bed, pretending to be annoyed. "Why do you talk to me like that?" she asked. "Do you speak to your wife in such a charming way?"

He shrugged. "She's dead. We don't speak at all."

"Well, some men like their women to take other men. Some even like to watch. Experience isn't a bad thing," she said, pouting prettily and refusing to take his insults to heart.

He pretended to mull his choices, then selected the leather he'd intended all along, knowing she'd hate it. Twenty inches long, with a buckle on the end, it had a fat, stuffed ball in the center of its length about the size of a small apple. He took it to her and saw her try to hide her distaste.

"Open wide," he crooned, with a small smile. "Can't have you screaming your delight out to the world when we're fucking."

Ella put a hand on his shirtfront, catching his eye. He was twice her age, with a mean streak. But she didn't mind. "You swear you'll get rid of her—the Patrizzi woman. Take her out of Lord Sevin's orbit for good?"

Smiling down on her, he said truthfully, "I will. This very night, as it happens."

"What are you going to do with her?"

He shook his head. "*Tut, tut.* That information isn't part of our deal. Just know you'll never see her again. Nor will anyone else."

She smiled, pleased. "Good."

He pressed the ball to her smiling lips, and after a brief hesitation, she opened for him. He stuffed it in her, then turned her, enjoying the way she protested when he yanked the buckled strap tight around her head, fastening it at the back of her neck. Then he turned her again to face him. Her eyes gazed docilely up at him as he checked the fit of the ball in her gaping mouth, making sure her screams would not be heard. They wouldn't be screams of passion, pretended or otherwise, this time around, though.

Although his excitement began to rise, he still kept his sex in his trousers, enjoying the pain of his strangled erection. He brought another, shorter strap and she obediently held out her hands, watching as he wrapped it around her wrists and buckled it tight as well. Stringing a long cord through that, he tied it off at the headboard, leaving her just enough lead string to put up a good struggle but not give him too much trouble.

Picking up the flogger, he showed it to her, wanting her to acknowledge his power. Once she had, he bent her forward again, arranging her just so, her forearms bent together on the mattress, the shift slightly lifted over her bottom. He was fully erect now, his cock ready to cram itself inside her. Not yet, not yet.

He went behind her and kicked her legs wide.

Whap! Whap, whap, whap!

She jerked under each stroke of the flogger. Her ass quickly turned a charming shade of pink for him. Now and then he let her rest as he carefully tested her cunt with the smooth tip of the flogger's wooden handle, going a little deeper each time. Then he struck her again and again, watching her ass go red and welted. She struggled, but he pressed her down with the flat of his hand at her back.

"Don't. It's not marking you," he lied. "You know I'm careful not to damage the merchandise." She calmed at his assurances, but he sensed her wariness now.

Signaling the next phase of things, he pressed the flogger's handle inside her again, so far this time that it tested her depth and made her wriggle with discomfort. When he pulled it out, it glistened with her natural feminine gloss. So beautiful. He laid it on the bed, next to her.

Excitement gripped him then, unbearable in its intensity. Shoving his trousers to his knees, he took his cock and pressed its tip just inside her. Head back, he rocked himself shallowly, groaning with pleasure. He waited until she relaxed and grew supple and unsuspecting. Then he drove into her full length and with more roughness than in their past trysts. She bucked under him in annoyance or perhaps pain, like some filly trying to shake off her rider.

In the past, she had always admonished him to make sure he didn't mark her. She hadn't yet realized what was in store. He loved the crisp, sharp moment when they did.

He held her ass with both hands, hammering himself into her. "Little whore, do you really think Lord Satyr will want you, even with Alexa Patrizzi out of the way?" he asked breathlessly. "He's many things, but he's also quality. And I imagine he knows quality when he fucks it."

His prey fought now, writhing and twisting in anger. But the leather ball in her mouth did its work, rendering her unable to screech at him. A half-dozen strokes and he felt himself nearing completion. Not yet, not yet. The timing must be just right.

He drove his fingers up her nape into her hair, yanking her head high and bringing her spine to his chest. Her face angled back toward his. She was flushed and her eyes shot angry sparks at him.

His thighs quivered and his balls jerked and twitched as he spoke in her ear, his words low, cruel, and horrifying in their simple truth. "You're going to die now," he said softly. "With me inside you. What do you think of that?"

Her eyes bulged and he heard her muted scream even around the gag. With a snap of her neck under his hands, he felt himself shoot off inside her. Long moments later, he fell to the bed with her and sighed, replete.

All had gone perfectly.

Unfortunately, there was no time to linger, so he dismounted and went to wash. Returning minutes later, he stood over her broken, lifeless body and stared at her dispassionately as he buttoned his trousers and his shirt. He took the gag and leathers from her, carefully washed them as well, and then packed them away. Then he restored his appearance, adding the wig, mustache, and top hat he'd used to disguise himself when he'd paid for the room an hour ago.

Hastily, he left the room behind and slipped out the back entrance. He'd reserved it for two nights under an assumed name. The *polizia* would never connect him—the esteemed Signor Armanno Tivoli—to this crime. Still, he was always careful to create an alibi. Just as he had last night when he murdered his own son. One could never be too careful.

As soon as possible, he would return home, change his clothing, and attend another function later tonight, making sure to be noticed. But first, he had another very important stop to make. Promises must be kept, after all.

Outside the salon, Alexa lucked into a carriage for hire and returned home, hoping to pack her bags and slip away as quickly as possible. She avoided her own bedchamber, not wanting to view the macabre sight she'd left there this morning. Therefore, instead of her own belongings, she stuffed her bags full of her mother's dresses and shoes. Fortunately, they were of a similar size.

Betrayal dogged her every step. In spite of Eva's encouragements, she should have known better than to trust Lord Sevin. Now she would suffer heartbreak on top of everything else.

More than an hour had passed since she'd left the salon. It was possible that he would come here after her. He was used to getting what he wanted, and didn't like to be thwarted. Still, he'd likely dally a bit with his harlot first. She ground her teeth. She almost wished she could stay here and fight with him when he arrived, for she was mightily angry.

But, no, she couldn't bear to stay in this house with Laslo lying upstairs. She lugged her bags downstairs, one at a time. She would wait at the ticket office until morning and then travel back to England. She had enough pocket money to last at least a year if she found lodgings in a London suburb. The Roman newspapers found their way north from time to time, and she'd watch for news of Laslo's death to see how the wind blew.

If she learned she'd been accused in his death, she would have to travel farther afield, perhaps to America, where she'd find employment under a false name. She was fluent in the English language, and was good enough with figures that some accounting firm might hire her on, she thought optimistically.

She dropped her bags at the foot of the stairs. She should go now. But her curiosity had been aroused by the book in Sevin's office, and there was one last thing she longed to do. It would only take a few minutes. Dashing to her mother's library, she dug through the books she had boxed up for sale. Finding the one she sought, she sat cross-legged upon the carpet with it on her lap.

This tome had been one of her favorite books as a girl, filled as it was with what her childish eye had imagined to be illustrations of fairy tale scenes and objects. Skimming through it, she found what she was looking for. A fountain. If only she had time to venture into the catacombs and compare this drawing to the actuality. It certainly looked the same to her untrained eye. Why was that fountain important enough to be in this book?

She peered at the text, wishing she had better light. According to the caption, the fountain in this illustration was located in Portone. She'd never heard of such a town in Italy. Maybe it was a village in the hill country, or—

"What's that you've got there?"

Alexa started violently at the sound of a man's voice, closing the book with a snap. Signor Tivoli stood in the library doorway. She'd been so intent on her reading, and his approach had been so soundless, that she hadn't heard him come.

"And why the luggage at the bottom of the stairs?" he continued. "Going somewhere?"

Pushing the book off her lap, she stood. Why was he wearing a wig and a false mustache and beard?

"You're trespassing, signor," she announced. "Please leave."

Ignoring her, he went to the liquor cart and made free with it, lifting one bottle, then another. He shuddered. "Whiskey—I hate the stuff."

Alexa's eyes went to the door. She lifted a shoulder. "Whiskey was my brother's drink of choice, not mine."

158 / *Elizabeth Amber*

"Where's the damned—ah, here it is." He procured two snifters and began pouring from a crystal decanter. Did he really imagine she would drink with him?

"If you're not going to leave, then I am." She stalked past him, her pulse tripping. Why was she so afraid of him? Perhaps it was that bizarre disguise. Perhaps it was the fact that his dead son lay upstairs, waiting to be discovered.

And then he was standing in her path, not three feet away. She stepped back, words bursting from her. "Why are you here—and why in disguise?"

He flicked his beard, smiling. "Do you like it?"

"Excuse me," she said. Twitching her skirt, she tried to step around him.

Again he blocked her. "Before you go, join me in a drink." He held one of the snifters in his hands out to her.

"I don't—"

"One drink. Then you may leave." He smiled. "In fact, I'll help you do so."

"Water, then."

He gestured toward the couch. "Make yourself comfortable." Realizing he wasn't going to budge, she did as he insisted. Keeping an eye on her, he returned to the cart and poured her drink of choice.

Then he brought her glass to her. Before she drank, he tipped his own glass toward hers with a soft clink. "*Salute.*"

She rolled her eyes, automatically drinking. She was thirstier than she'd realized and swallowed half of her water before finally setting the glass on the side table.

"Good-bye, signor." Leaping up, she made for the front door. This time he didn't pursue her. She found out why, soon enough. The front door was locked—its key removed! When she turned, he was behind her.

He showed her the key he held in one hand, then made a

show of dropping it into his pocket. From his other pocket, he pulled a pistol, aiming it at her. "And now we will stop all this foolishness." He tossed away his disguise.

Her eyes went wide, her heart thumping with fear. "What—"

He took her by the nape and shoved her roughly in the direction he wished her to go. Knocking his pistol hand aside, she drove an elbow into his stomach. Then she veered away from the stairs toward the back of the house again, not realizing he was herding her in that very direction. They wound up in the library again, where they circled each other with only a sofa and boxes between them.

"And so we are back where we began, *cara.*" He smiled. "Which will make matters easier for me." He shut the library doors, locking them.

There were three exits from the room, she knew. Those doors, the windows, and the door to the catacombs. Would he shoot her if she tried to escape? "What do you want?"

"Cooperation. I've had little enough of it from you since Venice. Although, back then, you were quite satisfyingly... malleable." He took a sip from his drink, considering her. "Poor Laslo, too stupid to realize what a tasty piece he'd wed."

"What does that mean?" Alexa's gaze scanned the room, searching for some sort of weapon.

"You really haven't guessed, have you?" He laughed. "About my son's attraction to men?"

"What? No! I don't believe it. If he preferred men, then how did he..." Her mind raced back to her wedding night, her brow knitting.

"Poor, *cara.* Can't work it out for yourself?" He eyed her, one hand holding the pistol and the other swirling the liquid in the glass he held.

She froze, her eyes on the snifter. Cognac *brandy.* It was this man's favored drink. She'd seen Laslo accept a glass of it now and then to hold as a prop in society. But she could never actually recall seeing him drink it. Had never smelled it on his breath until their wedding night.

A horrible notion crept into her mind. She tried to force it away, but as she searched Signor Tivoli's eyes she read the despicable truth there.

"Oh god!"

"Ah, so you've finally deduced the truth." He smiled at her. "What gave me away?"

She backed away from him, her gaze flicking to his drink.

"Hmm. My brandy, was it? Laslo never had the stomach for hard liquor. Or for women. I admit I looked forward to your wedding night. Figured you for a virgin, and was gratified to learn firsthand that I was right."

Alexa sidled her way toward the fireplace, sick with realization that it was this man who had attacked her in darkness and violated her so cruelly. Never had she been so furious and so terrified! She snatched up an iron poker from the fireplace and held it threateningly before her with hands that shook. "Get out of my way," she warned in a level voice.

"That won't be possible, my dear. Not now that you know so many of my family secrets." He lifted his glass, drinking.

She glanced toward the window. Perhaps she could smash it with her poker and leap from it to the street. Would he shoot her if she tried?

"You won't make it," he said. "And I *will* shoot you if I must. A murder-suicide would play well in the courts with you as perpetrator. And I'd still inherit everything."

"Did you kill him, you awful man? Your own son?" When he calmly nodded, she tried not to let panic choke her. She had to keep him talking in hopes that she could somehow escape. He seemed to be toying with her. Waiting for something. But what? "Poor Laslo, he was nothing more than your puppet, was he?"

"He knew his duty. He didn't fight your marriage. Appearances must be kept up. You know how it is in well-heeled families such as ours."

"Yes, I know," she snapped as they circled one another. "Like you, my mother was concerned with appearances, not with the happiness of her own children or with common decency. But why drag me into this?"

"It was this house. We all wanted it. Well, what's below it, anyway."

"We?" Her voice sounded tired. She *was* tired, she realized. And having difficulty keeping her eyes open.

"The Sons of Faunus," he replied. His voice sounded strangely distant. "And once you are convicted of my son's murder, this property will be mine."

"I didn't kill him!" she murmured.

"Doesn't matter. The evidence is sufficiently damning nevertheless. A carcass in your room." His eyes narrowed on her when she stumbled, seeming to weigh her strength, then he continued on. "I come from a family of architects, did you know? My grandfather built this house. I know every nook and cranny of it. Which is how I knew that there's a hidden stair leading from the catacombs to your bedchamber."

"What—?" she mumbled, unable in her confused state to make heads or tails of what he was telling her.

"Convenient for me," he interrupted, "since you'd locked the catacombs entrance and your Satyr had bespelled the perimeter of this house. Neither proved an obstacle since we never crossed the outer perimeter in order to gain entrance. The two of you did make my task more difficult, though. I had to lure Laslo into the catacombs and on to your chamber via that narrow stair on the pretext that I had finally decided to let you have your divorce and it couldn't wait. He came willingly, for a dissolution of your marriage was what he wanted as well." Signor Tivoli's lips curled. "Under the circumstances, my son was uncomfortable with the notion of his future husbandly duties, as you may well imagine."

The poker fell from her hands, hitting the floor. She stared down at it dully. "You're insane."

"You're the one who'll be judged so when my son's body is discovered upstairs." Briskly setting his drink aside, he then tucked the pistol into the waistband of his trousers. "But don't worry, you won't stand trial. What I have planned will spare you that."

"What's happening . . . ?" Alexa murmured. "You've drugged me . . . the water I drank . . ." Arms caught her as she slumped. The smell of brandy was strong in her nostrils, and she gagged, wanting to retch. But she was too tired even for that.

"Calm yourself, *cara*," Signor Tivoli crooned to the lax body in his arms. Lifting her, he took her to the sofa, then stared down at her. She looked lovely lying there, unconscious. He wanted so badly to fuck her here and now, like this when she didn't know. But he'd soon have his fill of her. Now was not the time.

Crossing the room, he pushed the lever that would allow him to open the door to the catacombs. "Like my father and grandfather before me, I was ordained into the Sons of Faunus. Over the years, I only practiced their rites on rare occasions, when I managed to get down here from Venice from time to time. However, the ranks of the Sons are dwindling of late, have you heard? Murders attributed to the ElseWorld lot." He laughed softly. "Cleared the way for me."

Going back to the sofa, he reached for her. "You'll be pleased to know that I plan to revive your family's business. There's money to be made in Bona Dea, and I intend to make it. And as one of the Sons, I am entitled to lie with any of its Daughters. . . ."

Alexa managed to lift her hand against him, but it fumbled at pushing him away. "No," she murmured in a woozy voice, her eyes still closed.

He made a *tsk*ing sound. "Come now. An anonymous message has already been sent to the *polizia*. They should be here shortly, so we must move things along. Wouldn't want them to find us here, where you murdered my son." Unconscious now, she made no reply.

Hoisting her over one shoulder, he made for the door that led to the tunnels. When she struggled, he smacked her rump. "If you were not so difficult, we could have formed an alliance. Alas. But you'll learn, my dear. Soon you'll take my cock when and how it pleases me. Within a few weeks of my tutelage, you'll be begging for—"

The lock on the library door suddenly gave under a great weight, crashing wide open. Tivoli whirled around, yanking the pistol from his waistband.

Sevin burst inside, his voice cracking like a whip. "Let her go, you bastard!"

Backing toward the portal that led to the tunnels, Signor Tivoli lowered Alexa in front of him so that she would serve as a sort of shield. Holding her with one arm locked around her unconscious body, he aimed his pistol at her head. "Lord Satyr! I see you continue to make overly free with my property," he chided. "But you won't be building your new salon here, I'm afraid."

"Who told you about that?" Sevin asked, trying to stall.

"Your little Romani whore. But I took care of her for you."

"What are you saying?" Sevin's brows rose in confusion as he carefully stalked the bastard who wanted to harm Alexa. "That you killed Clara?"

"No, you fool. Carmella did that. Jealous little thing. Thought if she did away with her elder sister, she could take her place in your affections."

"Gods," said Sevin, truly stricken by the news. "How did you come into contact with her?"

"I sold her the fey scent that allowed her to infiltrate your domain."

"In exchange for?"

"A few fucks. And she proved a fount of information regarding your business and family."

"And how was that of use to you?" Sevin asked, watching for an opening. Any opening. Just in case Luc didn't find the hidden stair. Tivoli was the true fool here, so anxious to brag on his own evil plotting that he had momentarily forgotten the urgency of his plans.

"To undermine your family," Tivoli said gleefully. "To fuel the flames of hatred, and thereby deflect any blame from me. But after the little explosive Ella set off in your salon—yes, that was at my behest—she knew too much."

"And so you killed her?"

"Just this evening, as a matter of fact." Nuzzling Alexa's cheek, he smiled. "Don't make me do the same to this one," he taunted as he stepped backward, taking her with him into the tunnels. "How surprised she will be tomorrow when she wakes in her new accommodations. I will fuck her there when and how I like, until I tire of her. And then I'll dispose of her as her mother did the others. Through the ancient sewer system."

Behind him, Luc silently stepped into view, making himself known only to Sevin. Waiting. Then Tivoli moved the aim of his pistol, pointing it at Sevin's heart. "But you'll be long dead by then."

Whipcord fast, Luc grabbed him and forced the hand holding the pistol to point at Tivoli's head. Surprised, the bastard let go of Alexa. Sevin leaped forward and caught her before she fell. At the same moment, the pistol fired. It was still in Tivoli's hand, but Luc's finger was over his, helping him to press the trigger.

Sevin held Alexa's lax figure against him, his arms around her. The two brothers stood over Signor Tivoli's dead body.

"You found the staircase from her bedchamber, I see," murmured Sevin.

Luc nodded. "His son is up there. Dead."

"So this will be a murder-suicide as Tivoli suggested, only with him as the apparent perpetrator. He drugged Alexa, expecting to kill her, too. That's how we'll frame this for the authorities," said Sevin.

"So his name is Tivoli."

"You know him?"

"He was involved with Bona Dea," Luc announced calmly. He nudged the man on the floor with the toe of his boot. "One of those nameless men who came to us in the catacombs."

Sevin stilled, his eyes searching his brother's face. Luc rarely revealed anything about his time in the tunnels, even under duress.

But Luc was hardly aware of his brother as he stood staring at the dead man, his mind returning to the past. "There was a girl down there once. She was younger even than I was. And so damned scared. We talked through the walls when she first came. She was sweet, innocent. I would have given my life to save hers, if only I—" He heaved a sigh, heavy with grief.

"Tivoli and one other man came one night," he went on. "I listened while the two of them brutalized her. Heard her moans and cries fade away over the hours they abused her. Heard the guard take her out afterward and toss her into the underground stream that ran below the catacombs. Within a week, another girl took her place. When the new one cried, I ignored her. I learned to be detached, not to care."

"Gods, Luc. You were surviving, the only way you could. But you're back with us now. Safe."

Luc stared at him a moment, his face expressionless. Then he looked beyond him, canting his head as if listening to some sound Sevin could not hear.

"We have guests," he announced. Bending, he dragged Signor Tivoli's body fully inside the library.

Sevin kicked the bookshelf door closed, obscuring the tunnel entrance. Luc turned the lever, locking it, just as the first of the *polizia* burst into the front door of the Patrizzi town house.

12

One week later

Something brushed Alexa's throat. Sevin's mouth. She angled her head, inviting more, and his lips traced the downward slope to kiss the ridge of her shoulder. For some reason, he was quite fond of the flower design she'd had inked there in Venice. How long ago that seemed. How happy she was now in comparison to those dark days.

Soft music floated to her on the fragrant air in the secluded grotto, mingling with the splashing sounds of water in the nearby pool. A bed of clover-like groundcover was under her back, its blanket forming the softest of cushions. Her body was flushed and pleasantly weary from Sevin's lovemaking, his hand warm on the curve of her waist.

They were celebrating tonight. He'd gotten permission from the Italian government to begin work on a second salon across Capitoline in her family home. Some of his female employees had visited various officials during the week as envoys, and she could well imagine what sort of bribery had led up to such an agreement.

The grotto was private, located in isolation and behind iron gates within the existing *Salone di Passione* for the use of the Satyr lords only. It seemed to her a paradise within a paradise, with its lush flowers and perfumed pools. Occasionally, the muffled sounds of laughter, conversation, and moans charged the air here, drifting to them from the main salon below. She wondered if those in the salon had overheard them as well. Her last fulfillment had continued for a full five minutes and she'd cried out numerous times under its passionate onslaught.

Sevin rose on an elbow to gaze down at her. "You never said how you came by this." He'd plucked a blossom from the grass and now drew it over her tattoo.

"It was an impulse. A backlash against my family's strictures. I wanted to make myself different from them, to do something my mother would despise and could not change."

"But why this particular flower?"

Alexa lifted a shoulder in a slight shrug. "For some reason, I was drawn to it in the inker's display of possibilities."

"It's the flower of my family's god, did you know?"

She shook her head languidly.

The flower moved over her, dusting its petals along her collarbone and lower. "It has always been specific to the worship of Bacchus, used in processions and incense devotionals to him throughout time." His floral brush teased her nipple. "It's an aphrodisiac to men of my blood."

Her nipple tightened and peaked under the flower's stroke and she gasped, covering her flesh with her hand. A dimple came and went in his cheek. Then the flower went lower still, over her belly where it traced an aimless pattern.

This reminded her of a matter of concern and she spoke of it. "I understand from Eva that you can only father children during your Calling." She slanted him a glance from under her lashes. "And I was wondering . . ."

"I was careful with you that night in the catacombs. As was Luc," he replied, catching her meaning. "Unlike human men, we can decide if our seed will be potent, if our mates will conceive."

"And three weeks from now, in your next Calling?" she asked, cupping his jaw in her palm. Already it was dusky with the beginnings of his evening beard. "Will you be as careful then?"

Sevin smiled slowly. His flower drifted to her thighs, running upward along the seam between them to tease at their apex. "Perhaps not."

She pulled his head down to hers. "Good," she whispered against his mouth.

The flower was tossed away and his body covered hers. An hour later, they clung together, in the pool now. He was seated on a slab of rock and she on his lap, facing him. Their bodies were linked in a slow undulation that had evolved into an extended, low-level orgasm that neither wished to end.

"We seem destined to make love in carriages, catacombs, and corridors," she said breathlessly. "And now grottos and pools."

"Why don't you wed me then and install yourself in my bed?" He smiled, the barest twist of those beautiful masculine lips, there and gone in a flash.

The sight of it sent a hard lick of lust through her, straight to her feminine core. She cried out softly as she came on him. For long moments, her flesh milked at his, yet he only held her through it and did not come himself.

At length, she pushed up from him slightly, disengaging. Standing, she turned from him slightly and studied him over her shoulder. "This bed of yours. Will we be alone there?"

He rose from the pool as well, and they stood there together, water streaming down their flesh. "Not always," he admitted slowly.

She nodded slightly, then she waded from the pool. She stood there combing her fingers through her tangled hair and considering his words and what they meant. She felt him join her and glanced up at him. His hands were at his hips, his face serious.

"So it wasn't just the situation we found ourselves in the other night in the catacombs," she asked. "Sharing is your common practice?"

"Only with Luc. Only during our Calling."

Understanding filled her expression. "It's because of his imprisonment," she guessed. "That's why he requires your presence." She shivered in the coolness.

Noticing, Sevin found toweling neatly folded within a cabinet that was cleverly concealed in a nearby stone wall. Then he pulled her slick body against his, and with his arms around her, he employed the toweling to slowly dry her back, her bottom. His hands worked on as he finally spoke again.

"Luc forgoes all carnal pleasure except when he is Called. And on those nights, he can't be alone. I don't trust him to do what he must. To mate."

He moved behind her, and wrapping his arms around her, began wicking moisture from her belly, moving higher. His voice was a low rumble at her ear. "I'll want you to join us, Luc and me, on those nights. I'll bring Shimmerskins into things in future, so that you'll spend most of your labors with me. But if you force me to make a choice between you and him . . ." He took a deep breath. ". . . you'll spend the Moonful nights alone." His hands found her breasts. The toweling created a gentle, stirring abrasion on her skin. "It's not what I want—"

She put her hands over his, then turned and wrapped her arms tight around him and lay her head on his smooth chest.

"I choose to be with you. And Luc."

"Gods." The toweling fell to the ground, and his arms came

around her. He buried his face in her hair, and she heard the relief in his voice.

She smoothed her palms up the long muscles of his back and down again, soothing him. "I would not have you abandon your brother for me. Your fierce loyalty to your family is one of the traits I most admire about you."

He gave her a quick squeeze, then his head turned, his mouth finding hers. "And there are so *many* traits to admire," he murmured, a teasing lilt entering his tone.

Her lips quirked. "Not the least of which is your modesty."

He kissed her deeply, his hands going to her waist. Cupping the rounds of her bottom, he lifted her against him in a gentle grind. "I need you. Can you go again?" She'd felt his hardness between them and knew what he was asking.

"Yes, my love," she whispered, her eyes smiling into his. "Yes."

As Sevin lifted her in his arms, neither of them heard his youngest brother's departing footsteps.

Luc closed the iron gate soundlessly. Nodding to the guards posted there, he left the grotto behind. He'd unabashedly eavesdropped on Alexa and Sevin just now. Had heard their lovemaking, her soft laughter, their plans to wed.

And his brother's request that she continue to include him in their lovemaking.

He'd departed before he'd heard her reply. It didn't matter. He wouldn't ask that of them.

In three weeks the next Calling night would come. Sevin's first with his new wife. Fool that he was, Luc hadn't fully considered what that would mean.

Now that all of his brothers were happily mated, he had no place here among them any longer. He had become even more of a liability, a problem.

On that first Moonful after his return from the tunnels, they'd all watched over him like clucking hens, making sure he took the elixir and that he engaged in the rites that began the Change. During his imprisonment, he'd already fornicated in every way possible, forced into every debased act by his captors, while under the influence of powerful drugs.

But none of that had prepared him for the onslaught of emotions he experienced during that first Calling. Untempered by narcotics, his need had been a terrible, uncontrollable thing inside him. When one of the salon employees—a fey female—had approached him, he'd panicked, rebuffing her roughly and frightening her. Frightening his brothers. And himself.

Dane had already been wed to Eva, but Sevin and Bastian had been with lovers. They'd immediately banished them from the chamber, bringing forth Shimmerskins in their stead. His brothers had then slowly and carefully drawn him into their circle, sharing their females with him. Instructing him on what must be done. Thus had begun his initiation into the ways of the Satyr at Moonful.

He well remembered that first push inside of a Shimmerskin. How soft her hair had felt fisted in his hand. How her body had cradled his. For the first time in his life, no one was forcing him, except the moon. And he knew he wasn't hurting her. His way had been eased by the prior spill of his brothers. And Shimmerskins could not feel pain.

But all that had been months ago. Why, after all this time had passed, could he not act alone with a female? Why this drive to partner with his brothers? It was a weakness, and one he must overcome if he wanted to live. *If he wanted to live.*

The sounds of the carousel were louder now, and he realized he'd reached the main salon. There were plenty of women here milling about. He gazed out over them. He could select one, woo her into one of the rooms tonight. His hands fisted, his heart pumping. Would he hurt her? He was capable of murder. He knew that.

His brothers thought he found it easy to forgo women in the weeks between Moonful. They were wrong. He craved fornication as much as they did. At times, he thought his unquenched need for carnal release would drive him insane.

Yet he didn't like to be touched. Abhorred the stroke of an unfamiliar hand. Even on Calling nights, he held his partner's hands carefully away, binding them above her head or behind her back. Anywhere where they couldn't touch him.

In fewer than three weeks, another Moonful would come. Sevin might be generous enough to welcome him into his marital bed, but he would not intrude. The thought of passing the Calling on his own filled him with dread. An attempt with Shimmerskins on his own seemed the best way forward.

He heard Bastian and Dane nearby, heard the splash and gurgle of the new Bacchus fountain. Sevin had had it moved here only last night from the catacombs below the Patrizzi house. His brothers were seated just outside the low wall that had been built to surround it.

He crossed the main floor toward his brothers. His head was splitting open. Another migraine. They came more frequently now. At least this one was not as bad as those that came in the hours leading up to a whole moon.

As he neared Bastian and Dane, he nodded and they returned the gesture. They were discussing the matter of the elixir and didn't notice his subsequent silence. They were accustomed to his strangeness by now. They worried over him, considered him a victim.

They had no idea what he'd become since his release. But humans did. A week ago, when they'd protested outside the salon, they'd called them murderers among other insults. They'd been right. At least about him.

How will we manage with the travel embargo in place? Bastian and Dane were wondering now. In three weeks, without the elixir, they would all die here. And in order to brew it, they needed grapes from ElseWorld to mix with the grapes they grew here in Rome. But the only interworld gate lay in Tuscany, where they could not travel.

This was their conversation, around and around.

As he stood listening a few feet away, Luc's face was calm. But his own thoughts were of mayhem. So far, he'd destroyed all but one of those responsible for tormenting him and the others in the tunnels. Only one final man still eluded him.

He hadn't killed them all only to salve his own wounds. No, he knew the sickness inside the hearts of these men who called themselves the Sons of Faunus. If they'd lived, they would go on hurting others.

But no matter how justified, each kill had sickened him inside, hardened his heart until he began to crave death himself, an end to remembered pain.

His brothers believed that the carefree child he'd once been was locked somewhere inside him. But they were wrong. That child was long dead. This brooding, taciturn shell of a man who'd been returned to them was all that remained.

His nights were full of horrific nightmares—his time in the catacombs relived. His brothers wondered why he would not talk of those days. He dared not for fear that it might send him around the bend. He had no aspirations to be locked away again, this time as a lunatic.

As usual, his brothers had no idea of his dark thoughts. He stood there, an island unto himself, gazing at the new fountain. Its waters flowed ceaselessly, splashing from the mouth of their wine god into a series of pools and then cycling away even as fresh water sprang forth again to flow from stone lips.

The gentle song of its series of waterfalls called to him, the sparkling showers holding him transfixed. There was something about this fountain that drew him, some secret yet undiscovered.

Portone. The word floated into his head as if on an ocean wave. He tasted it, rolled it around in his mouth. Then he spoke its meaning, softly so his brothers didn't hear. "Gate."

Hardly knowing what he was doing, he stepped over the low wall, wading closer to the fountain itself. Reaching out, he pressed his hand there upon its center. Stone seemed to liquefy under his touch.

He had to go.

There was something waiting for him on the other side of this gurgling fountain.

Shouts came from behind him. His brothers.

"Luc! No! Stop! What the—?"

But he was already moving forward. As if pulled by some magnet, he stepped forward into stone that would allow him, and only him, to pass through it.

It was so easy for him, this magical reshaping of molecules. This instantaneous travel that was impossible for others.

He would venture on, discover where the magic led. If it killed him, so be it. He was already dead inside.

Within seconds he was interred within the fountain, and then he found himself passing through and beyond it.

Transported.

Gone.

LUCIEN

PROLOGUE

Enclave a Roma in ElseWorld
1873

Though it was his fondest wish, Lord Lucien Satyr did not die as a consequence of thrusting himself through the gate within the fountain. Instead, on its other side, he emerged into another world and was cast into sleep, his mind void of dreams.

In passing from one world to another, his entire physical being was transformed. Flesh, heart, and soul hardened and became stone. He felt nothing. And in this, at least, he found the solace he'd longed for.

And yet all was not as he wished, for he only lay dormant in this state. He was close, so tantalizingly close to the ultimate release that death would bring. A release he would have craved if he could have mustered the energy to care.

Then one day, something came to tease at his mind. A female.

On all too rare occasions—ceremonial ones he sensed—this special female drew near. Near enough that her scent threatened to fill his hardened lungs like new spring breath. And then his soul would stir in his breast and fevered dreams would pulse at his mind. But when she moved away, his mind, heart, and body quieted again.

He, a man who'd eschewed the touch of all others, began to hunger for *her* touch. A touch that never came. *Why this sudden terrible need?* he silently railed. Surely this body of his had been cruelly handled enough in his youth and his mind abused sufficiently by the twisted appetites of his enemies!

Time began and ended, ended and began, becoming a fluid thing. And through it all, he waited. This female was wary, and never ventured near enough for stone and flesh to meet.

It was for the best. For she was not yet ready for him. Nor was he ready for her.

But the day eventually came when the gods decreed it was time. A time for healing. For reawakening. A time for him to find and know love. At last.

1

Enclave a Roma in ElseWorld
1882

With determined steps of her sturdy half-boots, Natalia threaded her way through tufted hillocks of wildflowers. Following the well-worn familiar path, she moved ever upward toward her forbidden goal.

The evening breeze pulled at the severe plait of her chestnut hair, tugging wayward strands from it and brushing them across her pale cheek. She had left the institute in a rush and hadn't yet changed from the uniform that marked her as an instructor there. Now burrs tore at her long, coarsely woven skirt as she went higher and higher up the moonlit hillside, away from the complex of academic buildings far below in the valley.

Somewhere in the distance above her, three female scholars—one of them her younger sister, Sophie—had a ten-minute head start on her. Foolish girls bent on mischief! But they were only eighteen, an age for foolishness.

Natalia was a decade older and had long since put such acts of rebellion behind her. It had been necessary in order to protect her sister after their mother had died a dozen years ago.

She heard muted voices just ahead. The trio of girls didn't know she was behind them, but she didn't dare call out for fear of waking the village below. Though she dreaded the prospect of venturing farther, she trudged on, determined to prevent a disaster in the making. Her gaze pierced the velvet twilight, searching. She could see the peaked roofline of the sacred temple at the crest of the hill now.

She could not yet see *him*. But soon.

Far below them, the institute's dormitory was in complete darkness. All the other students, instructors, and researchers would be in their bunks by now. It was against community law for females, both teacher and student, to leave the school after curfew. Yet here they were. Their mutual transgression tonight would be harshly punished if they were caught.

Sophie's voice floated back to her. "*Shh*. I hear someone."

Natalia lifted the hem of her skirts and loped upward. Just over the rise, her worried brown eyes caught her sister's hard green ones.

"Oh, it's only you." Sophie's lip curled, then she turned and continued on her way toward the temple. "Don't try to stop us," she threw back over her shoulder.

The other two girls, Leona and Rae, looked less sure upon seeing Natalia. She was an instructor, after all. But when she didn't make any dire pronouncements or expel them all on the spot, they seemed to realize they were safe and followed her sister. Natalia had a soft spot in her heart for all the girls at the institute. It was a fatal weakness that had kept her from rising from the pool of instructors to the more exalted position of healer, despite the fact that she was far more talented in the healing arts than others who had advanced beyond her.

"Of course I'm here to stop you. This excursion is a mistake," Natalia replied in a voice meant to carry just far enough. "Your medicinal herbals tests are tomorrow. All of you should be studying, or sleeping in preparation."

"What does it matter?" Sophie shouted.

"Quiet!" Leona hissed in wide-eyed alarm. "You're going to wake the entire institute!"

Reaching her sister's side at last, Natalia grabbed her arm. "Come back down the hillside. All of you. I'll use my master key to let us in the side entrance of the dormitory. No one need learn of this foolhardy errand."

Sophie yanked away and continued on her chosen path. "You go back. We didn't invite you here. But I took a dare. I'll follow through."

Natalia wanted to slap her, and would have if she'd believed it would've done any good. She'd been hard pressed to watch over her younger sister all these years since their mother's death from the Sickness. Since then, she'd made a good life for the two of them, the best she could. Yet Sophie always seemed to want more. It hadn't helped that the girl was a beauty. Everyone had spoiled her, and she'd grown stubborn and willful.

Reluctantly, Natalia silenced her protests, hoisted her skirts, and trudged after her sister and her two schoolmates. "Then hurry up about whatever you've planned so we can return home. Honestly, I don't understand you girls' fascination with the temple."

Sophie's soft laugh floated down the hill to her on the breeze. "It's not the temple that draws us. And you know it."

Yes, she knew. Every female in ElseWorld with a pulse knew exactly what drew them here. It was *him*. The infamous statue.

A bramble bush caught her, and Natalia bent to untangle her lifechain from it. The chain, which dangled from the belt at her waist, held twenty-eight beads now. She'd received the last one from the priests only this morning, on this birthday that marked a lowering of her worth in the eyes of the community. When she straightened again, she saw Rae's pitying glance.

A decade past her prime, Natalia was still husbandless, childless, bookish, and plain. It was an unforgiveable combination of attributes for a female in their village.

Since she had failed to conceive children during her ten years in the breeding program and failed to choose her own husband, she was to be herded in a new direction tomorrow. A brilliant scholar and healer, she was nevertheless now considered useless for little else but an arranged marriage.

A husband would be chosen for her in the afternoon tomorrow, toward the end of the annual festival. And tomorrow night—her wedding night—her lifechain would be forever removed by him. Thereafter, he would wear it around his throat to show his ownership of her. She would become his possession, bought and paid for.

Her lot was to become a convenience to him. A vessel in which he might relieve his lust when the mood moved him. A servant to keep his house. There would be no question of love between them. This she understood and accepted. But what if he refused to allow her to continue her work at the healing center? Or as a teacher at the institute? Her heart squeezed painfully at the thought. Her work in the healing arts was so precious to her.

She heard the girls' voices up ahead. They must have reached the temple. Lifting her eyes, Natalia saw it just ahead. Saw *him.* Quickly, she averted her gaze.

But *his* image was burned in her mind's eye.

He lay on his back, upon the sacred altar in front of the temple, his glorious nakedness enshrined in impenetrable stone. Under tonight's three-quarter moon and the lanterns that eternally burned here, it gleamed, giving off an ethereal bluish light.

He'd appeared from nowhere during a great storm the year

her mother had died. Natalia had been only sixteen then, and Sophie, six. And he'd lain here in this exact spot ever since.

The priests believed him to be a god. Claimed that he had the power to save this land of theirs, a land that was slowly dying. The hopes of the entire community had been hung upon him.

If only he would awake, they said. *He would save us all.*

Reluctantly, Natalia took the twelve granite steps upward. Out of habit, she and her charges dipped curtsies at the top of the temple stairs and drew the Sign of Respect across their chests.

The statue lay before them now at eye level, its pale marble as pristine as it had been the day it had first arrived. The rectangular altar that served as *his* eternal bed was hewn from the same fine marble and edged in gilt, and stood atop the polished granite stage that stretched out in front of the temple. The statue and stage were washed every morning and flowers placed in the vases by the temple doors. Pilgrims came here to the temple each spring from faraway lands to look upon him and to be anointed with droplets of the holy water used to bathe him.

Carved into the base of the altar he lay upon, in stark gold lettering, was the inscription:

WHO WAKETH HIM, SHALL SAVE OUR LAND.

Though the spring wind had not yet cooled with the evening, Natalia shivered and wrapped her cloak more snugly over her uniform. Coming here always unsettled her. Yet she was obliged to do so every Sunday as was the whole community.

"Do you think he's truly a godking? One come to cure our land of its ills?" Rae whispered into the silence that had fallen among them.

"The priests think so. That's what matters," Natalia said firmly. It wouldn't do to encourage disbelief in them. Punishment for questioning the old ways was severe, and as a healer, she could not bear to see anyone harmed, especially not her students.

"Just imagine if his eyes opened right now, and he saw us standing here," Sophie breathed in wonder.

"Do you think he might leap up and have his way with us?" whispered Leona. Her tone said she found the notion deliciously wicked.

Natalia's skin prickled. "Don't be absurd," she said sharply. Unlike the rest of the community, she didn't believe he would ever awaken or that he was meant to save them all. He was rock carved by the hand of an anonymous sculptor, nothing more. Her thoughts were heretical ones, and she didn't dare voice them.

The three girls approached the altar, but Natalia hung back on the periphery of the stage. She glanced back toward the institute. All was quiet for now, thank the gods, their mischief as yet undiscovered.

"I've never really understood it," Rae said, walking around the statue and eyeing it. "I mean, it's against the scientific principals we are taught in the institute to expect that he's ever going to come alive. No matter how many of us..." Her words died away.

"Fuck him?" Sophie supplied drily.

"Sophie," Natalia reproved. "Don't be crude."

Sophie peered at her through the darkness. "It's what we're all going to do. Why not say it? We're eighteen. It's our time to sacrifice."

Natalia wanted to weep at the truth of this—for her sister, and for Leona and Rae as well. Tomorrow was the anniversary of *his* arrival in their community. A festival would be held here on Temple Hill, and this trio of girls would be at the center of the spectacle.

It would be a day in which every girl in the community who had turned eighteen in the past year—which amounted to only these three—would be sacrificed in the performance of a pagan ritual. Not in the old ways of sacrifice, with their blood and entrails spattered. No, only their virgin blood was to be spilled on the morrow.

First would come the symbolic ceremony, a mock wedding in which these girls would be bound to *him* in holy matrimony. Afterward, under the direction of the priests and under the expectant gazes of the entire community, Sophie and her two companions would surrender themselves to *him*. Each in turn would ceremonially mount him and attempt to take his monstrous phallus into her body. It was said that the girl who finally accepted the entirety of his length inside her would bring him to life.

It was a ridiculous superstition and one Natalia believed the priests and government had conjured to deflect blame from themselves, for the poor state of things in the community. With all her heart she wanted to grab Sophie and run, leaving this place and its rigid patriarchal society far behind.

But where could they go? Surrounding communities were in dire circumstances as well, and females were scarce. Tomorrow would be a particularly dangerous time to wander, for males from other communities would scent virgin blood and come sniffing around, hungering for a mate. In these times, women were carnal prey, and they could easily wind up in a worse situation.

"Mistress Natalia, what do you say?" Rae asked. "We are women now, fully eighteen. Please tell us the truth. Do you believe in the prophecy?"

Natalia automatically slipped into academia mode, choosing

her words carefully. "While we may find it difficult to understand the role of faith and magic in what we know to be fact, as women of science, we—"

"You call yourself a woman of science?" Sophie scoffed. "You can't even look at him." She gestured toward the statue before her. She'd climbed the five steps on its opposite side and now stared across his still, carven body with narrowed eyes.

"What do you mean? I pass this way every Worship Day," Natalia protested. "And come down from there."

Sophie ignored the command, her pretty mouth twisting. "Yet you never look at *all* of him, I've noticed."

If Sophie has noted my reluctance, how many others have? Natalia couldn't help wondering. "Very well," she said easily. Under the pressure of her younger sister's gaze, she lifted her chin and forced her eyes to the statue.

He lay on his back in glorious repose, arms at his sides, biceps bunched, elbows slightly bent. His hands were huge. One was slightly open, its blunt-tipped fingers lifted as though it were seeking something.

Her eyes slid over the strong column of his throat to broad shoulders, and then she ventured on to the territory below, something she normally avoided. It wasn't that he was unpleasant to view. No, only that she considered him a temptation, one best avoided.

But now her reluctant gaze roved smooth muscled pectorals, each tipped with flat nubs. Then on to his ribs and the slight depression between them on the way to his pelvis. Bracing herself, she forced her eyes to linger over his most commanding and remarkable feature. Her heart thumped in her ears. Hastily, she moved on to brawny tree-trunk thighs, then to his well-formed calves and large feet.

She straightened and caught her sister's gaze, relieved it was done. "There. I looked. If you are satisfied, can we all return to the institute now?"

Sophie laughed at her, throwing her arms wide. "You are such a prude, Nat!" she declared, keeping her voice soft. "You can't even *look* at his male organ without blushing, can you? It's little wonder you've never been asked to wed with that sort of attitude."

Sophie was frightened and angry over what was to come tomorrow, and it was making her mean. That's all this was. Natalia refused to retaliate, and tried not to let it wound her feelings.

"Are you going to kiss him or not, Sophie? It's getting chilly out here," Leona complained, drawing her cloak closer.

"You came here to *kiss* him?" Natalia echoed. "To kiss a statue? That's what this is about?"

Sophie shot her a glance laced with defiance. "You don't think I could be the one to awaken him?" she asked coldly.

When did I become the enemy? Natalia wanted to ask. But she only shrugged, not wanting to egg her sister on. "Tomorrow will be soon enough to find out, don't you think?"

Her sister looked disappointed, as if she'd wanted a fight. But there was anger there, still simmering and waiting to boil over. It was so unfair that she would be forced into such an abhorrent situation on the morrow!

"Besides, it would take more than a simple kiss to . . ." Rae began.

"Hurry up. Mistress Natalia is right in what she said before," Leona interrupted. "I don't want to be caught up here."

"Girls, please—" Natalia begged. "Of all the pranks you've ever pulled in all the years I've known you, coming up here after curfew is the worst. Let's return now, while we still can."

Although Rae and Leona looked uncertain, Sophie ignored Natalia, kneeling on the altar at the far side of the statue. Touching the altar was a sacrilegious act in itself that made the other two girls gasp. Touching *him* was inconceivable, except during festival. Even the attendants who bathed him were careful to wear gloves.

They held their collective breath as Sophie laid a hand in the center of the statue's chest to balance herself. When nothing happened, Natalia drew a relieved breath. Though she hadn't realized it, some part of her had apparently feared that her sister might actually cause some change in him. After all these years, the community's superstitions had affected her as well, it seemed.

Sophie's hand slid higher, to his shoulder. None of them spoke now, but none could look away. The statue was so large and Sophie so petite by comparison that the two of them almost appeared to be different species.

As she watched the glide of Sophie's fingers, Natalia's fingertips tingled, and she curled them into her palms. A sudden shocking desire to trace his polished blue-white valleys and smooth the mounded marble of hewn muscle swept her.

"I wonder if he can feel me touching him?" Sophie whispered, her voice rough with suppressed emotion. As always, the forbidden excited her.

"What if he's ticklish?" Rae giggled nervously.

"Hurry, Sophie. Get it done. Before we're missed," said Natalia.

"Don't rush me."

Natalia recognized that stubborn tone. Now her sister would likely move at a snail's pace just to thwart her.

Sophie's other hand moved, caressing his face, tracing the hard smoothness of his jawbone. "I love a man with a granite jaw," she crooned, playing to her audience.

"Actually, it's a form of marble," Natalia said tonelessly.

Leona snickered. "Godking Marbelous."

Natalia glanced at her in surprise, and the girl's expression changed to one of chagrin "Apologies, mistress. But I didn't coin the nickname."

Natalia was aware of the ditties woven and sung about him in secret among the students, making sport of his astounding male proportions. But at the core of all the teasing was fear, as well as a supreme awe, and a belief in his ability to save them. "Best not to repeat them, however," she said. "There are penalties even for such minor infractions, as you know."

"You won't tell tales on us, though, will you, sister? Always so loyal and steadfast and good." Sophie traced her thumbs over his closed eyelids, then shaped his brow. A delicate forefinger traveled the carved blade of his nose.

She leaned down. But instead of kissing his lips, she ducked her head at the last minute and her tongue darted out and she swirled it around a distended nipple.

Natalia crossed her arms, immensely disturbed. "Don't," she choked out.

Sophie shot her a look. "Why not? I'll do worse with him tomorrow. Before a much larger audience."

Rae tittered nervously again, her eyes darting between them.

"Shush," said Leona, elbowing her. "There's no shame in the ritual," she reminded her, parroting the words she'd been taught all her life. "It's only a quarter hour or so of attempted mating, then you're done. You move on with your life."

Even though every fiber of Natalia's being rejected the necessity of the wedding sacrifice, she said nothing. Their religious education had indoctrinated them. They wouldn't try to escape with her even if she were to offer them the opportunity. They would only turn her in to the authorities for a heretic. And she wouldn't run alone—wouldn't leave Sophie behind.

She would be here to help her through whatever lay ahead. Tomorrow, all the other boys in her class—the entire community in fact—would watch Sophie fornicate for the first time in her life. Naked. In public. With a stone god. Sometimes Natalia understood those who resorted to visiting the drug huts before the festival.

"Then we can wed," Leona added, sounding thrilled at the prospect. Her eyes went to Sophie. "I know who Sophie would choose."

"Gentleman Cato perhaps?" Rae teased.

Titus Cato? Natalia looked at her sister, who was studiously avoiding their eyes. The boy Rae spoke of was one of her students, a senior in third-period Medicinals. At the institute, male students were properly addressed as gentlemen. But there was nothing gentlemanly in the way this boy behaved toward women, including her whenever they came in contact. He was a handsome, conceited ruffian, with few aspirations and even less intelligence. Could he truly be the subject of her sister's girlish dreams of romance?

As the only spinster over the age of twenty-seven in the community, Natalia was obligated to join in the marriage auction tomorrow night. Failing their attempt to awaken the statue tomorrow, these girls would be fair game afterward for the highest bidder who offered to husband them. However, they could refuse, and by doing so would enter the breeding program.

Leona glanced at her. "What's it really like, mistress? The sacred ritual?"

"I don't know," said Natalia. "I was excused."

"So you've never . . ." Leona gestured toward the statue.

"No," Natalia said firmly. "I was never a candidate for sacrifice. All must be virgins." The girls exchanged looks, which she assumed meant they wondered if she'd ever actually lain with a man.

"I was inducted into the breeding program at eighteen, a year before *he* came. Participants are regarded as tainted by other men's seed and therefore unsuitable, regardless of technical virginity."

Sophie had paused in her task to listen, and now Rae joined

in the conversation. "You must've had the seed of over a hundred men between your legs by now," she said with a youthful forthrightness Natalia found discomfiting. "What's *that* like?"

Although what went on within the program was not openly discussed with non-participants, these girls were of age now, and Natalia decided to speak to them more frankly tonight than she might have at any other time. Sophie and her companions might pretend sophistication, but they were frightened of what was in store for them.

"It's cold, clinical, like any other medical procedure," Natalia explained easily. "It's done with a syringe by one of the priestesses. Temple officials keep records so that brother will not breed with sister and that sort of thing. But donors are anonymous."

"It sounds awful," said Rae.

"That's what you get for refusing to take a husband," said Sophie. "I for one am always up for trying new things."

"Then why don't you pucker up?" suggested Leona.

"Yes," added Rae. "Get on with it. It's getting cold out here."

"All right," said Sophie. With dramatic flair, she flipped her golden hair over her shoulder, so the girls would have an unimpeded view of the impending spectacle.

Prolonging the suspense, she bent low to the statue's ear and murmured something low and soothing to him that the others couldn't hear. Then she finally, finally pressed her mouth to the uncompromising line of his lips.

Natalia's heart fairly stopped. Not because she was shocked, but because it seemed like a defiling. *Why*, she wondered, *when she doesn't believe?*

Leona attempted to appear unfazed, but Rae openly gaped, awed by Sophie's daring.

Eventually, Sophie's lips parted from his, leaving them wet

and glistening. She lifted her head and stared down at him. Natalia found herself, along with the other two girls, leaning in and holding her collective breath.

But his eyelids didn't flutter. His lungs didn't pump. His phallus didn't stir.

"I suppose you just don't excite him, Sophie," Leona murmured. She sounded almost relieved that he hadn't come to life.

Sophie shot them a saucy look. "It's not what I can do for *him*. The question is, what can he do for me!"

"Well, you'll get nothing from me if you keep stalling," said Leona.

"What do you mean?" said Natalia. "I thought she was just going to kiss him. She's done that. Let's go."

"Hush, Nat," said Sophie.

"There is more to our wager, mistress," Rae murmured.

More?

2

All eyes fastened on Sophie's hand. It cupped his cheek, then traced the thick column of his throat, ran over shoulders twice as wide as her own, then moved lower over his chest, down his ribs and flat pelvis.

"Surely you . . ." Natalia's wide-eyed gaze darted for the second time in her entire life to his most defining feature—his phallus. It was the size and length of her forearm.

In all the years she had passed *him* on the way to temple, she'd never once studied it for any length of time. Still, like every member of the community, she had been schooled on its exact dimensions. The girth of the shaft was precisely 7.6 inches in circumference. It was tipped with a crown swollen to 8.3 inches around. Forever tumescent with unfulfilled desire, it angled upward from his pelvis to an intimidating length of 9.252 inches.

Sophie's hand reached for it.

"For gods' sake," Natalia whispered frantically. "Wait until tomorrow. They'll give you sedative creams that will ease the difficulty. They'll monitor you, make sure you are not injured in your attempt with him."

She started forward, but Sophie whipped around with a hateful look. "You're not my guardian any longer. I'm eighteen now. An adult, ready to take a husband. If you can't keep quiet, then go back down the hill to the dorm."

Natalia's gut clenched as her sister's fingertips found the cool marble pillar distended from the apex of his thighs. "Don't," she breathed, her voice cracking. But her plea was whisper soft and whipped away by the wind.

Why did it matter so much that she not do this?

Because it seemed cruel. Wrong. Hurtful. To use him in this way without his permission. But he was made of stone, so this made no sense, and Natalia tried to shake the feeling. *He's a statue, nothing more. Statues cannot feel.* She repeated that mantra in her mind over and over.

Sophie's fingers had already slipped around his phallus. Her fingers circled the under ridge of the crown, and her thumb pressed over the slit that dimpled his tip. Then her fist began to slide slowly downward.

"I heard someone took eight inches once," said Leona, her solemn voice breaking the silence.

Rae nodded and supplied the name. "Elena Vidora. But it wasn't enough to wake him."

It doesn't matter how much of him you take, Natalia wanted to scream. *It's scientifically impossible for the ritual to work. Stone cannot be turned into flesh.*

"Well, if anyone can stir him back to life, it's definitely me," said Sophie. Releasing him, she fumbled under her skirts, then awkwardly stepped out of her underthings. She tossed the bit of institute-standard-issue white cotton behind her. Her pantalets snagged on the statue's big toe, to sway in the wind.

Rae giggled uncertainly. "Gods, Sophie, you are crazy."

"Oil," Sophie commanded, stretching her hand out toward them, palm up.

Leona produced a small jar from the pocket of her cloak and opened its lid. "Better use plenty."

Sophie scooped some out and carefully slicked it over the statue's phallus. "I know what I'm doing."

Natalia tried a new tack, desperate to dissuade her. "What about the ritual tomorrow? You have to remain pure."

Sophie snickered. "Don't tell me you actually think I've waited?"

Natalia stared at her, shocked. The other two girls shot her pitying looks.

"Everyone our age has lain with a man by now, mistress," Rae informed her kindly.

"At least everyone who's pretty enough," Sophie added, her voice laced with meaning.

Natalia knew she wasn't pretty, at least not in the same way as these girls with their curled blond hair and blue eyes and sylphlike figures. Although her own waist was small, her body had more voluptuous curves. And her hair was unfashionably wavy and lush. The priestesses had declared that her appearance was sinful, and as she'd matured, her body had therefore been bound with corsets and hair tamed into a plait.

"But what will the priests say when you turn out to be unchaste tomorrow?" she persisted.

Leona bit off a snicker. "My first time *was* a priest."

Natalia gazed at her, even more shocked, if it were possible. How could she have been so oblivious of what these girls got up to?

"Priests are just men under their robes," Leona confided in a superior tone. "They have needs. That's why the temple allows

198 / *Elizabeth Amber*

them to marry and have families." She shot Natalia a sidelong glance. "Haven't you noticed the special attention Lay Priest Baldassare pays you?"

Natalia shook her head, brushing off her words. "But the punishment for being unchaste is—"

"No one will find out. A sac of pig's blood tucked into our privates is said to fool the authorities," Rae assured her. "Instant re-virginization. It's what everyone does."

"Where in the world are you going to get pig's blood?" asked Natalia, astonished.

"The old hag who lives in the cedar stumps at the edge of the swamp doles them out for a price," Leona informed her. "We'll visit her tomorrow morning."

"But I thought you were all so frightened of the ritual," said Natalia.

"Well, we've never done it in front of a crowd!" said Leona.

"And never with any male sporting a member as big as this," said Sophie. She'd straddled him again and was now positioning herself to take him. With one hand, she flipped the back of her skirts out of the way.

Natalia glanced over her shoulder at the lights twinkling far below, terrified they would all be discovered. "This is no childish prank that will be forgiven. If caught, you'll probably be flogged before the whole community. Maybe even sold to the flesh peddlers on the outskirts of town."

Sophie flicked her a glance. Natalia read the wild determination in her eyes. "Don't watch if you don't want to. Go back."

Natalia seriously considered it. But someone had to smuggle these girls back into the dormitory, and she had a key, something they did not.

Sophie's knees spread wide over him to rest on the altar's surface on either side of his smooth abdomen. Her companions huddled together, shivering and waiting. Sophie lowered her head and lifted her hips, seeking impalement. Her hips sank slightly and she winced. "Give me that jar again."

Leona rushed forward and held the jar of cream out to her. Sophie scooped some out, then reached under her skirts.

Gingerly, she tried him on again. "Gods."

"What does it feel like?" Rae asked, sounding fascinated.

Sophie looked thoughtful, her enjoyment at being the center of attention overwhelming her discomfort for the moment. "Cold. Smooth. Like being stabbed by a—" Her hips raised and lowered in a series of quick jerks. "Enormous. Frozen. Sword."

Everyone fell silent for long moments as she squirmed, trying to take more of him. Her humor quickly fled as she continued the attempt. The silence among them thickened like the swirling mist sweeping in from the nearby sea.

Despite the chill, sweat beaded Sophie's forehead and she wore a look of concentration. Grimacing, she undulated her pelvis in a series of careful tilts. Then she let out a smothered cry.

"Give up?" asked Leona.

"Stop, Soph!" Natalia pleaded. She went to her and reached out a hand. "You don't have to do this. Not for some foolish wager."

Sophie batted her hand away. Their eyes met, and Natalia read her sister's unwillingness to give in in front of her companions. She'd unwittingly caused her sister to suffer simply by being here—somehow her presence had raised the stakes. Sophie was too proud and fearless for her own good sometimes. She'd kill herself on this damned lark before she'd admit defeat.

So Natalia made the decision for her. "Get off," she commanded, laying a hand on Sophie's thigh. It was quivering under the strain of her attempt. "Get off him. Now, before you kill yourself. If you don't come down, I swear I'll scream louder than the bloodiest banshee. The entire village will be up here in minutes."

Rae took several steps forward, her eyes gone wide. "No! Do as your sister says, Sophie. It's not worth getting flogged or sold to the flesh peddlers."

"Or worse," added Natalia, trying to truly scare them.

"Only if Leona declares that our wager is officially off," Sophie said stubbornly.

Natalia turned to Leona. "Do it," she ordered.

Leona let out a sullen huff.

"Do it, Leona, or I'll see you sold to the flesh peddlers myself," threatened Natalia.

Leona lifted a shoulder. "Very well then. Wager's off."

Sophie let out a relieved breath. She raised her hips, gasping. Natalia reached up to help.

"Thank you," Sophie whispered, so only she would hear. For this moment in time, she had reverted to the sweet sister from their childhood.

"Help us, girls," Natalia ordered. As she took one of her sister's arms, Leona and Rae ran to the other side of the statue and up the steps, taking her other.

Sophie gripped their hands hard, awkward as she began her dismount. Suddenly, she lost her balance, tumbling sideways.

Natalia caught her weight, immediately losing her own balance and falling forward. Her palm struck marble, bracing itself momentarily on the statue's ribs as she supported her sister. Under her fingers, the stone warmed.

Anguish, grief, torment, rage. The emotions beat at her, one tumbling over another in a blistering maelstrom, as if they'd been pent up and were only now breaking free.

Surprised, she snatched her hand away and righted herself as Leona and Rae pulled her sister upright. The emotions that had so overwhelmed her stopped instantly, as if a door had shut between them and her.

She took Sophie's arm and gazed at her with concern. "Sophie! Are you all right?"

However, once she was again on terra firma, Sophie was all bravado. "How far did I get?"

Leona studied the statue's phallus, noting where the moisture ended. "It appears that you took about six inches."

"Is that all?" asked Sophie, disappointed. She retrieved her pantalets and stepped into them, hoisting them higher under her skirt. "Are you sure—?"

Natalia put an arm around her sister and waved to the others, trying to herd them down the hill. "Come, girls."

"Oh!" Rae let out a little shriek and put a hand over her mouth.

"Hush!" Leona hissed.

But Rae's eyes were wide as she pointed at the statue's side. "But, look!"

They all followed her stunned gaze and saw—the impossible. There, branded on the statue's ribs, was a perfect imprint of a hand.

Natalia's hand.

"Gods, what did you do to him, Nat?" breathed Sophie, wonder in her voice.

"Nothing." Natalia backed away, shaking her head. "I didn't do anything."

"Nooo!" Leona wailed softly. "Now the priests are going to know someone was up here tonight. We have to repair it somehow."

"Oh!" Rae squeaked. "Where she touched him. Something's happening!"

Natalia and the others watched in fascinated horror as the handprint on his side began to glow. It was no longer an icy

202 / Elizabeth Amber

blue, but had heated to molten silver, seeming to draw color from the thin veins that striated the marble.

Abruptly, a chunk of stone in the exact shape of Natalia's hand fell to the ground with a muted thud.

" 'She who can make *him* flesh and bone will save our land,' " Leona quoted from the sacred tablets. Her eerie voice drifted to linger prophetically in the cold night air.

Natalia pulled her eyes from the phenomenon and saw the other girls staring at her in awed speculation. She spread her arms, forcing a smile. "You all look as if you think I might morph into one of the thirteen devils at any moment."

Sophie nudged Leona with her elbow. "She's right. You're being ridiculous. She didn't mate him."

"The prophecy isn't explicit about the necessity of that," argued Leona.

"No one really believes in the prophecy except the priests and the elders," Sophie said, reversing her previous statements about the validity of the myth.

"But maybe Mistress Natalia *is* the one," insisted Rae. She sidled as close as she dared to the statue and gazed into the convex handprint in the marble, appearing disappointed it didn't go deep enough to see any actual flesh beneath. "Just imagine if the myth were to finally come true!"

"I guess you'll have your own try at making it do so tomorrow, won't you?" said Sophie.

"There's little chance of that," Leona scoffed. "When they hear about this, the priests will have Mistress Natalia taking our places with him before you can snap your fingers."

"When they hear about what?" asked Sophie. "I thought we all swore that everything that occurred here tonight was to be secret."

"But—" Leona gestured toward the handprint, faltering

under the threat implicit in Sophie's stare. "They're going to notice."

"And they'll ask questions," said Rae.

"A new pact, then," Natalia suggested. "For the safety of all here, none of us will speak of this."

Leona and Rae looked uncertain.

Sophie took a threatening step toward them. "If either of you tell anyone, I will smear your reputations so badly that no father will ever allow his son to offer for you. Instead of wedding one of the boys at school, you'll wind up the brides of widowed elders. Now swear. Put your hands on . . . on *him* and swear an oath of silence on this matter."

Leona shook her head, backing away. "All right, I'll swear. But I'm not touching him." Not waiting for a reply, she turned and stalked off down the hill.

"I swear as well," mumbled Rae. Darting a wary look at them, she dashed off in the wake of the other girl.

Sophie and Natalia followed, solemn on the way back to the dormitory. Just before they reached their destination, Sophie whispered, "I'm sorry, Nat. This is my fault."

Natalia took Sophie's hand and gave it a quick squeeze. "All will be well, Soph. Don't worry."

Leona and Rae were waiting by the locked entrance to the dormitory. Natalia pulled out her key, and then they were all silently sneaking inside.

Back in her tiny, private bedchamber, Natalia bathed, washing her offending hand—the one that had somehow damaged the statue. No, it had been damaged long ago. Something terrible had happened. And when her palm had met a rib of stone tonight, it was she who'd been touched. She who'd been affected. By something beautiful—by a soul that had suffered unbearably and now raged for revenge. And yet was still redeemable.

No matter how she scrubbed at her hand now, an echo of the pain she'd borne witness to remained with her. And a need to heal it permeated her entire being, making her restless and uncertain of what to do.

And no matter how she scrubbed, she couldn't wash away the facts. Leona and Rae could not keep a secret for long. She would have to leave this place, and convince Sophie to go along with her. She pulled out her satchel and began packing.

3

_____

Natalia jerked awake the next morning with a feeling of dread. It felt late. Half asleep, she fumbled for her timepiece. Only ten minutes until her first class began!

She splashed her face with cold water from the basin, donned her uniform with lightning speed, and grabbed her satchel. She had to find Sophie. Tell her they were going to run.

She'd bathed last night, packed her belongings into her satchel, and then she'd lain awake for hours making feverish plans. At nooning today, the gates in the great wall would open so that the community could assemble outside the temple for the festival.

Although arrivals would be searched, anyone departing would not be. She and Soph had travel papers, and distant relatives in foreign sections of ElseWorld. They would visit them and ask to sojourn briefly in their homes. If the priests came searching for them, there were options, places they could run. Some of her friends had wed and relocated over the years. She could search them out.

But nowhere would be truly safe. They wouldn't be able to stay in one place for long for fear of endangering those who housed them.

She could already hear other students out in the communal room from which all their private chambers branched like spokes from a wheel's hub. Before she could open the door and join them in their morning bustle, Sophie burst in. Her face was tense, her green eyes wide.

"Leona broke her word," she announced.

Natalia's satchel hit the floor. "W-what?"

"This morning. Hoping to avoid her obligation to take part in the festival, she told the priests about last night." Sophie grabbed her arm. "Come on, you've got to get out of here. The priests—hells—the whole community is coming for you."

Natalia reached for her satchel.

"Leave it. You won't need it, and it will slow you down."

With dismay, Natalia realized there would be no class today. There would be no more classes for her to instruct ever, in fact. What did grades, students, and exams matter now? She wouldn't present her papers at meetings. Would never advance to the position of a professional healer. Her theories and research would never see the light of day. Because the priests had found out about last night, her entire life was about to change.

Taking charge, Natalia pulled their travel papers from her satchel and tucked them into her pocket. Then she leaned into the hall and looked both ways. "It's clear. We'd better go upward. Out one of the fire escapes, in case they're already here searching for us."

"We?" asked Sophie.

"We're related by blood. If I flee, they'll look to you as a replacement. Who knows what they'll do in their efforts to induce you to awaken that statue in my absence."

Sophie paled.

Natalia took her hand, tugging her from the room. "This way." Together, they flew from the dormitory and through the school's main corridor. Whenever they met students, they slowed, kept their heads down, and tried to appear as if nothing were amiss. No one seemed to take special note of them.

"Leona's revelation obviously hasn't spread everywhere yet," Sophie whispered.

Natalia nodded. "Thank the gods for small favors."

As they reached the second floor landing, Sophie abruptly shoved her back in the lee of a floor-to-ceiling window alcove at the front of the institute. Natalia peeked out and saw that at the bottom of the grand staircase, several of the male professors had gathered. She nudged Sophie and pointed upstairs. They detoured upward.

From the windows along the stairs, Natalia noticed that a mob had formed out on the school lawn. Among them were men dressed in crimson robes. Priests. They were assisted by temple guards dressed in drab blue jerkins and trousers.

Her heart thumped in fear.

"This way," she whispered to Sophie, taking her hand. They flew up two flights, and then dashed down a narrow hall toward the escape stairs that led to a labyrinth of underground tunnels created by the ancients to store the wine they made from the grapes grown in the community.

Sophie turned through a doorway at right angles to the hall, but before Natalia could follow, someone popped out, barring her way. She ran full tilt into a hard male body. Broad hands stopped her from falling.

"Aha!" a masculine voice crowed.

She glanced up into the face of Gentleman Titus Cato. "Excuse me," she said, trying to push past. "We're late for class."

Beyond him, Natalia watched as several of his cronies grabbed Sophie in an inescapable clench. "Stop that!" she heard

208 / Elizabeth Amber

Sophie say. Abruptly, her voice was stifled as someone placed a hand over her mouth.

"There are no classes held up here, mistress," Titus taunted. "Where could you be going in such a hurry, I wonder?"

Natalia lunged in her sister's direction, but her escape was cut off when two other boys joined Titus. Her view of Sophie was blocked as well, but not before she'd seen the jealousy in the girl's eyes. Did she honestly believe that Cato was enamored of her? Or she of him?

She turned a stern eye on the boys who'd waylaid her. "I suggest you and your friends let us go, Gentleman Cato. Or I will have disciplinary actions taken against you."

He laughed and Natalia found herself shoved against the row of wooden lockers, the boys on either side of her holding her arms. Titus's handsome face filled her vision. He pressed himself full against her, letting his forearms bracket her head.

Never had she been treated so roughly! What made them think they could behave in this way toward her? They must have heard the gossip. She and Sophie had to get away, and fast. She tried not to panic. "What do you want?"

"Heard you were up sniffing around the temple last night," said Titus. "If I'd known you were looking for that sort of fun, I'd have been glad to provide it." He plucked at her prim collar. "Truth is, I've been pining to see what you look like under this starched uniform, Mistress Natalia. We all have."

"Do you know what happens to the male physique when it's kneed in the groin?" she asked coolly. "It's rather unpleasant."

One of the other boys holding her snickered.

Titus glared at him. "Now, mistress, don't be nasty. Just give us a peek. Go on, there's a dear. Then we'll let you be on your way."

She gasped, struggling. "Don't you dare, you pit of foul deceit! I'll see you expelled."

"It no longer matters what liberties we take with you, mistress. You're the one who'll be leaving the institute shortly. I just want a look before you go, is all . . . and maybe a taste."

With that, Titus shoved his fingers under the placket of her blouse and yanked downward. Buttons popped off, pinging on the floor.

"Keep watch," he murmured to one of the others, his eyes greedy on the flesh her gaping blouse had exposed. With her arms held outward, her breasts strained at her corset and shift.

Natalia's head rolled to the side and she caught a glimpse of Sophie struggling in her captor's hold. Her eyes were furious above the white-knuckled male hand covering her mouth. If nothing else, at least this episode would serve to show her the true nature of the boy she'd once had finer feelings for.

One of Titus's friends glanced down the corridor. "Make it fast, Cato. Before we're discovered."

Natalia bucked against the wall, her face rouged with bright splotches of anger. "Would you want your own sister to be treated this way?" she hissed at the boy.

"My sister isn't a harlot like you and Sophie," he replied. "We heard what you got up to on the hill last night."

"So this is to be my punishment? You appoint yourselves judge and jury?"

"Shut her up," Titus told one of his friends. Immediately, a male hand covered her mouth, pushing her head fast to the lockers at her back. Titus's eyes were on his work as he yanked her shift down and opened her corset. Fabric fell away, and she felt the peaks of her breasts tighten in the morning chill.

All three boys leaned in, their eyes avid. Held mute, she stared fixedly at the breast of her assailant's jacket. Part of his institute uniform, it was emblazoned with a patch embroidered by the priestesses, which bore the school symbols of honor, tolerance, and piety.

"Gentleman Cato! Unhand the mistress—immediately!" a scandalized voice barked. All three boys jumped away from her as if they'd been scalded. Freed, Natalia swiveled toward the lockers, hunching as she straightened her clothing as best she could.

It was one of the masters, a professor of linguistics, who'd come to her rescue. Behind him, a crowd of men—many of them priests—began to fill the room. She glanced over her shoulder, searching out Sophie. She had been emancipated as well and now seemed to be trying to reach her sister's side.

Natalia frowned at her, shaking her head. She glanced pointedly at the far end of the hall, hoping Sophie would understand that she was to flee. Her sister stilled uncertainly. Hoping to divert attention from her, Natalia ducked between the boys around her and dashed toward the window. Executing a dive that was a credit to Mistress Marino's efforts in junior academy aquatics class, she made for the fire escape.

Her hands grazed the iron grate of the outside landing just as the window ledge drove the air from her lungs. Her ribs were bruised, but she'd made it halfway through. She clawed her way forward. Another few inches . . .

Somewhere behind her, hard fingers grabbed at her skirts, ankles, knees, hips. Her pursuers reeled her in until she was back inside, fully caught.

As they spirited her away, she searched the corridor for Sophie. She was nowhere to be seen. "Gods protect you," Natalia whispered under her breath. Then, she was cast adrift amid a sea of male authorities, and hustled off to the temple.

An assemblage of temple guards and priests flanked her all the way up the hill, then lead her up the granite steps to the temple stage. There, all made the sign of respect, including her, but she refused to look at the statue. At *him*. This was all *his* fault.

All around them, members of the community had begun gathering on the hillside, gossiping wildly, and clamoring for news. She glanced over her shoulder and searched the crowd for Sophie, and was relieved not to find her.

The high priest stood center stage. He nodded to the guards, who half dragged her to his side. There, under his watchful eyes, she was forced to confront the damning evidence.

In the stark sunlight, tiny veins of gold and silver sparkled within the alien marble that was *his* body. Her stark handprint still glowed softly at his rib cage.

"Come, mistress," the high priest said. "Give me your hand."

She folded her arms across her waist and tucked her hands under her elbows.

His brows pinched together. "Don't be difficult."

He motioned to someone behind her. Two guards arrived, and her hand was summarily forced into the hand-shaped depression. The remaining stone there heated again at her touch, but they didn't seem to notice and let her draw away.

She rubbed her palm on her skirt, worry snaking up her spine. *What the devils is going on here?*

"It fits," the high priest murmured, clasping his hands together in delight.

"Her hand! It fits! It fits!" someone behind her announced. Word spread through the guards to the crowd on the hill, gaining momentum. The excited whisperings grew louder.

"It proves nothing," Natalia protested. "A thousand hands would fit that print."

Just then, a group of guards arrived, taking the steps upward to them. One bore the hand-shaped chunk of marble that had fallen to the ground last night. It rested on a tasseled velvet cushion as though it were a precious artifact. They bowed, and then one of them spoke not to her but to the high priest. "It has been tested and conclusively bears her fingerprints."

"Then there's no doubt." The high priest's piercing black eyes swept her. "You are *his* chosen one." Natalia shrank back. His rule was absolute in the community, and everyone obeyed.

"Come, girl. I'll not hurt you."

Fearing the worst, she allowed him to take her hand in his be-ringed, pale one, and she breathed a sigh of relief when he only led her away from the altar. Together they approached the edge of the stage.

Facing the assembled crowd, he drew her to a halt, and nodded to the guards, who began calling for quiet. When silence fell, the high priest spoke. His voice rang out across their audience.

"You've all heard of the mark discovered only this morning on our godking. The stories of it are true."

Excited murmurs rippled over the crowd, drowning him out for a moment. She stood docile at the priest's side, but her eyes darted around in search of escape.

The guards demanded silence again, and then he continued.

"We don't know what it means, but we are hopeful. The mark was created by Mistress Natalia, one of our instructors at the institute. A healer."

His palm rested on the top of her head for a moment, then slid around to cup her face. "The ritual will take place as usual at the festival this afternoon. However, under the circumstances, there will be only one bride today."

"No! I'm not . . . ready," Natalia protested, shrugging him off.

The high priest quirked a brow at her. "Don't worry on that score. You will be made ready in time." Then he turned back to the crowd. "You may all return in three hours' time for the viewing of the ritual at nooning. Go forth now and spread the joyous news!"

*　　*　　*

Natalia found herself quickly handed off to priests of lower rank and ushered inside the temple, past its mammoth ancient doors, for preparations. Her mind flew wildly, grasping for a way out. Seeing none, she knew she must skew the situation as best she could.

Despite what had happened last night, she had no doubt she would fail at the task these men had set for her this afternoon. As a healer, she'd nursed dozens of girls back to health after they'd survived the ordeal of the sacrificial ritual. Tonight, it would be her own body she would be nursing, her own wounds the priestesses would soothe with salves and remedies under her instruction.

But as soon as she was well again, would these men expect her to take a husband? Would Sophie and the others eventually be inducted at next year's festival? She'd be damned if she'd allow that to come to pass!

When they reached the fountain in the nave, Natalia wrenched herself from her captors and folded her arms. "I'll cooperate on two conditions," she announced coolly.

The lay priest in charge of her seemed to be Baldassare. He brushed off her words, affronted. "We don't require your co-operation."

"But think how much more smoothly all will go if your godking's mate isn't shrieking in terror and cursing your heads."

He stepped toward her as if to strike her, then thought better of it.

"Females don't make conditions," one of the other priests murmured.

"Drug her instead," someone suggested.

"No, she's right," Baldassare relented. "We can't have her falling asleep or acting addled. It will detract from the sacred aspect of the ritual. The high priest would be displeased."

"Name your conditions," one of the priests told her.

Emboldened, Natalia spoke, her voice unflinching. "First, that I will be allowed to continue on as a spinster and will not be wed. And second, that my sister, Sophie, and the other two girls, Leona and Rae, will be permanently spared the festival ritual. That they will instead be allowed to choose their own husbands in their own time. I'll have all that in writing, witnessed, and set out in a public forum before the community, where all can see."

"Your conditions are predicated on the assumption that you will not awaken him," said Baldassare, gesturing toward the altar outside.

"Because that is what I assume."

"How can you know?" another demanded.

She only stared at them, silent. "Do we have an agreement?"

After a moment, Baldassare announced, "We agree to all but one of your conditions. If you are not the one to awaken the godking, you will consent to willingly take a husband. One who has already bid for you. You will agree to wed one week from tonight, after you have sufficiently . . . recovered."

Natalia sucked in a breath. "Who?"

He bowed slightly.

"*You?* You bid for me?" She stepped back and came up against the wall of the fountain behind her. "You don't even know me."

His colorless eyes swept her. "I've read your file. I've watched you. You will suit me."

So Leona and Rae had been right about his interest in her. She'd never even noticed he had singled her out. How long had he been watching her and waiting for this eventuality?

She shuddered inwardly at the thought of this man touching her. She wanted to argue the matter, but feared they might renege on the rest of their agreement. "But my other conditions will stand?" she clarified. "No matter what happens to me?"

He nodded.

"I'll want documents executed, stamped with your official seals, and filed in the courts before I begin the ritual this afternoon," she insisted.

Murmurs and gasps at her audacity in questioning their word whipped through the assemblage of men, but she held Baldassare's eyes. He nodded slightly, but she read his anger. Knew he would make her pay if she ever saw herself in his marital bed. She planned to try to escape during her recovery period that would be of one week's duration after the conclusion of today's spectacle. And she would take Sophie with her.

While the documents were drawn up, she was remanded into the care of priestesses. Once the priests departed as was customary, preparations began in earnest within the sacred coolness of the temple.

Within moments Natalia found herself naked in the center of a half-dozen clucking attendants, the last of her clothing having been stripped in shreds from her body, as though by the talons of eager vultures. None of what they would do to her here would be undertaken with any malice, but was only part of the tradition, she knew.

Their eyes dissected her, scrutinized her body, face, and hair. Their expressions were doubtful. *So this is his chosen one?* they seemed to silently wonder.

She quickly found herself held spread-eagle on a stone surface. The priestesses took care that every strand of pubic hair was lathered, then painstakingly shaved from her. Next she was led to the bubbling mosaic fountain in the chapel, where she was bathed by several pairs of gentle hands under the watchful stone eye of their patron god, Bacchus. Fingers darted inside her, cleansing her with a thoroughness that they believed would render her fit for a godking.

Their touches came, warm and gentle, as they rubbed her

skin with scented oils. Her hair was brushed and bunched high on her head in a cascading froth.

"I prefer my hair down," Natalia told one of the priestesses, reaching up to destroy their design. A hand stayed hers.

The high priestess shook her head and spoke directly to her for the first time since she'd come into the temple. "It's too long. You mustn't cover your body—it is written in the Tablets. The community will wish to view your sacrifice."

Natalia reached up and began removing pins from her hair. "But by whom was it written? By male priests? No god wrote it, that's for certain."

"Hush and obey, girl. A woman's place is subservient to the godking, community, and man. In that order."

Natalia gaped at her, appalled at this determined, dogmatic view espoused even by women themselves. She shook her head, using her fingers to comb out her hair. Then she gazed at the priestess in defiance. The woman only shook her head, *tsk*ing. "We are not your enemies," she murmured. "Nor are our men."

Natalia was left to ponder this for the next hour as preparations continued.

Eventually, when all was done and she was deemed properly sanctified, the wedding crown was placed atop her head—the one every girl wore on festival day as she gave sacrifice. It had been forged by a metalworker when the statue had first come to them, and was studded with precious jewels and delicate gilded stars that would sparkle in the sunlight when she . . . Natalia swallowed her fear.

They left the confines of the temple flanked by an assemblage of holy men and their guards. All wore their finest raiment for the occasion.

A shimmering, translucent gown covered her from head to toe, and a veil was clasped at her shoulders and left to trail behind her like a train. And beneath those, her lifechain with its twenty-eight beads remained, still encircling her waist. For it could not be lawfully taken from her by anyone but her husband.

The high priestess had touched it briefly before they'd gowned Natalia, tears in her eyes. "I pray that today *his* hands will remove it from you," she'd whispered.

4

Outside in the sun, Natalia's intended mate awaited her. A sea of humanity swarmed below, covering the hillside as far as the eye could see. It seemed the entire community had gathered for the spectacle, as the high priest had commanded.

With each step she took toward him, her unbound breasts swayed gently, reminding her that she was without her customary underthings. Practically naked save for her translucent sheathing. There would be no corsets or coarse skirts to hide her from avid eyes that would scrutinize her proportions.

She forced the thought away, and climbed the five steps that ran the length of the altar on this, its temple side. She paused on the top step, the statue at a level with her knees. Refusing to glance downward at it, she instead scanned the crowd. The sight of thousands jostling to gawk terrified her.

These were people who had seen her grow up from child to woman. There was the baker who had given her free bread after their mother had died. And the institute's counselor who'd helped her choose between a course in anthropology or mathematics when she was thirteen. And there—Leona's father.

Couldn't they see how she trembled? Her eyes darted in every direction, but found no haven in another's gaze. They all appeared so hopeful.

A lifetime of indoctrination made this rite acceptable to them. They wouldn't even consider an attempt to rescue her. Her fate seemed certain, and she stiffened her spine, resigning herself to accomplishing this act with dignity.

The priestesses had given her sedatives, both oral and vaginal. She would get through this. Ten minutes, maybe fifteen, and it would be over. And by this act, she would save three girls from defilement.

Afterward, she swore silently, she would run. This backward place was not for her . . . or Sophie.

She heard two priests take the steps and come to stand on either side of her. "Beautiful," a quiet voice said from beside her.

She turned her head and saw it was Baldassare who'd spoken. His hand smoothed stealthily over her hip, unnoticed by the other lay priest. She slapped his fingers away. "I don't want you."

"Do you think that matters to me?" he murmured. Staring straight ahead, so none would notice their conversation, he murmured his words, his lips barely moving. "I've waited a long time for you. I asked for you years ago when your mother passed on, and again every year after that. Yesterday, I was finally granted permission. In one week you will be mine. Think on that as you lie in your recovery bed."

The high priest joined them then amid great pomp, bringing with him two priestesses. Baldassare and the other lay priest stepped aside for them, watching as their leader dipped beringed fingers into the urn of holy oil that had been brought to him. They came away dripping. A ceremony began in which sacred unguents were used to anoint the godking's phallus.

It looked enormous from this vantage point, hard and glistening now with oils. Natalia took a shuddering breath.

High Priest was chanting verses from the Tablets now. Her stomach tensed. Her time was drawing near. His voice rang out, sweeping the crowd. "Before the gods and these witnesses I swear that I will be a faithful and true wife unto you."

"Repeat what he says," the priestess whispered to her.

Natalia kept stubbornly silent.

Baldassare stepped closer. "Speak it, wench. Or the bargain you wrought on behalf of your sister and her friends will be nullified."

She drew a deep breath, then spoke. "Before the gods and these witnesses I swear that I will be a faithful and true wife unto you."

"Louder, so the community can hear," the priestess urged.

Natalia cleared her throat and tried again. This time, her voice was stronger as she repeated the remainder of the words supplied to her. "Accept my humble offering, as this day, I give you my body, so that it may become your fleshly haven. So that it might give you succor. And so that I might awaken you and thereby bring an end to the suffering of this land and people."

The clasp at her shoulder was removed by one of the priestesses, and she was unveiled, left only in her long translucent shift. Red crept into her cheeks. She ducked her head, and her unbound hair swung to shield her.

Below, the crowd murmured, anxious for all to begin.

High Priest moved aside and watched as the two lay priests lifted her to kneel, straddling his belly. Just as Sophie had only last night. A lifetime ago.

"I'll count the days, wife," Baldassare murmured *sotto voce*.

"What if I don't fail?"

He snorted softly.

"You don't think I'll awaken *him?*"

He smiled and spoke close to her ear under the guise of assisting her. "He's only stone. No one can."

Shocked to learn that there were doubters even among the

priests, she could only stare after him as he and the other priest descended, leaving her alone atop the altar. From nearby, High Priest called out the words the ritual demanded, his officious voice echoing over the hillsides. *"Who waketh him, shall save our land."*

The crowd took up the chant, repeating it. Natalia had heard these words uttered countless times before as she watched others participate in this sacrifice. Attendance at the ceremony was mandatory in the community. Many of the women in this very crowd had taken *him* inside them—at least partially—before they'd each eventually been wed to another husband. She gazed at the audience and saw Rae crying for her. Leona stood alongside her, her face averted as if she couldn't bear to watch. No Sophie.

"It's time, mistress," the priestess who'd remained told her, her voice kind. "It's best not to think; just get on with it. Sit back now."

Tensing her thighs, Natalia lowered herself as instructed, taking care to keep her expression wooden. The cold hardness of him prodded at her private flesh. He was slick, as was she. Both had been plied with facilitating oils. Still she shuddered at the unfamiliar, intimate intrusion.

At last, she glanced at the statue's face. He looked so peaceful and oblivious of the havoc he'd wreaked in her life. Gravity took her lower, forcing the head of his phallus into her. She tensed her thighs, squeezing his hips between them to slow her descent. Where her flesh met stone, she felt the statue begin to warm. No! It wasn't scientifically possible for the touch of human flesh to melt stone. She said nothing, praying she was right.

"That's it," the priestess murmured in approval. "Press lower."

"It hurts." Her palms found the smooth bulges of his biceps, resisting.

"You're female. It's supposed to hurt," a male voice said.

Baldassare had returned. To ensure her cooperation? He stood several steps down, where he would not be visible to the crowd beyond her.

"She's taken the head, nothing more," the priestess observed. With painstaking slowness, Natalia bore down. The sedatives were doing their work, dulling the pain. When a sudden tearing sensation ripped through her, she flexed her thighs against him and drew away.

"He's drawn her woman's blood!" one of the priests noted. The joyful news that her virginity had been taken was passed from the priests to the crowd, where it spread from person to person like wind rippling over a field of wheat.

"Bear down," a voice told her.

She tried. For long moments, she struggled onward, then paused, panting. The pain of the impalement was growing worse. The experience was even more torturous than she could have imagined. She'd seen other girls crying and heard them begging to stop during the ritual. Eventually, they'd been allowed to give up.

"I can't. I ask permission to withdraw."

One of the priests cursed. Voices in the crowd bit at her as well. Angry accusations were hurled, claiming that she was willfully refusing the godking. She tried not to be angry at them. They were desperate, and their desperation had made them believe the myth the priests had woven.

"You're doing well," a voice encouraged.

"Better than some have before you," said another.

"But I can't go any farther. I swear it on the gods' names." The priests huddled, whispering.

"It won't do any good to kill the girl. She's taken all she can," she heard Baldassare argue.

"He's biased. He wants her for himself afterward," said another voice. "I heard him admit it."

"I say let her sit there and adjust," yet another voice suggested. "By law, she must try him on until sunset."

Sunset! That was many hours away. Natalia hung her head, shutting them and the crowd out. Ever since they were young, the priests had schooled them all on this rite of passage that would occur on festival day. She had heard students reciting the chants of obligation in the halls even as children. Now they ran through her head and she whispered them in nonsensical snatches, just as women in childbirth chanted their own mantras to soothe their pain. *It is my sacred duty ... it is my lot to sacrifice ... to save our land ... with all my heart I must try to awaken him ... to love ...*

The wind picked up, whipping her hair wild and free as she herself longed to be. If they would not give her leave to go, she would die here if she must. She had to persevere for Sophie and the others, so that they would not be subjected to this.

Tears brimmed her eyes and fell to *his* chest. They trickled over him, running over on to his biceps.

A sudden hush fell over the crowd. Natalia lifted her head, dully wondering what had happened. Something shifted under her. Suddenly she heard a strange sound, as though heavy millstones were grinding. The marble beneath her shuddered.

Then, impossibly, she saw the muscles of his chest flex before her eyes. Saw his elbows bend. Saw his arms curve. Felt his hands come around her waist, hard and cold. Where marbled muscles flexed, the stone encasing them cracked and exploded in small bursts, then fell away to crash on the stage.

Her eyes flew to his face. His eyes remained closed, his expression unaware. Except for his arms and torso, he still showed no sign of life. *Life?*

"No. No. This cannot be happening," she whispered. Natalia pulled at those hands, squirming to get away, flexing her thighs in an attempt to relieve herself of him. His hands only clasped her waist more tightly. Fingers pressed, dimpling her flesh and bruising it.

She reached out to the priests, but they backed away, eyes round and fearful. "Cowards," she railed. "Help me. Please," she called. Frantically, she searched the crowd for a friendly face.

"He lives," the onlookers whispered reverently, bowing down.

Only part of him. The rest of him was still stone, still slumbering. Something told her she had better escape before his eyes opened.

The stone hands squeezed, and she felt herself being pushed downward, her body being forced to take more of him.

She beat at him with her fists. Members of the community gasped, shocked at her audacity and the spectacle. The penalty for touching him without authorization was severe. No one knew what the penalty for striking him was. But not even the priests dared come closer to chastise her.

"Oh gods. No. I can't," Natalia whimpered, panting and slapping his marble chest. "If you can hear me, stop. You're killing me. Stop!"

With a hard jerk, the hands suddenly reversed direction and lifted her away, disengaging their bodies. Distantly, she heard herself scream at the sensation of suctioning and abrupt loss. Then spots filled her vision and all consciousness fled.

When she swam back into awareness, she was no longer impaled. Instead, her pliable body lay draped over a chest and belly made of unforgiving stone. Her legs had separated and slid down to dangle on either side of statue and altar. Her cheek was on his breast, the top of her head tucked in the crook of his neck.

Masculine hands held hers—*his* hands—moving them over smooth marble with infinite slowness. Everywhere her palms touched him, the stone slowly heated, cracked, disintegrated.

This could not be happening!

Suddenly, his chest swelled under her. She heard the sound of a great, sudden gust of breath being drawn in by lungs long unused.

She pushed up on her elbows, her gaze seeking his face, and then watched as his lashes fluttered for some minutes, struggling to break free of the stone. His hands lifted and took hers to cover his face. Marble cracked and he let her go, ripping away the blinders of stone himself. Eyelids flickered. And opened.

Silver irises gazed at her from eyes framed with stone-dusted lashes. They were blank at first. But in an instant, they filled with wary confusion. Hard muscles bunched and tensed. With a mighty roar, the creature under her lunged upward, to crouch atop the altar.

Natalia howled as she fell to the stairs. She landed hard on one shoulder. Then she slid and bumped her way down the rest of the steps to lie in a crumpled heap on the stage.

Above her, he crouched on the altar, surveying the priests and the crowd below with fierce suspicion.

Lucien Satyr lay atop a block of marble, fighting the blinding pain that threatened to split his skull. Blood pulsed sluggish agony through his veins. He was half naked, his cock hard and throbbing with the need to come. He was inside a woman. Fucking her. Who she was, he didn't know. But fucking her felt good. Better than good. He lifted his hands, pulled her closer.

Others were moving around them, surefooted and purposeful.

They had an audience.

Through the pain that burst in his brain, his thoughts gathered and congealed to a burning pinpoint of hatred. Somewhere among the onlookers, his enemy lurked. His final enemy. The last one of those who had tortured him and the others imprisoned in the catacombs.

The urge to kill swamped him. He tried to rise, but something was inhibiting him. He wore some sort of coat that was as heavy as a lead weight. Had that bastard restrained him? *No! Not again.*

If he could just fight free of it, he might have a chance of getting to his enemy. Of tearing him limb from limb. This was the one he'd long sought—the one who'd favored young, fresh meat. Male or female, it hadn't mattered. He'd taken what he wanted, and now Luc would make him pay.

The woman in his arms struck him. What the hells? Was she that devil's minion? He disengaged from her and she lay over him. Even that felt good. Warm.

He lifted her hands and laid them on his flesh, wanting to feel her touch. Craving it. He, who hated to be touched, even by his own kin.

Breath filled his lungs.

He tried to open his eyes. Found he could not. Panic filled him. He was blind. He reached up to his face and felt the mask that encased it.

Ripping it away, he then blinked at the woman who rode him. She was beautiful. And terrified. He sensed the man he sought was escaping. He had to get to him.

He pushed her away and rose to a crouch, careless of the strange woman's fate in that moment. His eyes scanned the crowd around him. Where was the evil one?

He swayed on his feet. Gods, what was wrong with him? He was weak as a baby. And covered in . . . plaster?

Natalia hunched on the marble tile at the bottom of the steps, trying to gather within herself the wherewithal to stand. Atop the altar above her, the statue rose to his full height, a monster that was half marble and half flesh. Blood—her blood—dripped from his phallus, bright scarlet on gleaming white stone.

There was pandemonium among the holy men and women around her. No one knew whether to applaud or run. Some bowed low and were trampled by the fearful trying to get away. Meanwhile Natalia mustered her strength. Pushing to her knees, she cried out at the sharp pain between her legs and sank again.

His head swiveled in her direction.

Oh gods! She'd drawn his attention. His brows drew together and his eyes narrowed. The emotions she'd sensed the previous night when she'd first touched him now blasted out at her from him, stronger than ever. Wariness. Terror. Rage! She cringed away, whimpering under their force.

He stared at her, accusing, as though he believed her the cause of his disorientation.

She shook her head in protest. "I didn't . . . I'm not . . ."

He snarled, a low animal sound. In another burst of crushed stone, he leaped, catlike, from the altar and came toward her. His gait was awkward, hindered by the marble that still clad parts of him. Wherever his body flexed, great plates of it shattered and crashed to the temple stage.

Natalia inched away on her back, then got to her knees again, crawling, trying to reach help.

Masculine fingers threaded her hair. She whipped around at the same moment he tugged. The tiara, which the priestesses had perched on her head, came away in his grasp. He stared at it in bewilderment.

A hysterical giggle threatened to escape her, but she smothered it. Taking advantage of his distraction, she scrabbled across the tile, desperate to flee. But he reached for her again, showering her with tiny shards in the process. She ducked away, shielding her face. Taking her arms, he hoisted her high over one broad shoulder.

Turning with her, he moved decisively toward the temple. In a dozen steps, they were inside it. Behind them, gargantuan ancient doors that hadn't moved in a century slammed shut. And he hadn't even touched them.

"No one can move those doors," Natalia whispered into the black.

Luc ignored her, his thoughts a riotous jumble as he moved up the nave past rows of seats. The smell of fresh irises was sickly sweet in the air here. It made him want to throw up. Every minute that passed was a fight to stay on his feet.

His mind screamed with memories banging against his skull as if to break free and make him confront them. Torturous memories of the miscreant he'd scented outside. Of the cruelty he'd perpetrated on Luc and all the others who'd been held captive in the catacombs all those years.

No, he stuffed the memories deeper. He couldn't afford to think of them now. He was too weak. He had to get his bearings. To rest and collect strength before he faced his adversary.

The woman he carried delivered a particularly vicious kick to his belly and he grunted. Ignoring her protests, he moved on, half blind from stone dust and the surrounding murk. A moment ago, he'd been lying on a sacrificial altar outside this place. With her.

Five minutes before that, he'd been in Rome with his brothers. He remembered he'd eavesdropped on Sevin and Alexa. Then he'd gone to the main arena of the *Salone di Passione*. Bastian and Dane had been there, worrying over something.

He felt a sense of urgency, as if he had some mission that was as yet uncompleted. But what?

Why couldn't he think? His gods-damned head was set to crack wide open with the pounding inside it. And the woman's infernal struggling wasn't helping matters. He would let her go eventually, but first he needed answers.

There were furs hanging on the wall behind the main altar

ahead. He continued up the nave and went for them, tearing them from the wall and tossing them on the floor. Then he set his burden to lie on them.

Natalia landed on something soft and bristled. "The sacred furs," she murmured in surprise. "You can't—"

When her captor moved away, silence fell. She cocked her head, hope rising in her as she listened to the stillness. Had he gone? No, she heard a sound. But it was a distance off. This was her chance. She reached out and gingerly pulled herself up against a wall.

From somewhere nearby, he let out a soft curse. It sounded like he was trying to light a lamp.

Ignoring the cramping in her abdomen and the cruel bite of pain in her shoulder and between her thighs, she pushed herself to her knees. Then she stood and limped toward escape. She wouldn't be able to budge the main doors, so she tried another route.

She'd been in this temple hundreds of times, had hidden in its nooks and crannies as a child playing hide-and-seek. Finding her way largely by feel now, she made for the choir chamber, the closest exit.

Her hands found him before her mind recognized what she was touching. His flesh was as hard as the rock wall. But unlike the smooth wall, remaining patches of stone marred him, making him feel damaged and strange. She was in no condition to run, but she tried anyway. He caught her. Light sprang up between them. He'd gotten the lamp working.

Wordlessly, he hooked an elbow around her waist and picked her up under one arm, holding the lamp in his other. He trudged back to the altar and then let her go.

She tumbled to the furs again and he stood over her, glowering. "What is this place?"

When she didn't reply, he nudged her with his foot. Bits of

white splintered and puffed in the air all around him. He reached up and ripped away a piece of it as big as his hand. "And what is this damned plaster?"

She scooted backward, her gaze wary.

"Speak," he demanded.

"It's marble. And this place is a temple," she murmured. As if her voice had been a physical stroke, he arched his spine and shrugged those broad shoulders, sending another chunk of marble crashing to the floor.

Luc brushed a layer of lingering dust from his shoulder, eyeing her suspiciously. Her Siren's voice eased his tension, relaxed him, making him want to lie down beside her on those furs. Making him want to hold her close. He, who abhorred being touched. Whatever magic she employed, he fought it off. Now was not the time.

"Where? In what city, what world?"

A pause. "Enclave a Roma, parallel two fourteen, Else-World."

"ElseWorld," he grunted. Her tone had told him she thought him addled. Perhaps he was. "Sleep," he commanded.

In response, a strange lethargy stole over her. "What did you—?" she mumbled. And then she slept.

Natalia woke sometime later. She moved gingerly, somewhat surprised to find that she still lived. Her body felt battered and muscles she hadn't known she possessed ached and protested. But she didn't seem to be actively bleeding anymore. In fact, she didn't feel any pain at all inside where he'd mated her. Incredibly, that intimate flesh was the only part of her body that actually felt good.

She looked at him, barely making out the shape of his face in the darkness. He was awake, sitting with his back against the wall. "What are you?" she whispered. "I don't believe you're a god."

A harsh laugh left him, sounding like it had issued from

deep within some ancient abandoned tomb. "Maybe you're the one who's addled."

Her brows rose. "The prophecy. Do you know it?" She gestured toward the nearby sanctuary.

Somehow, Luc got to his feet and lumbered over to view what she was pointing at. His head was swirling with a strange sort of exhausted delirium. He braced himself on the sanctuary's altar when he reached it, trying not to topple over. There were gold letters carved into the altar's side, he realized. Writing. He turned away, unable to read it and too embarrassed to admit to his lack of education. "My vision is blurred. What does it say?"

" 'Who waketh him, shall save our land.' "

He tried to make sense of that through his dizziness, and failed. Confused, he ran his fingers through his hair and they came away covered with a fine white dust. His thoughts where whirling in a maelstrom. He'd come here to this world hoping to find something. What? Something urgent. For his brothers.

She spoke again. "The priests say you were sent here to save our land. They claim you're a god."

He laughed, his voice cracked and ravaged. "They're wrong. I'm no god. Far. From. It."

He saw her lips move in reply, but he could not hear her above the buzzing in his ears. Going lightheaded, he fell to his knees, then collapsed onto the sacred furs beside her and passed out.

5

Healing Center, ElseWorld
Day one

Three days later, Natalia stared through the one-way glass window at her new patient. He lay on his back, his body largely covered by a white sheet. He was tall—so tall that his feet hung off the end of the single iron bed he'd been given. His muscled brawn tested the bed's strength, and his shoulders spanned almost the entire width of its mattress.

His wrists and ankles were tethered to the bed frame, tension evident in every line of his body. Even though he slept, even through the glass that separated them, Natalia could feel his silent rage.

She forced herself to study him objectively. He wasn't physically wounded. No, his were wounds of the soul, and they had festered and boiled over into this terrible anger. He was young, darkly handsome, his muscles well-toned despite years of stasis, and if she wasn't mistaken, he was—

Natalia felt her face flush and her startled eyes jerked from the sheet tented over his belly. She stared sightlessly at his file, then her gaze fell upon a single word written there. Abruptly, she turned away from the glass, setting the file aside on a desk and shaking her head.

"No. I don't want him," she told the man seated there. "I can't take on this assignment. Find someone else."

"Why not?" he asked. His eyes darted nervously to the other man in the room, who stood with his back to them, gazing outside from the only exterior window.

"I don't have to give a reason, Physician. I feel no connection," she lied. "I can't heal him."

"No connection? But you're wed to him."

"So are hundreds of other women in the community. It doesn't make me special."

"Ah, but you are a healer, the first of your profession to wed him. And he's already responding to you."

Natalia blushed. Surely he wasn't being so indelicate as to refer to the tented sheet?

"Before you recovered enough to come to him, he was restless and struggling," Physician went on. "See how calm he is now that you're here? Your presence soothes him, even from a distance, even through walls."

She shook her head, adamant. "He's not within my client profile. I work only with women and children. And there's my research at the institute to consider. Along with my teaching duties, they already consume my time—"

"That part of your life is finished." This from the other man, who'd finally turned to address them. His clothing identified him as an Advisor, a government official. "I'm pleased to tell you that you are advancing in position, as of this afternoon. By taking on this patient, you will achieve the official rank of Healer." He executed a slight bow. "Congratulations."

Joy welled up in her, and frustration. If she were to take this patient, and delve into his secrets, the risk was too great that her own secrets would be discovered.

"No, I'm sorry," she said, shaking her head. "I'm sure you'll find—"

"I understand your sister is of an age to enter the breeding program." Advisor lifted his hand, showing her a file he held. It bore Sophie's name.

She drew in a sharp breath. "Is that a threat?"

"It's an opportunity. I'm on the program committee and I can ensure she is excused. Permanently, even if she marries."

"What do you want in return?"

His eyes flicked to the patient in the adjoining room, and her gaze followed.

"Do you still believe him to be a godking?"

"No."

She considered that. "Then why is he so important? What goal have you set for me with him, other than seeing him mended?" she asked. "I won't hurt him for you."

"Even though he has hurt you?" Physician put in softly.

She steeled her spine, ignoring the oblique reference to the events of the festival three days earlier. With remarkable speed, she'd recovered from it physically. However, her plans to escape had come to nothing, for she'd been heavily guarded. Even now, there were guards out in the corridor who'd brought her here from her temporary room in the Recovery Unit next door.

Today she'd braced herself to fight an effort on their part to give her to Baldassare. Instead she'd been brought here. "You want me to elicit some sort of information from him?" she persisted. "Is that it?"

Advisor perched on the edge of the attendant desk, which sat just outside the one-way glass window, saying, "We want to know how he came here, by what means of travel. Who he is. What he wants in this world. Anything. Everything."

"Why?"

"You just do your job, Healer. Don't think beyond that. We want him well enough to remember. Do whatever it takes, as quickly as possible. You have ten days." He smiled slightly. "If you agree."

She turned back to the one-way window.

"He'll wake soon," Physician told her after a silence passed. "Will you begin now?"

With an inward sigh, she gave them a curt nod. "After you depart." She looked to the physician. "Both of you."

The men didn't move.

"He'll know if you're observing."

"Someone will be at all times. He'll have to get accustomed to that. And I'll expect daily written progress reports from you." Advisor tucked Sophie's file under his arm and thrust a clipboard into her hands.

"And when my work day is done? Where am I to make my bed, Advisor?"

"Your quarters will be here, in the Center from now on. Physician will have you escorted to your chamber later."

She breathed an inward sigh of relief. Even if they planned to marry her off to Baldassare in future, taking on this client meant more time to plot an escape.

Inside his cell, Luc slowly swam back to consciousness. An all-too-familiar voice sent a surge of rage laced with terror skittering down his spine. His every muscle went rigid with the instinct to fight or flee. He yanked at his arms. He was restrained! *Oh gods. Not again.* He forced down the panic that threatened.

"Wait," he heard a woman say. Her voice was soothing and somehow familiar. His mind latched onto it as if it were a bridge to sanity. "Why is he here?" she asked the devil outside. "And not with the other patients?"

The devil replied, "We've sequestered him. He's dangerous."

"And drugged him?"

"Of course."

"If I'm to be his healer, I'll need autonomy in his treatment."

"You understand speed is of the essence?"

"You understand he could be harmed if we move too quickly with his therapy."

"Just get it done. Ten days."

The door opened, and Luc turned his head to stare at the woman who entered his cell. He recognized her instantly, but not just from the altar. From the way his cock went hard.

She was holding a clipboard, her back to him as she shut the door. Luc caught a glimpse of the markings she was making on the paper it held, but was unable to decipher them. Years ago, while other boys his age had been studying, he'd been imprisoned in the bowels of the earth. He couldn't read.

She set the clipboard aside and glanced at him, smiling slightly. "You're awake. How do you feel?"

He saw the exact moment that she noticed how his prick tented the sheets. She flushed pink.

His lips twisted. "Guess that's obvious. I feel like fucking."

She went silent. To him, this was a punishment. He wanted to hear her voice again.

"My body seems to be slowly gearing itself back to life," he said more civilly.

"That's good to hear," she said, the smile back in her voice. "I imagine this bed isn't helping. I'll try to see that you are given better accommodation."

He closed his eyes, letting her voice wash over him. It was beautiful, like some incredibly soothing balm. "Keep talking."

"What?"

He must sound like an imbecile. He forced his eyes open again, then narrowed them to slits. The light pained him.

She immediately dimmed the lamp, as if she'd guessed.

"You're a healer?"

"Yes, how did you know?" She gazed at him in surprise.

He shrugged, then moaned at the pull of the few last shards of marble that stubbornly clung to his flesh.

She came closer. "I'll try to get the rest of this stone off you. If you'll allow me to."

He struggled at his bonds, made of some material he couldn't defeat. "Remove these restraints, and I'll do it myself."

"I'm sorry. I can't release you."

He wanted to howl, to beg her to do it. "Then the stone stays," he said through gritted teeth.

A small quiet fell and she moved about the cell fiddling with things here and there and arranging items to suit her.

"How long have I been here? Wherever this is," he asked at length. "They wouldn't tell me."

"Three days in this Center. Twelve years in this world."

At the news, Luc felt stricken. Gods, back in EarthWorld, his brothers would all be a dozen years older now. Had he aged as well? He felt a thousand years old. "A mirror," he demanded. "Get me a mirror."

"I'm sorry. We don't keep them in patient rooms."

"Then tell me—how old do I look to you? What age?"

She angled her head. "Twenty-one?"

He grunted, perplexed. He was eighteen, but his build had always made him appear a few years older. Yet if twelve years had passed, shouldn't he now appear to be thirty?

"What year is it?"

"Eighteen eighty-two."

His brows rose. "But . . ." It had been 1882 when he left Rome in EarthWorld. It didn't make sense. Unless . . . had he traveled backward in time? "You say I have been here twelve years?"

Natalia nodded.

"No. That can't be," he said. "Let me go," he said hoarsely. He yanked at his restraints. He had to get back to his family. They were all he had. Without them . . .

"*Shh.* I can't let you go. You need to rest."

He turned his face to the wall. "Then leave me. Get out."

"All right," she said gently. "An attendant will be in to see to your needs soon. I'll return tomorrow and we'll talk again. Try to sleep. If you need pain medication—"

"I won't."

No! Don't go! He didn't want to be alone. He wanted to beg her to stay and talk to him, help him—free him—but he remained stubbornly silent.

He had always prided himself on the fact that he'd never once begged his captors. Never once broken during all those years in the catacombs.

And he would not beg now.

Day two

"Mistress Natalia Lattore," her patient announced the minute she entered his cell the next morning.

She smiled, drawing his eyes to her mouth. "You know my name."

"Wasn't hard to learn it." A corner of his mouth lifted as if he were proud of his sleuthing. He was sitting up in the bed today, the sheet turned down to his waist. Still in restraints.

Turning away, she set her clipboard on the counter and gathered some instruments, but that first glimpse of him was burned into her brain. His torso was a brawny landscape of hard, sculpted flesh, his silver eyes framed by dark lashes, his hair blue-black. Attraction flickered in her, but she squashed it down, appalled. He was her patient, and such feelings were inappropriate.

She'd never worked with a male patient for any length of time before and felt foolish, at her advanced age, for being drawn to one so young. But, gods, he was so beautiful it almost hurt to look at him. Her eyes dropped to his chart, touching that single inflammatory word that had made her refuse him as a patient yesterday.

Satyr.

Ten days, Advisor had given her to tame him. Moonful came in eleven. During his Calling he would be vulnerable as were all of his kind. Did they plan to use him for some nefarious purpose during his time of weakness?

"And will you tell me your name?" she inquired at length.

A hesitation. "Just Luc."

She glanced at him.

"Well, Just Luc, maybe when you trust me a little more, you'll tell me the rest."

Luc's gaze slid over her, weighing her. "Why did they choose you for me?" She was wearing a long, drab skirt that emphasized her small waist, a blouse that failed in its attempt to disguise her lush curves, and the beautiful glossy hair he recalled from the temple had been restrained in a severe plait. "Not that I'm complaining."

She hesitated, holding the clipboard tight to her chest as if unconsciously trying to hide from his intent study. "Because they believe I have some effect on you and . . ."

He nodded in the direction of his prick. "Obviously." In spite of the fact that the attendant had wrestled a pair of loose drawstring trousers onto him earlier, there was a sizable bulge under the sheet at his crotch. One that had hardened upon her arrival.

Her voice became irritated, but her gaze refused to venture

below his waist. "A *calming* effect. You need healing, I'm a healer. End of story."

"You know what I think?" He nodded again, this time toward the glass window. "I think that someone out there wants you to pry information out of me."

A guilty silence fell.

He closed his eyes and laid his head back on the mattress. "No, don't stop. Keep talking. It helps my head."

"You have a headache?"

Her voice came closer and she rested a light hand on his forehead. He drew away, a kneejerk reaction. No one touched him! Even the attendants here had figured that out after he'd given them enough bruises.

Her hand lifted away. Their gazes clung, each searching the other's face. Hers was kind, intelligent, her features strong. Her brows and lashes were naturally dark. The skin at her throat was a pale gold. His eyes traveled lower. A good Italian woman with curves in all the right places.

"If you want to get out of here, you need to cooperate. Let me treat you. Your treatment won't proceed well if I'm not allowed to touch you."

"If you want to soothe my aches, start with the one below my waist," he said crudely. He was shocked to hear himself make the suggestion. He, who abhorred touch. Was he actually encouraging her to—

"Your headache. Can you describe it?" Ignoring his suggestion, she'd moved to stand behind him at the head of his bed, where he couldn't see her without straining. "Common headaches produce a dull pain around the front, top, and sides of your head, almost like someone stretched a vise around it," she went on when he didn't reply.

"But a migraine is different." As she spoke, her fingertips came, stroking his temples in small, light circles. When he didn't object, she moved on to his cheekbones, then his head, combing her fingers through his hair to remove more of the marble that still clung to him here and there. He tensed, waiting for the customary crawling feeling to assail him. Incredibly, he instead felt himself relax under her touch. His eyes drifted closed.

Her hands moved to the sides of his neck, stroking the long tendons, releasing the tension. "Symptoms include throbbing and aches on one or both sides of the head. Do you feel dizzy or sick to your stomach?"

"Mmm-hmm."

Her hands stilled. "You do? Now?"

"No. But sometimes, with the arrival of these damned headaches."

"You have them often?"

"Only since . . . after an accident I had back in my world. I saw ElseWorld physicians some months ago in Enclave a Toscana for treatment. They couldn't help. You won't either."

Another silence passed, and Luc felt her curiosity. But she didn't inquire about his *accident*. Her hands went lower, working on the muscle of one shoulder, then down his arm. He felt her brush away more of the bits of marble that still stubbornly clung to him. Her voice came again. "I'll describe more of the symptoms of a migraine, and you can tell me if any are familiar."

"Mmm."

"The heart pounds faster, breath quickens, muscles tighten, your senses become sharper."

"Mmm-hmm."

"These physical changes are nature's way of increasing your strength and stamina. Your body is preparing you to defend yourself against a danger that doesn't exist."

"Or for one that does," he murmured.

He felt her consider that. "Do you believe yourself to be in danger? Were you when the headaches began?"

Yes.

Unlike his previous ElseWorld doctors, she didn't seem to mind when he didn't answer her questions. When she didn't badger him, it made him relax further. She'd folded the sheet aside in a clinical way that revealed one of his legs but kept his prick shielded. The heel of her hand rode the length of his thigh muscle.

"Mmm. That feels damn good," he told her. After working that leg, she covered it and worked her way around to his other one.

His lashes lifted and he watched her through slitted eyes. She was intent on her work, a small frown of concentration on her sweet face. He was melting into butter under her hands. He wanted nothing more than to lay her out on this bed and slide his cock inside her.

This time without an audience. And with him on top. He'd thought her a harlot when he'd first awakened at the temple. A professional temptress like those in Sevin's salon, who were free with their favors for payment. Those women would not blush at carnal suggestions, and would have taken him up on the offer of sex in a heartbeat. This was a different kind of woman, one who for some reason fascinated him.

"Why were you with me on that altar?" he asked and felt her hands falter.

"I was coerced."

His eyes went hard and his wrists tested his restraints. "By whom?"

"It's hard to explain."

"Try."

She sighed. "What happened was a tradition. Part of a festival that centered on you. When you appeared so suddenly twelve years ago, seemingly out of nowhere, everyone believed you to be some sort of god."

This woman who hid her body behind a clipboard and

would not even peek at his male parts when she thought his eyes were closed was not the sort to engage in such a ritual without extreme enticement. "Did I hurt you?"

She folded the sheet firmly over his legs again, not looking at him. "Yes."

Luc frowned. "Gods. If I'd known . . . I'm sorry, Natalia."

She only nodded and changed the subject and he let her. "These headaches. Do they increase your sensitivity to light, noise, or particular smells? Do you experience blurred vision?"

"All that. They're at their worst during my Calling."

At last, something sent her eyes up to meet his again. "C-calling?"

"A rite performed in the worship of Bacchus, my family's god."

Natalia's hands left him. She went for her clipboard, making notes and hoping he didn't see how they shook. His file was accurate, then. He'd as much as admitted he was a Satyr. That must be the reason she felt so drawn to him, she reasoned. Why she'd always avoided the statue. Because of what *she was.*

Would he guess her long-held secret? And if he did, what would he do then? One thing was certain. She must make absolutely sure that neither she nor Sophie was in his vicinity when he was Called. It was imperative that she learn whatever Advisor wanted of him well before her deadline.

He groaned and she turned back to him, her brow knit.

"Are you feeling ill?"

"No." He sighed, obviously lying.

She patted his arm, and reached for a syringe. "Your body has been through an ordeal."

"You have no idea," he said obliquely, and she sensed a hint of self-deprecation in his voice. Was he teasing?

"You need to rest. I'll give you something for the pain."

"No."

She soothed him with words. "You're going to be fine. Stay calm. I can take your pain away."

He felt something prick the vein in his arm.

Then sleep came.

Day three

The healer was back. Sitting in a chair alongside his bed, she was scribbling notes on her infernal clipboard. Luc stared openly at her, enjoying the prim way she held herself and the serious expression on her face. And thinking how much he wished she were naked.

Her eyes met his and she canted her head slightly in that intriguing way that displayed the soft skin of her throat. "Do you know how you came to be encased in stone?"

He shook his head. It had been pounding this morning. Within minutes of her arrival, the pain had virtually faded away. "I'm guessing it was caused somehow by my crossing into this world."

"How did you accomplish that exactly?"

He shrugged. "I don't remember."

"Liar."

He smiled. "Some healer you are." She was right, though. He was close to remembering how everything had come to pass. He could feel the memories lurking around the edges of his mind, now that it was clearer.

"Why did you come here?"

"Revenge."

This got her attention, and he saw the surprise in her gaze when it lifted. "Against whom? Or what?"

"That's my business."

"A word of caution then. Be careful what you wish for," she

told him softly. "Revenge may not prove to be as sweet as you believe in the end."

"Oh, I think it will be very sweet."

"Truly? If you destroy whomever or whatever you hate so desperately, will you be completely happy then? What happens after you do so? Have you considered that? What will your goals be then?"

She was questioning the reason for his very existence, and it made him mad. "Release these fucking restraints. I have to piss."

She stood with an irritated twitch of her skirts. "I'll call an attendant."

"No." Luc's voice lowered. "Hells, Natalia." His head fell back. "I don't need to relieve myself. I just want you to . . . release me. To trust me."

She hesitated, glancing over her shoulder at him. "Why should I? You've been rough with the guards and attendants. It's in your chart."

"I don't like anyone touching me without my permission," he admitted slowly. "I don't like being locked up. Would you?"

Her eyes narrowed. "You're not making my job easy here."

"Is that what I am? A job?"

Avoiding his question, she tapped her pen on her chin and then seemed to reach a decision. "All right." She went to the door and locked it. Coming back to him, she released his restraints. Almost immediately, the door began rattling, those outside wanting in.

He leaped up, all male bluster, looking ready to do battle against them.

"I have the only key," she informed him, unfazed. She turned to the glass, signaling to whomever was outside. "It's all right," she called out.

The doorknob stopped rattling.

246 / *Elizabeth Amber*

She turned back to him. "I don't believe you'll harm me, but those outside aren't so sure of you. If you act calmly, they'll leave us alone."

"How's this?" Luc stood with his back against the door and folded his arms, looking pleased with himself that he'd convinced her to do as he wished. Then he reached out a hand to her.

She stepped back before he made contact. "Stand where the attendant can see you. And you're not allowed to touch me, do you understand? I can touch you, but not vice versa."

He put his hands on his hips, looking annoyed. But in the end, he nodded and did as she asked, moving to lounge against the countertop. Picking up her clipboard, he stared at the indecipherable writing on it.

Coming to his side, she took it from him, turning it facedown on the counter. Then her gaze slipped over his chest and she began rummaging through the drawers in the cabinet below the counter.

"Now let's hope these cabinets are stocked with a robe that fits you," she said. "Otherwise, we'll soon have every female in the building flocking outside that glass to gawk."

Days four and five

Natalia's next session with Luc passed uneventfully save for a single admission on his part that his surname was Satyr. There were none in the community—hadn't been for decades—but they were legendary for their licentious behavior and stories of their carnal feats still circulated. Just one week ago, she could never have imagined she would now be keeping company with one!

She left him in the early afternoon. On her way from his cell, she copied her notes and delivered the duplicates to Physician's office as she did every day.

Since the institute was some distance from the Center, it would occupy most of one day to visit, and she made arrangements to travel there the following morning. She hadn't heard from Sophie since the festival.

As she struck out from the Center the next day, guards flanked her carriage. "I don't require protection," she told them, and was summarily informed that their accompaniment was mandatory and they were under Advisor's orders. This was unsettling, and she pondered what it meant all the way to the institution. How long would she remain so carefully guarded, and how would she ever manage to escape if Sophie agreed to her plan?

She found Sophie in the institute's dining hall at nooning with a group of friends that included Leona. The latter girl looked chagrined to see Natalia and didn't speak. The others noted her guards and then stared at her as if she were a bug on a pin. In fact, the entire hall seemed to be staring. After the events of the festival, she was infamous.

"Sophie, I would have a word with you," Natalia said.

Looking irritated and slightly embarrassed by all the attention, her sister nevertheless rose and went outside to walk with her. The guards followed at a respectful distance.

"What is it?"

"You know I'm working at the Healing Center now?"

Sophie nodded. "Congratulations. It's what you've always wanted."

"I've had papers signed by Advisor to the effect that you won't be inducted into the breeding program. And the priests issued documents that you and Leona and Rae cannot be co-erced into marriage."

"Rae has already wed."

248 / Elizabeth Amber

"What? Did she—"

Sophie shrugged. "Gentleman DiPietro offered for her and she agreed."

"I see. And what are your plans?"

"Private."

"Sophie," she said carefully. "I hope you saw Gentleman Cato for the cad he is, when he attack—"

"He said you'd been flirting with him."

Natalia put a hand on her arm. "No!"

Sophie shook her off. "Why are you here? What do you want?"

Natalia glanced back at the guards. "I want to know if you wish to leave the community. With me. If I were to go."

"What do you mean if you go? You can't just go, not without permission from the Advisors. Or . . . oh, are they planning to trade you to another community for a female who isn't barren?"

Natalia gasped at her thoughtless words.

But Sophie's attention had wandered. "If that's all, I have to go."

Glancing ahead Natalia saw a group of boys emerge from the adjacent building. One that included Titus Cato. "Sophie—"

Sophie gave her a quick hug. "Farewell, Nat. I wish you well in your new position. You've always aspired for greater things and now you will have them. But I'm content here. I fit in, as you do not. So please, don't keep pushing me to want what you want. Just be happy for me, as I am for you."

With a sinking heart, Natalia watched her only sister join the group of rowdy boys just ahead and then split off to stroll in tandem with Gentleman Cato.

6

Day six

"Where the hells were you yesterday?" Luc demanded in a surly tone when Natalia entered his cell the following morning. "I was locked up in this cage alone, strapped to this bed again, with nothing but imbeciles around me. They drugged me and shaved my face. Gods know what else they did."

"Your new look suits you," she told him, as she unlocked his restraints. When he continued to glower, she admitted, "I went to the institute. To visit my sister, Sophie. I was a teacher there until the afternoon that you and I . . . until recently."

She let her words die away, embarrassed to have mentioned the matter. She was rattled, was all. Sophie was back to being her stubborn self again. The fact that she'd taken up with Gentleman Cato had Natalia worried. But she pushed all that aside for the moment.

"Do you have any family yourself?" she asked him, moving away now that he was released.

He glared at her, rubbing his chafed wrists as he sat up.

Today he was wearing a fresh pair of the drawstring trousers that were a stock item at the Healing Center, and nothing else.

"No, you don't," he said, still sounding grouchy. "No turning the conversation into an interrogation. I'm not in the mood."

"Very well, then. You may direct our conversation instead." She set a robe beside him on the mattress, hinting.

But as she took his vital signs, Luc only lifted her lifechain and silently toyed with it. She'd begun allowing him to roam loose in his cell during her visits, but now she eyed his hand pointedly.

"Technically, I'm not touching you," he said. "Still within your rules."

She didn't reply, which gave him tacit permission to examine the chain.

He rolled one of its beads between his fingers. "What is this?"

"My lifechain," she told him, pressing the metal disk of her stethoscope to his breast.

"What is it for, I mean?"

"If you must know, it reveals a woman's age." She jotted down the measure she'd taken of his pulse.

He cocked his head at her. "Not all women wear them though. Sometimes men do. The attendant, for instance."

"You're observant. In this community a woman gives her lifechain to her husband upon their marriage." His other measurements taken, she started to ease away.

"Wait. Explain the custom to me." He held fast to the chain, wanting to keep her near.

"It is forever removed by her husband on their wedding night. Afterward, he then wears it at his throat as a necklace to show his ownership of her."

"Ownership?"

"She becomes his possession, a convenience to him. A vessel

for his lust. Keeper of his household." Her matter-of-fact tone gave no indication of her feelings, but her slender foot was tapping.

A graveled chuckle left him. It felt rusty. "And I thought I was cynical about love."

"There is rarely any question of love between a husband and wife here." She tugged at the chain.

"Technically, this chain is mine."

"What?" she asked in confusion.

He smiled slowly. "Your memory is short . . . wife."

She pushed at his hand and yanked, and he let the beads slip through his fingers.

Turning, she went to the counter and slapped her stethoscope and clipboard onto its surface. "I'm not your wife."

"I distinctly recall a promise, one about giving yourself to me for all time, or something along those lines anyway."

"You heard?" She reached for her clipboard and pen. "What else do you remember from that day?"

He crossed his arms. "You agreed this would not be an interrogation."

She stopped writing. "Yes, I suppose I did," she said reluctantly. "And you're quite correct. I am legally wed to you. So are half the women in the community."

"But you're the only one I want."

She looked at him, abruptly speechless, then quickly recovered. But her cheeks remained a telltale pink. She was attracted to him, he realized in satisfaction.

"I rather imagine that what you *want* is to deceive me with your flowery words, so that you may escape this cell." She sidled away, clearing her throat. "You're understandably restless."

"Hells yes! I've been cooped up in here for a week."

"What I mean to say is that I know that you've gone for some time without . . ." She stepped to the cabinet and carefully set her clipboard on it. "That is, if you'd like a female companion to sojourn here with you overnight, I can arrange for one." The pink in her cheeks deepened. "Or more than one."

The smile that stretched his lips felt unused and strange as it formed on his face, but it felt good. "Thank you for the very kind offer," he said, humor in his voice. "But . . ." He came behind her, close enough so he could feel her body's warmth, but still not touching.

Luc wanted to bury his face in her throat, in the silken fall of her hair, to hold her and join his body to hers. It was a thrill beyond compare to actually desire physical closeness with another being. For the first time since the catacombs, he saw more than desolation in his future. Because of this woman. He planted his hands on the countertop on either side of her waist, effectively capturing her.

"You're the only female I want to *sojourn* with."

Natalia whipped around, her eyes going wide with alarm when she saw how close he'd come, and she pushed at him. "What are you . . . no." She darted a glance toward the glass and lowered her voice. "Please move away from me, Luc. There's always someone watching us. It may be just an attendant, but it could be a government official or even an Advisor."

"I don't care."

"I do."

He frowned toward the glass. "Why? What makes me so important to them?"

"You tell me."

Straightening, he jerked his chin toward the glass. "And if I do? Will you write it on your little clipboard and deliver the news to them?"

Her silence damned her.

"Do you know what a miracle you are to me?" he asked, gazing down at her.

Her brows rose and something akin to fear crept into her pretty brown eyes. She shook her heard slowly.

"Back in my world, I could not bear to be touched. I didn't fornicate except on nights when my Calling drove me to it. But with you, it's different. I want you to touch me, Natalia. Lia. I want you to lie with me. Be with me." He leaned toward her, his eyes on her mouth. His unfettered hands rose toward her.

But she ducked away. "I'm flattered, of course," she said stiffly, once she'd put half the length of the cell between them. "However, do you realize how that sounds? After less than a week?" She took a fortifying breath. "You have to understand something, Luc. It's perfectly natural that you've formed an attachment to me. And you're not the first patient to do so while under a healer's care. I'm your whole world at the moment. Your touchstone. Soon enough, these feelings you think you have for me will pass."

Luc stared at her, slowly shaking his head. "You disappoint me, Healer. You really do."

Natalia studied his expression, surprised at what she read there. Had her rejection truly wounded him? "How old are you?" she asked in exasperation.

"Eighteen."

Oh gods, he is even younger than I suspected. She lifted the length of her lifechain and held it out to him. "There are twenty-eight beads on this chain."

He raised and lowered one powerfully muscled shoulder. "So?"

"So I'm a *decade* older than you are."

"So you're twenty-eight. What does that matter?" Then, "You believe yourself too old for me to want you?"

"I've lived longer than you, experienced more. I could almost be your—mother."

He laughed, and for some reason that made her angry. "You know nothing of my experience of life," he informed her. "Believe me, I've lived through hells. And I feel far, far older than you'll ever actually be."

He turned his back on her. "You can go now."

She folded her lips inward, biting them, not sure how this conversation had gone so wrong. "Tomorrow, then."

Natalia waited for his nod, inexplicably relieved when the acknowledgment came. Then she unlocked the door and left the cell, relocking it as she departed. A few steps farther, and she drew up short.

Along with the usual attendant, Advisor was seated there. He looked as if her sudden early leave-taking from the room had caught him by surprise. Had he been here every day observing, only to steal away moments before she came out? The thought made her skin crawl.

"Interesting little scene," he commented. "Our lunatic seems to have progressed under your devoted care."

"He's not—" Grinding her teeth, she turned to the attendant. "I'll need privacy for my work in future. A curtain is to be hung inside my patient's cell so that I may draw it over the glass on occasion. When certain treatments require it."

The attendant glanced toward Advisor, but the latter didn't quibble. A healer's methods varied, sometimes involving erotic massage or even fornication with a patient. She had neither in mind, but she needn't share the reasons for her request. She herself wasn't even sure what they were.

"Your methods don't matter to me," Advisor said briskly. "Just make sure they work. Four more days. Use them wisely."

She nodded and started to move past him.

"How is that sister of yours? I understand there's a romance budding between her and one of the gentlemen at the institute."

She kept her expression carefully blank. "I see you have spies everywhere."

"I do. Keep that in mind, Healer."

"Good day, Advisor," she said coolly, and then she swept from the room.

Day seven

"I've brought a peace offering," Natalia announced as she entered his cell that afternoon. She'd left him alone and unfettered for the first time during her mysterious absence. There was a curtain hung now at the cell's only window, but he hadn't pulled it shut while here alone, knowing the attendant would object.

Instead, he'd paced the cell, searching it with his eyes and surreptitious nudges of his fingers, for something he might employ as a weapon when he attempted an inevitable escape. He was strong enough now. Just waiting for an opportunity. And a chance to convince his healer to go with him. As far as he could see, this world was a dying garden, and she its only flower. She deserved better.

When she'd entered just now, he'd still been pacing, trying to remember something, anything. He'd sensed the evil one lurking outside his cell last night and it had made him edgy and frustrated, and had incited his killing instinct. Now he turned toward Natalia, staring at her. At what she held. A bowl. One that was full of grapes.

Grapes.

Elixir.

The gate. The Bacchus fountain in the salon had been a gate! Like a lamp switching on in his mind, he remembered the moments just before he'd come here to this world with exact clarity.

Bastian and Dane had been worrying over the need to obtain grapes from ElseWorld in the face of the new travel embargo in Rome. Grapes from both worlds were necessary to create the elixir used to initiate their Calling. Yet travel to Tuscany and the only known interworld gate in existence had been summarily cut off.

He took a handful of grapes from Natalia. Munching them, he began pacing again. And thinking.

The full moon appeared in this world with the same regularity as it did in EarthWorld. His body told him it would rise here within a matter of days. Three or four at most. His enemy must know how vulnerable he would be then. His body tensed. His incarceration must end before Moonful.

But how to escape? He'd somehow gone backward in time when he'd come here. Which meant he had been given the gift of time in which to return to his family bearing the grapes they would so desperately require come Moonful. But would time reverse again when he traveled back?

The elixir would save his brothers' lives. If he made it back to them in time. If he could find the gate again—the one he'd apparently used to transport him here.

He scooped another handful of the fruit from her bowl. "These are from vineyards in this community?"

She nodded, and began gathering the paraphernalia she used to do her incessant monitoring of him each day. "The grapes are the only fruit that still grows here. I picked them wild just now. Other crops have withered."

"They taste different from the grapes in EarthWorld," he said.

"Different how?"

He eyed her intently, then turned so his back was to the window. "Why don't you come to my world and find out?"

Sudden tension thickened the air.

Natalia went to the door and locked it, then drew the curtain she'd had installed over the window so his attendant could not play voyeur. She came to him, her expression urgent. "Is there a gate here in this village? One that leads to your world?"

"You tell *me*."

"The only gate I'm aware of is in Enclave a Toscana, miles from here," she said honestly. "The beneficial effects of the sharing of grapes between worlds are no longer felt this far north. It's why this land is dying. Why the priests hoped you were a godking sent to save us. When you appeared so inexplicably, they thought you might have come through a local gate. Here in the community."

"I did."

She leaned forward, breathlessly. "Where exactly?"

He considered her briefly, then his expression changed to an interesting mixture of guilelessness and cunning. His arms went overhead, and his body stretched mightily. "Do you want to know what I need?" he asked her. "A bath. A real one. Not some cold sponge running over me. Is there a public bathhouse nearby?"

She nodded dubiously. "There's one here in the Center. Is this to be in exchange for an answer to my question?"

"A bath would definitely make me more malleable," he told her. "And less foul-smelling."

He wasn't at all foul, and he knew it, but she was eager for answers. This was the very information the Advisor sought. It would buy safety for Sophie and herself. She pushed away the niggling reluctance she felt regarding the matter of supplying such information, once gleaned, to the authorities.

She'd sought escape for so long. And now a new idea was born in her mind. Sophie had never seen another way of life. If Luc could be convinced to take the two of them through this mythical gate to the adjacent world, maybe her sister's feelings would change. Maybe she would realize that her happiness could be found in EarthWorld instead of here with men like Titus Cato.

"I'll make arrangements," she told him. With that, she opened the curtain and left the cell. A half hour later, she returned. Instead of locking herself inside with him this time, she held the door wide. Outside it stood a half dozen armed guards. When they insisted that Luc wear restraints, Natalia replaced the irons at his wrists and ankles.

Wearing only manacles and a pair of the drawstring trousers that were freshly supplied to him each morning now, Luc stepped outside the room that had been his prison for over a week. Minutes later they found themselves the sole patrons at the Center's public baths. Their guards positioned themselves at every exit, where they stood waiting with their eyes averted.

The floors and benches in the bathhouse were travertine, and in the middle of the rectangular room there was a long oval pool bounded by enormous stone columns. She avoided the main bath for now, since its cool waters were meant only for rinsing off. Instead, she drew her patient into one of the private nooks framed by towering Corinthian columns, where he might enjoy a solitary bath.

A female bath attendant followed them, but Luc stubbornly refused her ministrations.

"You'll need help at your bath, wearing those restraints," Natalia pointed out.

"Then help me," he said simply.

"Do you promise me answers afterward?"

He nodded, his expression a little too innocent to suit her.

As Natalia stepped behind the screen in the corner of the nook, she heard him take the steps down into the circular bath. *You can do this,* she told herself. She'd given baths to both male and female patients during her training at the institute. When she stepped from behind the screen, she wore only the long linen gown that was the traditional garb of a bathhouse attendant.

Luc was already seated on the stone bench within the subterranean bathing pool. A fog hovered over the surface of the pool, steam rising from its warm waters to obscure all but his head, shoulders, and upper torso from view.

His eyes slipped over her as she waded in to join him, a worrisome gleam in them.

"This will be a bath, nothing more," she informed him severely. "Afterward you'll rinse in the main pool, which is cool by contrast."

Nodding solemnly, he took her hands and placed them on his chest, moving them over him in a circular motion.

She kneeled before him. "This is a mistake," she told herself under her breath.

"Hmm?"

"Nothing." Briskly and efficiently, she washed his chest, slicking soap over him. Under his arms, she felt tufts of hair, but his torso was as smooth and well formed as the marble it had once been. She washed his back, thighs, calves, and feet. Everywhere she touched, any last vestiges of rock returned to flesh. He groaned now and then as she ministered to him, and she wondered what such a transformation must feel like to him.

She pretended not to know what she'd left out, but he eventually pulled her hands there to his phallus and wrapped her fingers around it. It was hard, swollen, and straining from him—hotter even than the surrounding waters. This sort of physiological change had occurred in patients before during her training as a healer, and was one of the very reasons she no longer accepted male clients. However, she had agreed to take this particular man as her patient, so she merely washed him as her job required.

Still, she'd never been attracted to another patient. And the very fact that she was attracted to him lent an intense intimacy to the act. Her hand trembled as it encircled him. Her other palm gently coddled his testicles.

His head fell back, the tendons of his neck going stark. "Gods," he swore through gritted teeth. His hand closed over hers, pushing her soap-slicked fist slowly down his length, then upward, then along the same course several times more. His visceral enjoyment was so easily read in his face that she could only stare at him raptly as she worked him, her lips parted.

Without warning, his eyes slitted, catching her gaze. The rich black of his pupils dilated, overtaking the silver of his irises. Hands covered her breasts, cupped them, squeezed in an arousing rhythmic massage. His thumbs brushed her nipples.

Forgetting the manacles, he tried to embrace her and then cursed softly when he could not. Instead, she rose higher in the water before him and laid her palms on his chest. There was some great secret pain buried deep within him. But he was strong. He'd been hurt but not broken. At this moment, no cost seemed too high to see him whole and content, as she sensed he had once been and could be again.

And he was open to her now like he hadn't been before. She would give anything to heal his heart. Even herself, though in the giving she herself, or at least her heart, might be broken instead.

"Natalia." Luc's hands framed her face, the chains of his bonds forming a bizarre sort of necklace at her throat. "I've been a carnal creature for more years than I care to count. I've fornicated in order to survive, but never—never in my eighteen years have I made love." His voice was gruff, welling up from some place deep inside him where he'd hidden away a wealth of horrors. "Let me love you now, Lia. My Lia."

His lips came closer. His fresh breath stirred hers. Something leaped between them—a dangerous attraction akin to heat lightning flashing from sky to ground.

In her true heart, she had known this would happen if they came here. Had yearned for this. For him. Something in him drew her. Had drawn her for twelve years, even as he slept.

Her hand curled around his nape and she angled her head slightly, brushing her mouth over his. He was Satyr. Everyone knew what that meant. They required regular carnal activity, she rationalized. A healer's mandate included the offering of physical surcease to a patient in need. And even though she knew she could not maintain a proper clinical distance in the giving of it, her heart thumped with anticipation as she whispered to him, "Yes."

Immediately, she heard the clink of chains. Then the loop of his chained arms lifted over her head, encircling her until his cuffed hands found the small of her back. Her knees separated around him as he pulled her close upon his lap. His body strained for her, his cock hot, slick, and hard. Her private flesh convulsed gently for want of it. Only the wet linen of her gown separated them now.

"Mistress?" One of the guards had apparently grown concerned and now stepped into the nook. She blinked at him over her shoulder.

Luc snarled, low in his throat—a male animal repelling another male who threatened to separate him from his mate. "Leave us!"

"Do as he says," Natalia told the guard. "I'm fine."

The guard nodded and stepped away, lingering just outside.

"First at the temple, now this. Must there always be an audience at our amatory engagements?" Luc growled. His hands curved over the rounds of her bottom, and he spoke at her ear, hot words of wanting. "I want out of this place. And I want you to . . . come . . . with . . . me." Those big hands of his moved her now in a rolling motion that plowed his length along her furrow without yet plowing deep, his rhythm matching the pace of his last three words.

"The soap," he whispered urgently. "You're small. I don't want to hurt you."

Realizing what he wanted, she snatched the soap up from where she'd set it on the edge of the pool and slicked it over his vein-roped length between them. His hands went lower under her bottom, lifting her. Fingers parted her folds, opening her to receive him. He pushed.

A small cry left her at the sensation and she put her hands on his chest. A harsh, ragged groan came at her ear, an erotic sound low in his throat as her flesh accepted his plump, slick head, and began to take more. He was enormous, yet her body took his as readily as if she were a candle mold and he, molten wax.

Her lips parted in a silent cry as he slowly penetrated her, plowing deep, so wonderfully deep, and deeper still, filling her as completely as a man could. "Gods, it's good. So good. My Lia." The very second that her bottom met his thatch, his grip on her seized and he bit off a strangled shout. Hot semen blasted from him. Her body jerked under its strength. Another pulse came and with it a ragged groan and another vigorous spurt of cum. And another, flooding her tissues with his thrilling passion.

Her eyes squeezed tight, as she sought to find what he had found, sensing it was close. The hands at her bottom tilted her then, and he moved her against him in just the right way so that each slow, downward stroke of her slick flesh against his exposed her clitoris to the delicious rub.

And then she was coming as well, her blood pumping and fizzing, her inner tissues fisting on his. The hard rhythmic squeezes went on and on and on until she thought she might faint under the glorious pleasure of it.

Yes! Oh yes!

Oh gods!

What have I done?

7

Minutes later, she was behind the screen, dressing, and then they were on their way back to his cell.

"What's wrong with me? With the idea of us?" Luc demanded.

"There's nothing wrong with you. You are doing well. Healing nicely under my treatment."

"Your *treatment?*" he sputtered. "Is that what you call it?"

"Lower your voice, Luc. The guards. And I'll tell you what's wrong with *us* in any long-term sense. You're too damn young. Too damn handsome. I am plain. I've always been so. No, don't try to flatter me," she said when he tried to argue. "We would make a ridiculous pair."

He smiled, making a *tsk*ing sound. "Two curses in one speech. My, my, Mistress Natalia."

His eyes roved over her, noting the bruised shadows under the sweep of her lashes; the chafing his evening beard had left on her pretty neck; and her lips, red from his mouth. He'd been greedy with her, rough. His body still wanted hers. Wanted to

264 / Elizabeth Amber

kiss her, fuck her, love her. It clamored to press itself to her warmth again, to inhale her goodness, her kindness.

His lips curved. And she thought herself plain?

As they reached his cell, she entered, but he balked, bracing both arms on the doorjamb.

"Stop it, Luc. Come inside."

He did.

Once the guards backed off, she murmured to him. "As of tomorrow, I'm relinquishing you to another's care. Another healer."

"No!"

"Please don't worry. I'll weigh in on the selection of my replacement and make sure you are in good hands."

He grabbed her arm, suddenly desperate. "They want you to cull information from me? All right. You want to know how I came here? All right. I came through a gate, from the other world. I'm guessing they want to know where it opens on this side, in this world. So that they can exploit it. I—"

"No! Don't tell me where it is." She fled, ignoring his roar of protest.

"He doesn't know anything," Natalia told Advisor the next morning. "He's not from another world. He simply wandered in from an outland and fell under the spell of some inexplicable magic. I see no point in continuing on with him. As you'll see by my recommendation, I believe he can be released into the general population."

Advisor tapped his pen on the desk, staring at her where she was seated opposite it. "Nonsense. Try again. Three more days."

"I'm telling you—"

"If you won't, I'll get someone else. You're uniquely suited to this case, but not irreplaceable."

"What do you mean?"

He lifted a brow. "I mean that there are no other maenad in

the community or anywhere nearby. But we'll make do with an inferior counselor. Is that what you want for him?"

Natalia's heart fairly stopped in her chest. No one in the community knew what she was, not even Sophie. Her mother had known and told Natalia the facts of her breed and that it must be kept a secret. Maenads were the carnal worshipers of the Satyr.

Their mother had been wed, but when she'd proven barren, her husband had bought into the breeding program. His seed had sired children in not one but two program participants. Therefore Natalia's and Sophie's mothers had been different, neither of them the woman who'd reared them. But it was tradition that a husband's issue from the program would be mothered by his wife as if they were her own.

"How did you—?"

"I've known all along. Mistress, why do you think I chose you for this task in the first place? We have the documentation regarding your biological mother. She died in the Sickness shortly after you were born. But she was a maenad. The only one in the community. The only one in all of Enclave a Roma, as far as is known."

"I don't understand why this matters."

He leaned forward, his eyes avid. "The whole moon comes four days from now. The Calling time for those of Satyr blood. And for those with the blood of the maenad. Like you."

"He'll be vulnerable. You'll be in a position to bargain with him."

"With my body."

"As you did in the festival. Is this so different?"

"Yes."

"Are you refusing to cooperate?"

"The Calling has never affected me before," she said doubtfully. In these outlands, its effect had lessened to almost nonexistence in most inhabitants.

266 / *Elizabeth Amber*

Advisor's eyes gleamed. "But then you've never been around a Satyr either, have you? All we're asking for is the answers to a few simple but very important questions. The first being the location of the gate he traveled through. And then the details of transport. How he accomplished it. Whether he can go back."

"I'll consider your request, Advisor."

"Do that. And remember the stakes while you're considering it."

"For my sister?"

"And for him. I can summon other healers who may work less effectively with him. Do more damage. Think about it."

Day eight

"You're maenad."

Oh gods, now even Luc had guessed her secret. This was bad.

Natalia's fingers tightened on her pen. She was back in his cell this morning, and they'd begun as if the events of yesterday had never happened, neither of them broaching it. In fact, they had been having a perfectly civil conversation suited to their roles of patient and Healer. And now Luc had to say something like that to ruin it.

At her sour expression, one side of his mouth lifted and he laughed. "I'm right. The immediacy of our attraction makes more sense now. Your kind is meant to worship mine."

She wrote something on her clipboard.

He leaned over her shoulder, pointing to what she'd written. "What does that say?"

"Patient is an ass."

Another smile tugged at that beautiful mouth. "Are you teasing me?"

She searched his eyes, and realization struck her. "You can't read, can you?"

"I can read you," he said. He turned his back to the window so the attendant couldn't read his lips. His hand found her hip, low where the touch could not be seen by their watchers. "And your body language is saying you missed me last night. You should have been with me." His hand stroked her thigh, the clandestine nature of his touch making it all the more thrilling. "Imagine how nice it would have been to share a bed. All night long. To have each other as often as the mood strikes."

She glanced at his narrow mattress.

"Not that bed. Yours."

Advisor would probably whoop for joy at the idea of a torrid, public liaison between them, his prize Satyr and maenad. She shook her head. "Not possible."

"Close the curtains."

When she didn't move, he clucked at her with feigned solemnity. "Your kind is supposed to worship my kind, Mistress Maenad. I can see you'll need some lessons in what pleases me."

Reaching beyond her, he whipped the curtains closed himself. Then swinging her into his arms, he set her on the desk, knocking her clipboard to the floor. He popped the buttons of her blouse open and unfastened her corset.

His hands took her waist and his mouth fell on the peak of one breast. Teeth tugged at her nipple. His gently rough tongue laved her there, and she felt the sensation pulse at the private flesh high between her thighs. Her head fell back, and she wove her fingers into his hair, holding him. She moaned.

The doorknob jiggled. "Healer?" The attendant.

His mouth lifted. "Annoying bastard. Tell him it's all right."

"Luc . . . I'm not sure this is wise."

His hand went under her skirt, finding the slit in her pantalets. Two talented fingers entered her. A thumb brushed her clit. The fingers began to move. "Tell him."

Her body bowed upward and she gave in, gasping and calling out in a strained voice, "All is well, attendant."

"Take your hair down for me," Luc whispered. He hooked her legs over his shoulders, the fingers of his hands still moving in her, gently testing her body's slick feminine clasp.

Her arm lifted and she began removing pins from her plait as if she were in his thrall and unable to disobey. Satisfaction filled him as he watched her do his bidding, watched lush waves of chestnut hair tumble around her shoulders. In her chaste gown, she looked so beautiful, endearing, fuckable.

Lovable.

Heat churned through him and with it came a fierce longing, stronger even than the one he'd felt yesterday. A longing to hold her. To ease her loneliness and his. To make her come for him.

"You're wet, mistress," he murmured, kissing her belly. Her legs relaxed for him, sliding slightly farther apart.

"That's it," he coaxed, his voice dark and low. "Offer your pristine body to me, maenad. It's what we were meant for."

"Pristine?" She gave a sad sort of laugh.

The rhythm of his fingers slowed inside her. "What does that mean?"

Her hands gripped his arm, and his fingers pulled from her. She came up on her elbows, struggling to get away. Their eyes met.

"Tell me."

"I don't come to you untouched," she admitted, sounding ashamed. "I took part in the community's breeding program. A duty. There were monthly clinical inseminations. Ten years. A hundred and twenty chances, but no children came. I'm barren."

"Not with me, you wouldn't be." It was a soft promise, one that made her heart squeeze with foolish hope. She was stupid. In what world did she imagine they could be together? Not this one. And there was no way to reach his unless . . .

A hand came around her, bringing her against his body as it loomed over hers. With a quick shove of his free hand, drawstring pants sagged low on narrow hips. She felt him tilt the angle of his cock. Felt him find her opening. Felt him stretch her, felt the virile strength of his entry. She was still tender from their joining yesterday, and it heightened the sensation now. Her spine arched, her chin lifting, she drew in a long, shuddering breath.

Her entire being was concentrated on his stroke, their joining. On the long, slow glide of his hot, ruddy thickness moving inside her, filling her, claiming her as his.

His growl colored the air, harsh and possessive, as his flesh took from hers and gave. He drove deep, only to suction from her and slam home again. He leaned over her so she half lay on the counter under him, bracing himself on a forearm, one hand going under her ass to tilt her as he liked. As she liked. His hips rode hers, moving sensuously, grinding and rotating. With the perfect ardor of a salacious symphony, the slash of his spine arched and bowed as muscles bunched and slackened. His balls thudded against her bottom, sending a fervid thrill through her.

Under her hands she felt the shallows formed in the sides of his rear cheeks as muscles drove him deep. She wrapped her legs around him, reveling in his powerful, rolling rhythm.

Ruddy color now suffused his cheekbones and a shadow of coal-black bristle dusted his strong jaw. Silver glinted from beneath lowered lashes as he gazed at her with brooding intensity.

Last night had been a thrilling, dangerous exception. He'd lost control of his wits and been at the mercy of his physical desires. What was it about this world—about this woman—that had held him in such thrall?

"Come with me," he whispered. "Come with me. Through the gate. To my home. Wed me again, in my world."

"Yes." Already she could feel her flesh fisting gently on his, gentle pulses that built higher and higher, stronger and stronger. His arms gripped her, hard, and she felt him come, in scalding shots of semen that made her writhe and twist with pleasure.

She cried out. "Yes!"

The doorknob rattled.

They both ignored it. A pounding began. "Mistress?"

"It's all fucking right!" Luc bellowed as she called out something along the same lines. The banging stopped.

Eventually, their coming eased and she laughed quietly—at the earlier disturbance that had interrupted their passion, and simply because she felt, well, happy. He gave her a disgruntled smile. "It's not funny. I want you all to myself next time."

Her fingers threaded his hair, enjoying its rich texture, both of them loath to separate. "What did you mean before, about my not being barren with you?" she asked him, her other hand smoothing down his side.

"During our Calling, under the whole moon, we can choose whether our seed is potent. We can decide if the women we mate bear our children."

She came up on her elbows as an insidious thought came to her. "So that's why they want you under their control! Oh, Luc, they're going to keep you here. Use you as a breeder of females. Starting with me. It's why Advisor chose me in particular. Why he has thrown us together."

He frowned. "Explain."

She pushed him away and he lifted her down, helping her to straighten her clothing.

"I was sent to get information from you. To find out how you traveled here, so that they can use your gate themselves. I see now that they are testing you with me this Calling, seeing if your seed will prove fertile in a barren woman. And if you manage it, afterward you are to be put out to stud. We have to get you out of here."

His hand caught hers. "This Advisor you spoke of. What does he look like?"

She gave him a brief description. "Why?"

"Because I came here for revenge. Against him. He's one of those who came to the catacombs," said Luc. "His surname is Arturo. He liked them young. Liked to make the hurt last. Male or female, he didn't care."

His story spilled from him then. It was a tale he'd long kept buried, one he had carefully hidden away from other doctors, from his brothers.

It had been a Moonful night thirteen years earlier when all had gone so awry. Their parents had gone out to the family's olive grove to celebrate the rites, leaving the four boys in the care of servants. Dane had recently become curious to learn something of these mysterious rituals in which the Satyr engaged under a full moon. And he had sneaked out, hoping to spy.

Unbeknownst to him, five-year-old Luc had followed. Both had been captured and held in the catacombs as sexual slaves at the behest of the Bona Dea empire. Dane had escaped, but Luc had remained for years.

He asked no pity now of his solitary audience and his tale was told calmly. But he felt some of its poison leech from him in this first telling of it.

And in his narrow bed, his beloved lay with him, holding him, weeping for the boy he'd been, for the wounded man he'd become. She curved a soft palm to his cheek, touched gentle fingertips to his mouth.

"Few men could have survived what you did," she told him. "A lesser man would have found his relief in narcotics or in the

272 / Elizabeth Amber

taking of his own life. But don't look back. Move forward. Behind you lies revenge. If you seek it when we try to escape, all may be lost. They might recapture you. Keep us apart."

"And that matters so much to you?"

"Yes, gods, it matters. Listen to me, Luc. Whatever happens, know this. Believe it. You are a good man, a strong one. A man worth loving."

Love for her welled up in him, chasing away hate. "Then love me, Lia. Love me. You are the one I want."

And with her kiss, he felt himself begin to heal. At long last.

Day nine

Natalia smiled at the attendant on duty outside Luc's cell as she arrived the next morning. "I've brought something for you." She tugged back the cloth covering the basket she held, revealing a small bottle and some freshly baked bread. "Wine. From grapes I picked two seasons ago."

She set them out on his desk. His eyes lit up.

Leaving him to it, she entered Luc's cell, carrying a satchel and another basket.

Reaching into the satchel, she pulled out some tailored street clothing and handed it to Luc. "Put them on. Hurry," she told him. "I've drugged the attendant. And this morning, I've done some sleuthing. There's a private sanctuary used only by the priests within the temple you took me into when you woke at the festival. There's a fountain dedicated to Bacchus. At the very temple you arrived at twelve years ago."

Luc yanked on the clothing she'd brought. "Damn. That explains the reek of irises. It must be the fountaingate. I was so close that day."

When he finished dressing, he took her hand and made for the door. "Take me there."

Nodding, Natalia peeked outside. Seeing the attendant slumped forward on the desk and hearing the soft buzz of his snore, she tugged Luc after her. She'd plied the guards on duty with the same tainted wine so their escape was easy. "I have a hired carriage waiting a short distance from here," she told him.

An hour later, they were walking up the hillside above the institute. Cresting a rise Luc gazed at the devastation all around them. Hills of dry grasses stretched out on all sides, in every direction. Only the ancient grape vines grew green, sprawling up stakes.

The two of them quickly reached the temple. The altar where he'd lain all those years stood empty of statuary now, all the bits of marble that had once encased him swept away.

"I know a back way into the temple," Natalia told him. "We used to sneak inside it and play there as children."

And then they were in the temple. And sneaking into the priests' private sanctuary. Standing before the fountain within it.

"Yes. This is it," Luc breathed, instantly certain. He reached for her hand, frowned when she handed him the basket of grapes she'd brought and backed away.

Natalia drank him in with a hungry sweep of her eyes. Noted the solid strength of him, the watchful silver gaze, the sapphire highlights in his dark hair. He wore a dark coat and trousers now instead of the Healing Center uniform. He looked self-assured, dangerously attractive. These last minutes might be the last she would ever see of him.

"Take the grapes to your brothers," she told him. "Make the elixir. I can't go with you. My sister, Sophie, is here. She has no one but me to guide her."

Luc reached for her again, this time taking her arm in a hard grip. "Now, you listen to me for once. This world is every bit the anathema my brothers led me to expect. Nothing good can come of you remaining here."

"I was born here," she argued. "As were you."

274 / Elizabeth Amber

"But I left this world when I was young. Because my parents somehow guessed what it would become. They sensed the coming of treachery and war and sickness. Gods, Lia, you don't belong here." He smoothed curls of luxuriant hair back from her face and throat. "You'll wither and die, just like everything else. You deserve better. You deserve love, happiness, protection. I'll do my damnedest to give them to you."

Natalia wanted to weep, but she held tears back, shaking her head. "I can't leave my sister. Go now. Return to me if you can. Only if it's safe."

His embrace swallowed her. "You've made me whole," he whispered, his voice ravaged at the thought of losing her. "Made me want to live again. Plan a life. We are not done with this world. I can open the same trade here as the Toscana gate enjoys. Regular deliveries of grapes between the worlds. I'll open negotiations with your government immediately."

Tears filled her eyes now, spilling over on to her cheeks. She wiped them away. "Oh, Luc. Thank you."

"We've been discovered in the human world. There are many ElseWorld kind there who need the help of a healer of your talents. Work with them, if you like. Or don't. Only come with me now, and I swear we will return soon to visit your sister."

"Oh gods, yes, Luc." She threw her arms around him and kissed him.

"Thank the gods." He murmured the heartfelt oath against her mouth. And then they were stepping toward the gate together.

"Stop them!"

At the sound of this voice he hated above all others, Luc hesitated, started to turn back. A long-held familiar call to revenge momentarily threatened to consume him.

"Forward," Natalia whispered, laying a hand on his arm. "Remember?"

The need for revenge warred with the need to take her home to his world and keep her safe. Then she smiled encouragingly at him. He put his hand over hers and squeezed it. And together, they stepped into the light emanating from the center of the fountain. Within it, voices whispered for his ears only, imparting the mysteries of it. Teaching him how to use it, how to bend time to suit him. Whispering that this particular gate only afforded passage to those who were worthy. Only to the Satyr and those they escorted.

Behind them, the last of his abusers leaped into the gate in a desperate attempt to learn those very secrets, only to be caught there in torment for hours that felt to him like an eternity, before he finally disintegrated in transport, never to be seen again.

And on the gate's other side, in EarthWorld, Luc and Natalia emerged whole and unscathed.

Luc burst through the gate into the salon, his face wreathed in a beatific smile and his hand upraised with the basket of fruit. "I bring you grapes of ElseWorld!" he announced to one and all. "And my new maenad wife."

Only an hour had passed in this world since he'd left it. By now, Bastian and Dane had been joined by Sevin. All three brothers were there in the salon just as he'd left them that day he'd first entered the fountain. They welcomed him eagerly, and with open arms they embraced Natalia.

Luc put his arm around the woman at his side and gazed down at her with all the love he felt for her. He would never tire of her touch, her embrace, her kiss, her voice. He would make a home with this woman, a life for them here in the bosom of his family. It would be a long life filled with joy. They would make a home together. And children. And for him, peace would come at last.

There would be a Calling night, come tomorrow. It was to

be a night in which he would worship his family's god through a carnal ritual that would last from dusk to dawn.

And for the first time in his eighteen years, with this woman alongside him, it would be a joy. Already, his body was quickening in anticipation.

He looked forward to it.